Mark IV

James Ostby

Crime, brutality, corruption . . . . When all conventional means of confronting such evils fail, there's a secret organization: **Ragnarök.**

Web page: **www.jimostby.com**
E-mail address: **jimostby@gmx.com**

Other books by James Ostby:

Men With Broken Faces: A literary WWI
novel

Jake Miller's Wheel: A Dostoyevskian work

Rat-Tail Curves: A creative nonfiction study
of physical, philosophical, spiritual and other
general human limits

1

Part I

2

Chapter One

Ragnarök

Dereck Bors got out of the car, shifted his white cane to his left hand, and adjusted his wrap-around sunglasses. His eyes were taped shut underneath. Alecto took his upper arm, clutching it firmly. "Keep your hands away from your face," she said, her voice hard and metallic. Alecto, one of the three ancient Greek Furies: *Unceasing Pursuit,* whose duty was to punish crimes that lie beyond the bounds of human justice.

Bors felt the weight of the totality of his life press down on him; baggage born into a new animate existence from which there was to be no turning back. He would leave behind the tattered and useless mental artifacts of his old life, but it wasn't easy to repudiate the past. Perhaps it was at best problematic, but he would try. Actually, he had been trying for a long time.

The car drove away, and Alecto guided Bors along a sidewalk. "Left," she said. She smelled musky, like she wasn't wearing any deodorant. An attractive smell. She was exquisite, with short, boyish, blond hair and deep, intense, blue eyes, and she didn't like him much. Some sort of negative imprint: the kind you either try to overcompensate for, or you say to hell with.

The air was damp and cool; perhaps they were near water. "Nice day for a stroll," Bors said, and he instantly regretted it: the flippancy, but mostly the banality. He disdained banality more than anything. He couldn't stand stupidity either, because he wasn't stupid; and he couldn't tolerate ignorance, because he wasn't generally ignorant, and anyway ignorance isn't direct stupidity. He could live with his psychical foibles and irrationalities-- the ones he couldn't shake off--because he had to, and because sometimes they were strengths. But he could not tolerate banality, most of all in himself. Whatever else he was, he would not be banal.

Alecto only tightened her grip and walked faster. Fortunately her fingernails were short; any longer and he would have been bleeding. "Left," she said. They turned, and Bors heard footsteps coming. Alecto nudged him slightly to the right, then forward again.

"You move well for a blind man."

She said it harshly, but it was the first unnecessary thing she had uttered since they had met near the Empire State Building.   That was some improvement.

"Thanks.   I'm new at it."

Sir Bors de Ganis--cousin of Sir Lancelot du Lake--had been his Arthurian hero.   Sir Bors--one of the three peerless knights--who had joined in the quest for the Holy Grail, and had witnessed Sir Galahad fulfill that quest. Bors was renowned not for his strength as a fighter, but for his nobility and purity of heart. He died in defense of the Code of Chivalry.

"Five steps up."

Alecto.   Sometimes she called herself Atropos: one of the ancient Greek Fates. Atropos, the Inexorable, who carried the dread shears to cut the thread of life at the appropriate time.   Indeed she hoped to do so; to cut some threads of life.

As Bors took the first step a truck or some other large vehicle passed behind them. When they reached the top they waited, and after several minutes a door squeaked open and they went in.   Alecto kept her grip while someone closed the door and then she led him into what--from the reverberations of their footsteps--could only be a large room.   Their guide walked away.

"Here," Alecto said, and she let go. Bors' arm was sore, but he didn't rub it.

They waited, and all Bors could hear was Alecto breathing.

Someone came in and murmured, "Alright."

Alecto removed Bors' sunglasses and took his cane. "Now these," she said, and she ripped the medical-tape patches from his eyes, both at the same time.

"Ow! You didn't have to do that!" Bors cried. He rubbed his eyes. "Do I have any eyelashes left?" He peeked through his fingers, but his vision was blurred, and his eyelids felt as though they had been stretched like rubber bands, then snapped back against his eyeballs.

"Quit sniveling."

"I'm not----"

"Welcome to Ragnarök," came a low voice from far in front of him. "I am Rhamnusia."

"Rhamnusia," Bors repeated. "She whom none can escape."

He massaged his eyes with his fingertips, then looked again. It was a large room; more like an old auditorium, or a theater, but with only a dozen folding chairs now. On a low stage, standing in front of an antique walnut desk, was a lean, athletic, dark-complexioned, beautiful lady. Her long, straight hair was the darkest of black, and her aquiline nose--a mannish nose which would have been a flaw on any other woman--made her all the more becoming. In contrast to her hair she was light-complected, her eyes were pure blue, and her stare penetrated Bors. She had Alecto's eyes.

"We apologize for the clandestinity. And the eye patches. Please take your time."

Bors' vision blurred again. He thought she had directed the part about the eye patches somewhat caustically at Alecto.

"You know your ancient Greek mythology," Rhamnusia said, giving Bors more time.

"Some." Bors blinked, and his vision returned.

"Please, sit if you like."

Bors shook his head. Alecto sat.

"We've done the necessary checks Bors," Rhamnusia said. She leaned back and rested against the desk. "Or shall I call you Sir Bors?"

"Bors is fine."

"Before I begin, do you have any questions?"

"Am I in?"

"Of course you're in. Alecto has no doubt told you that. You were in from the moment you saw her, and from now on there's no way out. Well, there is one way." She

worked a smile across her face, then became
impassive again. "Joining Ragnarök is like
becoming a 14th-century nun: it's for life. Any
other questions?"

"But what happens when we get too old
to work for Ragnarök?"

"You will still be in but you will be
inactive. Anything else?"

"Where am I?"

"You're not ready for that yet."

"You said I'm in."

"What does it matter? And why do you
keep asking trivial questions? Our information
on you tells us you are bright enough."

The place smelled foul and rotten.

"Who's this?" Bors asked, pointing back
down at Alecto, who muttered an obscenity at
him.

"She's you partner."

"Partner? I didn't know we were to have
partners. For how long?"

"Perhaps forever."

"Don't we have any choice in----?"

"No. Why?"

"Because she could use a good, hard kick
in the ass."

"Calm down. She could save your own
ass someday."

"Splendid."

"What else, Mr. Charm?"

"Then what about the organization of Ragnarök, and----"

Rhamnusia waved her hand. "Later. First, tell me again why you came to us. You're in, deeper than you seem to realize, but I'm still curious. I think there's more than what's on your application. More than what our operatives have found. A hell of a lot more."

She was fishing. As Bors collected himself he became aware that there were no windows; only dim overhead lights hanging from the high ceiling: large, yellow, fly-specked bulbs beneath what had once been white, glass reflectors. Gold-painted Florentine scroll work adorned the faded-blue stucco walls where they met the ceiling. The waist-high oak wainscoting was old and the hardwood floor was worn and patterned with holes that had once anchored rows of seats. The holes were filled with years of grime.

"I suppose I've always been an idealist," Bors began. "Even a moralist. I hate chaos. I value order, and I believe Homo sapiens can advance, but only if the most intelligent lead the way. But I often abandon all hope for humankind; the stupidity, the religiosity, the ignorance."

"Then why are you here if you have abandoned all hope?" Rhamnusia broke in.

"I said *almost* abandon."

"You said *often*."

"What's the difference?"

"The difference is obvious.   I hope you aren't going to be difficult.   Have you any deeper concerns?"

Bors flinched internally, and considered. "I think we in Ragnarök should be operating worldwide instead of messing around with----"

"First, what causes you to think we are *messing around*?   And second why do you assume we are not working worldwide?"

"Are you?"

"Never mind.   Well, not yet."

Rhamnusia fell silent, and Bors started again.

"When I left the CIA----"

"When you were booted out."

Alecto got up and slapped Bors on the back of his head.   He winced mostly in surprise and glared back at her for a moment.

"When I left--because I couldn't stand the limitations on their activities--I realized two things.   First, that the most serious injustices committed against humanity are perpetrated by two classes: the exceedingly intelligent, whose obligation should be to help create a better world, and the dim-witted.   Some in each class can be so monstrous and immoral that they'll never be brought to justice by normal means. Actually there's another class in between: the clever. Alexander Hamilton said something to the effect that *clever men are never intelligent. They are the worst.*"

"Clever men and women, whatever your so-called classes," Alecto barked as she sat back down. "At least you recognize women's abilities."

"Well," Bors continued, ignoring Alecto, "for all that, personally I don't have high regards for the average person as they lump along unthinkingly through life guided mostly by societal habits, traditions, or customs. And most important laws are toothless," Bors continued. Alecto was getting on his nerves; tapping her fingers on her seat and muttering indistinctly. "Themis--the Lady of Justice--has become a feeble, corrupt, ugly crone. The scale of justice in her left hand is weighted, and the sword in her right hand has been turned against the virtuous. We are in a new world, but like the old Montana Vigilantes, the only way to fight immorality is with immorality. But that's not as depraved as it sounds. There are mobs, hate groups, drug smuggling rings, terrorists, vile and ruthless leaders--all kinds of evil organizations and personal corruptions-- why not a good counterpart that also exists outside the law? Why not----?"

"Thank you," Rhamnusia cut in. She lifted herself from the desk on which she had been leaning and stepped to the front of the stage. "Now I'll talk."

She seemed amused. Or pleased. Bors couldn't tell for sure, but maybe neither. Not angry though. Maybe it was something else. Anyway, she was fascinated with him; he sensed that. Behind him Alecto shifted impatiently in her chair. He tried to fight back his attraction for her, despite his annoyance.

"As you know," Rhamnusia began as though she were starting a college history lecture, "in Ragnarök we are all anonymous. That way if you're *encouraged* to talk, you will never compromise our organization. The only one who knows your real name and background is Z, and I have never seen her. Or him, or them."

A large, gray rat scurried across the stage behind her.

"You need a cat." Bors said.

"What?"

"Them? That's all you know about Z?"

"Most of us think Z is a triumvirate."

"Why Z?"

"Originally, Z was Phoenician for *sword*."

"A tad melodramatic, don't you think?" Bors heard Alecto move agitatedly in her chair again and he rather enjoyed annoying her. If she were to be his partner it was going to be an interesting relationship.

"I suppose so," Rhamnusia shrugged. "Anyway, all of our directives filter down to us. I'm at the third-lowest level. You're at the lowest. Now for the Codex. You're familiar with it? It's been published in newspapers and shown on media all around the world."

"I know the three principle points. The raison d'etre of Ragnarök is to enforce moral laws, to combat evil, and to oppose philosophical and religious meddling in people's lives whenever possible. And to work outside the laws if necessary. I guess that means outside the laws of any country."

"In your own words, but close enough. And you're still fishing. I have already refused to tell you whether or not we work outside of our country."

Bors smiled. "I thought you had."

"And always remember, one main tenet of the Codex is to follow orders."

"Thank you."

Rhamnusia smiled a real smile and narrowed her eyes as she leaned forward slightly to further study Bors. Alecto muttered something so softly that Bors couldn't make it out, but the nuance was not encouraging.

"You have been assigned to work with Alecto because she is a good match for you," Rhamnusia said. Her smile was wiped away by some inner solemnity.

This time Alecto's disdain was palpable, though Bors wasn't even looking at her.

"You know our *mark* system?" Rhamnusia asked.

Bors, distracted, attempting to discern the reason for Alecto's contempt, didn't answer.

"Let me review," Rhamnusia said. "Mark I is a public warning, Mark II is a personal admonishment, and Mark III is a violent remonstrance." She paused.

"And Mark IV is death," Bors finished.

Rhamnusia held up her hand. "No. Mark IV is the one that only makes you *wish* you were dead. There is another mark: Mark V. It is death. Slow death. That is why we will never speak of it again."

"But isn't the *slow* part a little cruel and unusual?"

"You said it yourself: we're in a new world; one of technological and other advances that have left conventional law enforcement agencies unable to cope with too many elements of crime and corruption. We are opposed by two organizations: the FBI; and a covert group called Scorpion, working under the Terrorism and Violent Crime Section of the Criminal Division of the U.S. Department of Justice. Scorpion was established by shady politicians, wealthy industrialists, and moral con artists. Be careful of the FBI. They're mostly okay, but they work under too many restrictions. Beware of them, but fear Scorpion. Its leader, Demetrius Eppers, is obsessed with cracking Ragnarök, and he has no constraints. Part of Scorpion's muscle is a former Russian KGB agent's son named Zabov; a cunning sociopath. Fear him most of all; he kills, but he kills leisurely and meticulously."

Bors wasn't afraid.

"Oh, I almost forgot, as far as we know only Scorpion and the FBI agents know about Mark V, and they're not in a hurry to publicize it."

She scrutinized Bors until he felt he had to say something.

"Oh."

"Alecto will tell you the rest. Don't worry, we'll break you in slowly, on a *need to know* schedule." Rhamnusia backed away from the edge of the stage, turned abruptly, and disappeared. More melodrama.

Bors looked around again and the mouse dirt and other perfumes overpowered him.

Alecto stepped in front of him with her tape.

"Enough with the tape," Bors snapped. "I'm in now, officially, and we're equals whether you like it or not."

Astounded, she stepped back. "We may be partners, but we're not equal."

"I can't help it if you're not up to my standards," he countered.

She had slapped him earlier, and this was his return slap. Her face flushed with anger, but she bit her tongue. When she had regained control she threw the tape on the floor.

"Okay, I guess you have a point, but that puts me in a bind. I was to bring you here, and to leave here, with you blindfolded."

Bors thought for a moment. "Alright, how about if you put small, loose patches on my eyes, and I wear the sunglasses? Then when we get to the vehicle and down the street, or road a way, I take them off. I owe it to you to be reasonable from now on."

"Good. Thanks."

But he knew she still didn't like him much.

When they were outside and were being driven away by a hard-looking Ragnarök flunky, Bors pulled the small tapes from his eyes. He turned to Alecto and said, "I believe you will find me easier to get along with than you think, and loyal and trustworthy too. And if there is ever anything you want to discuss or confide in with me, I'm prepared to listen. If not I know how to mind my own business."

He detected a slight flicker of surprise in her eyelids.

Chapter Two

Alecto

Central Park. Bors felt more in need of his *accouterments*, his weapons, there than anywhere in New York City. An irrational feeling perhaps, but he hated Central Park as a facade, foisted on the residents of Gotham. A dangerous, dirty, polluted, inorganic, overcrowded imitation of the pristine nature he had known as a child in Montana. Possibly he was wrong, to some degree. Anyway, he also felt like a country clod.

Dereck Bors--once upon a time Uther Pendragon Montgomery--had felt, since an early age, that the spirit of the original Sir Bors de Ganis looked down on him as a guardian angel looks down on a cleric. Therefore the contemporary Bors had to think that he too was a cleric, though of a different and somewhat more malevolent persuasion, and to sundry degrees.

Sir Bors--the only knight to survive the quest for the Holy Grail--was the first of all knights to uphold the code of honor of the

Round Table: to respect ladies, to avoid treason, to defend the rights of the weak, to fight for the sake of one's country, ... Something of an irony that he had picked that alias: he was reasonable with women, avoiding treason was yet to be determined, he was not much concerned with the weak, ... But one thing he was sure of: he would fight for the sake of his country and for the betterment of humanity in general.

Bors had found a park bench with a mostly-open view. He knew Zabov, and Zabov knew him. But Zabov had the advantage. It had come down from Rhamnusia that one of the top disguise artists in the country--who had done work for the CIA--had quit, and was working exclusively for Zabov. An offer the artist couldn't refuse. That meant Zabov could come right next to someone, unrecognized, with anything from a new nose to a completely different face, and you wouldn't know it was new unless you looked at it from two feet away; and no one wanted to get that close to him. Nor would they and live to tell about it if he had it in for them. No wonder Alecto was uneasy.

Bors watched, through the periphery of his vision, a half-dozen teenage boys approach a pretty, young mother who was pushing a baby stroller. As they passed her one of them--an almost-albino with a crew cut--glanced at Bors, nudged the youth next to him, and they both snickered and stared, but they continued walking. Bors pretended to ignore them. He had more to worry about than a bunch of piss-ants. A lot more.

Bors felt a hand on his shoulder and someone shouted in his ear. "Yeow!" He jumped up, twisted in midair, and came down facing Alecto. "Jesus, mother of . . . ! God damn, don't do that to me!" His head throbbed as it always did at such sudden intrusions.

Alecto laughed a genuine laugh; a rarity. "You move like a cat!" she said. "If you were thrown from a three-story rooftop you'd land on your feet. Sorry, but I couldn't help it. It's my nature."

She was officially his permanent partner now, assigned by the higher-ups in Ragnarök, the organization named after the ancient Norse vision of *the final battle*, their Judgment Day.

Bors and Alecto were partners for life: until death, or until they could no longer function; and they had had no choice in the pairing.

"It's my nature to----" But Bors stopped to let his palsied head and hands stop shaking. After a few minutes he continued. "It's my nature to, without stopping to think about it, kill people who do that to me."

"What if I had been Zabov?" Alecto asked, almost gaily. She sat on the bench and patted the place beside her.

Bors glowered at her, but sat down. "If you had been Zabov you would have been dead."

"More likely it would have been you who were dead." Alecto was still smiling. "You say you're a Buddhist at heart, if not in fact or temper, so mellow out. Have you heard the one about the ox and the rooster? A Chinese farmer had taught the ox to pull the plow by himself, and one day as the ox plowed, the rooster, who was sitting on a nearby fence----"

"Cut the crap."

Bors glared at her, then at the teenagers, who had returned and were ogling Alecto as they passed. The first time by they had been an annoyance, but now Bors was surly, and he wished they would start something.

"I must say," Alecto teased, "as a Buddhist you sure have committed yourself to a life of violence. How do you resolve that contradiction?"

"I don't. Suffice to say, nonviolence is in my past, and probably in the past as regards humanity in general. We're reverting to our basic natures."

Several joggers sweated by.

Both he and Alecto were girded. Bors' girding included his leather, Kevlar-layered gloves, with a sprinkling of lead bird shot impregnated over the knuckles and along the knife edge. The *shuto* edge of his hand. He put his left hand over his pants pocket and felt the ninja throwing stars in their Velcro-enclosed pouch; and he put his other hand into his right pocket, down through the open bottom, and grasped the seventeen-inch handle of the telescoping samurai sword strapped to his leg. He had studied the subtle--and often not-so-subtle--art of ninjitsu since college. Kendo and Aikido too, for which he possessed unique mental and physical abilities; he was big, strong, and fast, and he had superb coordination. Alecto had gibed him for his passion, likening him to martial arts movie characters. It was the thing for movie writers and directors to be addicted to hand-to-hand fights, sword fights, and all similar nonsense now in modern times. Pandering to youths and not-so-smart adults. But he had made a concession to her, retiring his puny Colt .25. He now carried a .40 caliber Beretta 96. At almost thirty-five ounces--unloaded, with no accessories--it was big enough to beat people to death with. As good as he was at martial arts, he was a terrible shot, and he had chosen the old Beretta mostly for its heft. Feeling it

hanging heavy in his shoulder holster was a
comfort to him. And there was always the
chance that, with the optional laser pointer, he
could hit something. Regardless, it was
unlikely that he would be involved in anything
like the shootout at OK Corral.

Alecto carried her regular Para-Ordnance
.45, and when they were on especially-
dangerous assignments--like now--she wore her
double-action, .40 caliber, two-shot derringer
high on her inner thigh, tied with cotton string
so she could reach inside her pants and jerk it
loose. She'd have to be close; almost close
enough to put it into someone's mouth. And
she was the kind who would put it into
someone's mouth. He had no doubt of that.

"You're a gem, Bors. When Ragnarök
got you, they got a real diamond. A rough
diamond, but I think you have----"

"Okay," Bors said. Despite his surliness,
he detected a rare compliment. He had
suspected she was gay, but maybe she wasn't
gay after all, though what that had to do with a
compliment was a bizarre thought.

"I've got the rental car," Alecto said,
lowering at the teenagers, who had stopped.

"We're nothing more than slammers,"
Bors grumped.

"Slammers?"

"Back in Al Capone's day the mob muscle men were called slammers."

"Just the other day you were telling me how you liked it that way.   Just do the job, and all that."

The young toughs approached and fanned out.   There were more of them than before and the almost-albino one leered at Alecto.   "How's it goin' pussy?"

Bors didn't wait for any movie-style banter.   He stood, withdrew his black leather-wrapped sword handle, slid off the safety, and pushed the release button.   Two blades shucked out one after the other and snapped into place.   He lowered the tip of the slightly-curved katana to ground level--in salute--then he lifted it over his right shoulder.   Alecto had accused him of using a blunderbuss when he should be using a pump shotgun, but in public how could he start blasting around with a gun; any kind of gun?

The katana wasn't as good as a real, solid katana, and at thirty-six inches it wasn't as long as he would have liked, but he wasn't fighting bandits in the thirteenth century either.   Just young hooligans who may or may not be dangerous, but again, Bors didn't really give a darn.   His black moods came more rarely, but they still came, and when they did he was capable of anything, and right now lopping off an arm or two would be a good start, and he hoped they would stay and put up a fight, but usually punks like them just shit their pants. Or pulled guns, and he would close fast in case they did. He had to go for the one most likely to draw first, and he did; the half albino. Bors knew Alecto had her Para halfway drawn, and she would take care of the rest. Maybe take care of them all. Bors felt the rage wash over him, and his vision narrowed as he rushed forward.

"Holy crap!" one of the youths screeched, and they all ran, scattering in different directions.

Bors chased the albino for a little way-- close in case he started shooting--then he stopped, and again his head hammered. He lowered the katana, hung his head, closed his eyes, and let the blackness fade. He felt Alecto's hand on his shoulder again, hard. He compacted his sword and put it back into it's leather holder on his leg. A small group of people had gathered but they kept their distance, then Bors saw a police officer come running like a Keystone Cop. Bors and Alecto kept their hands in sight and tried to appear composed.

"What's the trouble here?" the officer asked. His hand was on his holster.

Bors worked up a smile. "Bunch of punk kids making trouble." He held the smile.

The officer looked skeptical. He was heavy and ruddy faced. "They said you have a sword!"

"Does it look like I have a sword?"

"No, but----"

"I think they're high on something," Alecto said. "Those kids."

The officer relaxed his arm and called to the group of spectators, "Anybody see this guy with a sword?" One man shook his head, and they began to disperse. Either they thought the troublemakers had gotten exactly what they deserved, or no one wanted to get involved.

"May I?" Bors asked. He slowly lifted his right hand, indicating that he wanted to reach for the inner breast pocket of his jacket.

The officer tensed. "Take it slow," he growled as he put his hand back on his revolver, and this time he flipped loose the restraining strap.

Bors slid his hand under his right lapel and pulled out a card, holding it loosely between his index and middle finger. He held it out. "FBI."

"FBI? The hell?" The officer took the ID and looked at it, then up at Bors, then down, then up again. "Got a badge?"

"Never carry one. That's Hollywood stuff these days. Call the number on the card if you like." There was a Ragnarök member available at the phone just in case.

"Huh." He squinted at Alecto. "Who's she?"

"Just a friend," Bors winked.

The officer's shoulders sagged as he relaxed. "If I call in your name is it gonna check out?"

"Absolutely," Bors answered. "As I said, call if you like."

"Naw, that's okay. I've been on the street long enough to read people. You're okay."

"Built-in lie detector, eh?"

"Yeah. Sixth sense. Some have it and some don't. It's been my experience that most don't."

"Really?"

"Yeah. Well, I suppose you've got enough to do. Be careful out there." He smiled at his allusion. "I've gotta get back to my rounds. I've had trouble with that bunch before. Those *kids* as you call 'em. I call 'em rotten little mother----" He took off his hat and smoothed his thick, black hair straight back. "But whatcha gonna do?"

Bors watched the officer's tired shuffle as he walked away, and he felt Alecto's aura sear his back as she came close behind him.

"That was really great," she said softly. Her voice hissed like like that of an asp, if asps hiss.

Bors' impulse was to turn on her, but he remained still. Alecto further chastised him by her silence as he kept his back to her and waited for his blackness to finish lifting. He closed his eyes and imagined wild Montana prairie flowers; crocuses, sweet peas, bluebells, coneflowers . . . . And prairie roses; his great grandmother's favorite, from her homesteading days. He felt the steady, cool wind in his face, and he could smell the richness of newly-plowed fields, as only someone raised on a farm could----

"You clodhopper," Alecto seethed. "Where did you get that----?"

"I can speak Bumpkinese too." She muttered something unintelligible, then, "Sometimes I think you should have stayed on the farm. Been a farmer. A pig farmer, or a sheepherder."

Warm rage rose on the back of Bors' neck, like the redness in a thermometer. He and Alecto silently fought each other.

Then, "Let's go," Alecto said.

Bors turned, but already she was walking away. He followed, and as they came to the edge of the park she stopped, turned her head to one side, and looked up, as if studying a treetop.

"What?" he asked.

She didn't appear to hear him as she stared upward and turned in a circle, muttering to herself; something about being targeted.

Bors put a hand on her left shoulder--not her right, in case they were in imminent danger--but she shrugged him off roughly.

"Don't do that!"

"What"

"Interfere with me when we are being threatened."

"We're being threatened? I don't see----"

"Of course not." She lowered her upward gaze and frowned at him. "You're new. It takes time."

"But there's no one around, and certainly not up there in the treetops!"

Alecto studied him contemptuously. "Lord do I have my work cut out for me."

"Well I'll give you the benefit of a doubt," Bors responded, "but either me or thee is crazy--as the old philosopher said--and I suspect thee."

She started to say something, but clamped her jaw shut, and Bors saw a tear in one eye. He backed off and tenderly motioned her to follow.

Alecto did follow, meekly, and Bors felt his heart melt. They left the park, and as they did he reconsidered. Was there something to her alarm? Had she been looking for drones or some other deadly weapons?

It was a nice, sunny, warm day, and it would have been much nicer, sunnier, . . . , were it not for their portion.

A drunk approached them for a handout but they ignored him. Next was a poor idiot jabbering to himself or to some invisible being. Both were elderly, filthy, hairy, . . . , and well beyond either physical or mental redemption.

Bors' mind wandered, as it was wont to do, and the two wretches brought to mind a conviction he had come to a few years ago: that how the devil can democracies survive, much less thrive, given voter stupidity? Most people he told that observation to reflexively asked what system is better? He always replied that maybe anything else would be. He didn't believe it, but the looks he got were worth it. Nonetheless he could have suggested a lot of changes. Some qualifications to be met before being allowed to vote. The growth of Ragnarök in itself was evidence of the shallowness of voters; the regular justice system was failing. Impotent. And how could working for the good of humankind be morally depraved?

Bors softened, and indicated for Alecto to sit on a clean patch of grass, which she did. He sat close to her and she didn't recoil.

He began slowly and softly, and approached her from a different conceptual angle, without looking at her.

"You know, for all of my tough talk and my rough appearance and demeanor, I have more private, internal weaknesses than you may assume."

He paused, waiting for a response, but there was none.

"I'm speaking somewhat out of character. Where I grew up men didn't talk the way I'm talking to you. It doesn't come easy; boys-- even girls--were brought up to stifle their most inner feelings."

He elbowed her softly, but there was no response. Some youngsters walked by and he thought he recognized one of the boys from the group of miscreants they had just tangled with, but the kid didn't seem to remember him. Bors peeked at Alecto and she had gone from staring into space to watching a squirrel.

"Now for the real hard part," he began again. "I think I'm starting to like you."

At that, Alecto blinked three or four times and looked down.

"Don't think I'm mocking you or ridiculing you. That's the last thing I would do right now.

Alecto turned on the grass to face him, and she seemed puzzled, yet she remained silent. The squirrel came cautiously toward her.

Bors pressed on. "I want to help, if you ever need help. We have to help each other now that we are bound, and I hope we do so not out of obligation, rather out of respect."

"You're leading up to something," she said softly, "and I think I know what it is."

"Of course you do, but if you want me to stop; to ask later, or never, please say so."

"Go on," she whispered, looking away again.

"Back there, when you were peering up into the trees, or wherever, when you said we were in danger, what was it? Or----"

"It was nothing," she cut in. "I realize that now."

"You just thought----?"

"Yes, but not now. Ask me later." She moved closer and rested her head on his shoulder and closed her eyes.

He did nothing.

Chapter Three

Mark I

Bors had followed Alecto down the long, dark corridor of the abandoned building. It seemed that his eyes hadn't fully adjusted as well as hers so he followed the bob of her blond hair. Then he saw she was guided by a small, round, stained-glass window at the far end of the hall. Behind them were two thugs-- *helpers*--carrying a wooden crate. Inside the crate was Lord Edmund, television evangelist. Edmund had changed his given name from John to Lord.

Bors felt years of filth beneath his shoes as he soft-footed down the hall. Small jobs first, *until he was sure of himself*, he had been told, but it was really until he proved himself. He was as sure of himself as he would ever be, and that surety was certain. He had found his calling, and he knew full well that he would be good at it. He was no wimp, and he had the requisite intelligence and mentality. Although he did feel a slight queasiness of stomach.

They entered a windowless inner room where the thugs dropped the crate and took battery lanterns from their belts. One thug set his lantern on the floor and began removing the lid of the crate with a small pry bar while the other stood with a slight, wide-lipped, crooked-mouth smile, shining his lantern down. The two were rough looking, but not large. Huge only in their shoulders and backs, like fighting bulls.

While the first thug finished removing the lid, Bors and Alecto pulled rubber Halloween masks from their back pockets and put them on. Alecto was a witch; he was a half-human monster with hideous gashes and bloodshot eyes. Then she took two costumes from a small bag. She put on a black cloak and he donned Frankenstein garb. He felt foolish but he contrived to believe she knew what she was doing; presumably that their object would be so stressed that he would succumb to their simple devices.

Bors' eyes had fully accustomed themselves to the gloom and he saw empty wine bottles scattered about, and the room stank of dust and rat droppings. The only indication that the place had been a hotel or apartment building was a closet in the center of the far wall, empty, with the door hanging from one hinge. Not an auspicious start to his career with Ragnarök. He thought back to his grade-school days in Montana; how he had always disliked disorder, chaos, and injustice. And how he had so often been the butt of injustices, like in fourth grade, when John Gear had made a habit of beating him up. Not actually beating him up, but intimidating him through pushing, arm twisting, taunting, ... The usual bully stuff, and how he had been too small to fight back, and too proud to ask for help, which wouldn't have done any good anyway. Now he was on the other end of the stick and he found latent satisfaction in it; a higher-level remediation.

Edmund stood shakily in the crate, like a ludicrous Jack-in-the box, with his hands bound behind his back. The first thug pulled the medical tape from Edmund's mouth.

Lord Edmund was a tall man in, perhaps, his mid fifties; wide in the middle, with narrow shoulders and hips. His almost-black hair was receding in front, but because of his low forehead his balding wasn't all that noticeable. "Who are you?" he asked. "What's going on?"

The thug holding the lantern moved it closer to Edmund's face.

"This is outrageous," Edmund shouted. "I demand to----" The other thug slapped him hard. Not a woman's indignant 1950s B-movie slap after she's been kissed, but a hard, vicious thwack that came close to putting Edmund back down into the crate. The thug slowly put his index finger to his lips.

"If you please, Mr. Edmund," Alecto said, "we'll explain everything. Let me start by reminding you that you have already, a month ago, received Mark I."

"Mark I? You're with Ragnarök? I thought Ragnarök was only a----" The thug whapped him again, harder, and he swayed back and forth, and Bors smelled urine wafting from the crate. Bors' nostrils tightened.

"This is Mark II, Mr. Edmund. You and your fellow con men have bilked your followers out of millions, and now it stops."

"I resent that implication. I run a legitimate ministry----" The thug slapped him again, and his head went back, then he bent forward at the waist and sagged over the edge of the box with blood dripping from one corner of his mouth. He groaned softly, like a small child sitting on a pot.

"Save the crap," Alecto rumbled quietly. "You've been fleecing your flocks for years. Retirees, widows, the infirm, the feeble-minded . . . . Now, you will stop." She let her admonition soak in for a minute, then, "Will," she repeated sternly.

In the short time Bors had been assigned to work with Alecto he had learned only one significant characteristic; she meant every word she uttered, and she didn't waste words. In her case his man's instinct had utterly failed him, and all he could ascertain was external, like her shortness with him, and her seeming disdain for humanity in general. And, uniquely, her almost phenomenal strength. Once she had come up behind him and had tried to lift him off his feet by his belt. If he had weighed less than his two-hundred twenty pounds she would have succeeded. Seemingly she had wanted to make a point with her monster wedgie, which point evidently had something to do with him singing falsetto for the rest of his life. But after she had made whatever forceful signification she had intended, she relented--to a degree--as perhaps a master violinist who first breaks a beginning student of all bad habits; then, when the breaking is complete, reluctantly allows the student some modest hope.

"You will," Alecto intoned, "announce your retirement from the ministry." Edmund straightened up. His mouth started to move, but he stopped it, and kept quiet. "You will dissolve your ministerial organization, and all of its tentacles, and you will donate all money and assets--except for fifty thousand dollars, which you may keep--to the American Red Cross."

Edmund was again upright, and silent.
He seemed to be trying to glare, but Bors saw a
tear in the outer corner of one eye, and his jaw
quivered.

"In case you are tempted to cheat we will
know, and your attempt will automatically incur
Mark III.   Though we are fully aware that you
are by nature perfidious, believe me when I say
you do not want Mark III.   You will wrestle
with your greed, lust, and immorality, and you
will win, or you will face the unimaginable."

She spoke the last measuredly, and Bors
would have thought it an affectation were she
not so deadly serious.

Edmund looked surreptitiously around the
room, at the litter on the floor, the loose,
hanging plaster on the walls, and all of the rest.

"Take a good look, Mr. Edmund," Alecto
said, almost pleasantly.   "When you're through
please kneel."

Edmond stopped looking and grimaced at
Alecto.   Thug number two tore off a piece of
tape and slapped it roughly over Edmund's
mouth.

Edmund's eyes flashed in the darkness,
and he remained standing.   Alecto slowly
reached out her arm, pointed between his eyes,
then gracefully she bent her wrist downward.
Bors was sure she was smiling behind her mask.

"We shall see," she murmured.   "We shall see."
Still he stood.

One of the helpers moved behind Edmond
and put one hand over his eyes while holding
him tightly with the other arm.   The second
man came in front and pressed something with
two probes to Edmond's privates, and he let out
a long, screeching, horrible, unearthly howl for
a full ten seconds.

Bors felt faint.

Edmund sank slowly into the crate.

After the thugs had left carrying the crate,
Alecto lingered.   It was the first time she had
wanted to talk, or maybe she wanted something
else.   "You okay?"

"Who were your friends," Bors asked,
referring to the two thugs.

She shrugged.   "Our higher-ups provide
them."

"Aren't they a security problem?"

"They're well paid, and they know that if
they ever betray us----"   Alecto's hand brushed
the pistol under her shirt, perhaps
unconsciously.   "Not what you expected?" she
asked.

"If that was Mark II I'd hate think what
Mark III is.   I thought Mark II was just a
personal admonishment."

They both took off their masks.

"We have some latitude. Occasionally a little extra emphasis is required. All part of the dirty work." She pulled a penlight from her shirt pocket, and from the other pocket she took a package of cigarettes. She put one of the cigarettes in her mouth and returned the package to her pocket.

Bors felt his cheek muscles tighten as they always did when he was irritated. "I didn't leave the CIA because I couldn't stand the----"

"I know. You were booted."

"I keep telling you I didn't quit because----" He stopped and waited for Alecto to take out her matches, but she only toyed with her cigarette, licking it, and rolling it in her mouth, smiling. "You have it backward," Bors said. "I wasn't afraid of *dirty work*, as you put it. I felt compelled."

Bors' mind drifted. He was compelled to transform chaos onto order. A diagnosed obsessive-compulsive. Not perpetual hand washing, or checking to see if he had left his kitchen stove on, but obsessed with societal integrity. He had been cursed, but, like many obsessive-compulsives, the curse wasn't the compulsion itself; rather the realization of the full implications of it. Moreover, through the course of his life he had been an observer, of himself, and of everything external. The degree varied. Sometimes he hovered directly overhead; sometimes he was on a cloud, looking down. And at times he floated in space, and he could see the universe. And he was always aware. The only times he wasn't aware was when he was drinking, and he had quit drinking. Mostly.

Alecto spat a shred of tobacco on the floor, and continued toying with her cigarette. She spat like a man.

"I don't have any matches," Bors said.

"I don't smoke. I quit five years ago."

"That's when I---- Then why are you licking on that cigarette?"

Alecto held the cigarette sideways and ran her tongue along it teasingly, but she didn't answer.

The stench of the place had been overwhelming, but as Bors regarded Alecto his sense of smell adapted, and he detected some new odors. Alecto had put away her penlight, and the only luminescence came dimly down the hall from outer rooms. Bors halfway expected bats, and he listened for their rustle.

"What about Edmund?" Bors asked. "Have you been at this long enough to have a feeling for what he'll do?" He was as much interested in finding out how long Alecto had been at it as he was in what Edmund would do.

Not long, he guessed, or she'd be higher up in Ragnarök.

"We'll see Edmund again," Alecto said.

"Even after he peed his pants?"

"Even after. It happens all the time. Some of them are like monkeys. It's said that natives in the Amazon jungle used to put treats in clear bottles and tie the bottles high in trees. Monkeys would reach in and grab a handful of nuts, or whatever. They couldn't get their hands out unless they let go of the nuts, and they wouldn't let go, even as they were being captured. I don't know if that's true, but I think it is."

Bors didn't want to leave. "Seems to me Lord Edmund is small potatoes. How far will he take us? Surely not Mark IV?"

"Perhaps. Don't underestimate human greed. And most of them think we're simply humbugging them."

"Despite all of the notoriety Ragnarök has achieved?"

"Yes."

Bors considered for a moment, then, "Have you been in on any Mark IVs?"

Alecto crushed her cigarette and threw it on the floor. "One," she said. "A mobster. Two months ago."

"Any Mark Vs?"

"One. He died of natural causes." She smiled wryly.

"I never heard anything about that."

"We don't talk about them."

"Why not?"

The question seemed to surprise her. "I don't know."

When they were back outside the building Bors saw relief on Alecto's face. Up until then, for as long as he had known her, she had been unreadable, except for her lapse in the park when she had seen something invisible. Nonexistent most likely, and he would, when the time was right, press her on that. There was much more to her than her cold bearing revealed. She was tough, but there was an inner weakness.

Chapter Four

Continuation

"Tar and feather?" Bors scoffed. "You want us to tar and feather the sonofabitch? What's his name? Langtree? They actually want us to tar and feather a corporate crook? Hell, there are so many corporate and political crooks we'll run out of tar! We don't have the manpower. What in the---?"

"You're ranting," Rhamnusia said quietly across the table. She threw a worried look around the restaurant. "Will you please rant quietly? And we have women power. And we're growing. Women, that is."

Alecto smiled at both Bors' and Rhamnusia's discomfort.

They were in a little place called *The Restaurant II* or something on 43rd Street. It reminded Bors of the restaurant on the old Seinfeld television show, but it was untidy; crumbs on the floor, half-clean tables, dirty windows, ...

Bors clamped his mouth shut and glared down into his coffee cup. The waitress came

for their orders, eyeing him and smiling in the
way women had always smiled at him. She
was blond and not-so-bad looking in her short,
white skirt and a starched, too-tight red blouse.
She would have been better looking were it not
for the large wart on her chin. She took out her
pad and pencil. Bors looked into his cup again.

"Hamburger and cheese, small fries,
small diet cola," Rhamnusia said.

"Same," Alecto said.

The waitress looked at Bors. "Nothing,
thanks," Bors mumbled. She hurried away.

Though he was looking down, Bors could
see Rhamnusia studying him, and he grudgingly
admitted that she had class. She had never
come on to him in any overt way, and he didn't
think she ever would. She was the kind who
would never demean herself, and he admired
her for it. And lord she was elegant. She
could have been a fashion model if she had
been vain. Or a movie actress. Plus she had
an hour-glass figure that set the standard for
hour-glass figures.

An old man in a gray sweatsuit, smelling
of body odor and urine, passed their table in a
trance. He staggered toward the counter and
managed to climb onto one of the stools. He
was a dieter's delight; anyone would lose their
appetite around him. Someone should bottle

the odor and sell it to obese people to dab on their cheeks morning and evening.

Bors felt Alecto's leg brush his and it was electric. She must have felt it too, because she flinched almost imperceptibly and drew away. Rhamnusia sensed something and seemed amused, but there was a hint of something else beneath the mask of her smile.

"You should know," Rhamnusia began softly, "that tarring and feathering is not the comical, cartoon-like punishment you may think it is. Back in antebellum days--and later--down south, tarring and feathering was one of the most severe forms of punishments that could be meted out. People sometimes died from it. The tarring was bad enough, but usually they'd have to ride the rail too. Can you imagine being tied to a split-rail and left there? The rail was wedge-shaped, and the more you squirmed, the deeper it---- Well, you get the idea. So when you start bellyaching about how we're going soft, keep that in mind."

"Why us?" Bors grumbled. Still he refused to look up.

"Quit pouting," Alecto said.

"Because Langtree has a vacation home in Montana," Rhamnusia answered. "More like a vacation mansion, up in the mountains west of Livingston. And he's there now, with his girlfriend. He and his wife are having problems." She picked up a French fry and bit off the end. "And I hear they still have rail fences out there," she added, talking and chewing. She leaned her head sideways with her ear almost to the table, and winked up at Bors. "John Langtree, CEO of Langtree Mining Associates," she whispered. "Mark II."

———————

Bors turned off the interstate on the east edge of Livingston. He hadn't been there in a long time. When he got downtown he turned left, then right onto Callender Street, and Alecto seemed intrigued by the old-west style brick buildings. He assumed she hadn't been out west before, from the way she had been taking everything in since they had crossed the Mississippi River.

Ragnarök had provided them with a 1989 Ford Econoline; a big, gas-guzzling E-150, but it was in good shape and it couldn't be traced. Fake Montana plates and registration, fake insurance slip, fake driver's licenses and social security cards for both of them, fake everything. They'd even changed the vehicle serial numbers. Montana everything because if worst came to worst and they did get pulled over their chances were better than with out-of-state plates and documentation.   They were John K. and Sarah M. Merryfellow from Billings.

"Where are the cowboys and Indians?" Alecto asked.

Bors couldn't tell if she was serious, but he guessed she was.

"There aren't any cowboys anymore. The only ones left just think they are.   The whole cowboy thing lasted only a few decades in the late 1800s, and from then on it's been mostly a big myth.   And the Indians are another story.   Tell you about them sometime. Better yet, take you to one of the reservations, and you can see for yourself.   It's not pretty, and it's getting worse.   It was genocide."

Bors stopped at a red light and a long-skirted artsy-craftsy lady crossed in front of them.   She was in her mid thirties, wearing gaudy 1950s western movie clothes; the kind that get you laughed at behind your back by the locals.   Movie stars and such sometimes came there to live part time, and reportedly people who had to escape from something for one reason or another lived there full time.

Alecto chuckled at the lady.   "That's even too much for me."

Bors started across the intersection.   He and Alecto had been sleeping in the back of the van for security reasons.   Less of a trail to follow.   They would just pull into a secluded place. One night he had woke up with his arm across her, and--god dammit anyway--for some reason he'd left it there. After a while he realized she was awake, so he pretended like he was tossing and turning in his sleep and rolled over the other way. They both knew he was full of it. What was the matter with him? They were getting along better though. She had confided to him her vision as they had been leaving Central Park. She had called it her *reverie*, and she had hinted that it came infrequently. Her admission had disconcerted him. *Some reverie* he had thought.

Langtree Mining Associates had very little to do with mining; still Bors was queasy about their mission. Probably their object would survive the Mark II, but----

"You have everything?" Alecto asked.

"Yeah."

They had parked their van in a secluded area a half mile away from Langtree's country home. Outsiders usually went for log homes.

"Tar?"

Bors looked at her wryly. "That's what we came here for isn't it?"

"Rope? Pulley?"

Bors didn't answer. Now she was needling him.

"Where did you get the feathers?" she asked.

"Cheap pillow," he growled. "Let's unload, then go to town."

They hid their equipment nearby.

They parked in front of a bar and waited for Langtree's girlfriend; an attractive blond. A California type who stood out from the locals like an orangutan would have.

They got out of the van and stood leaning against it while pretending to talk to each other. After a few minutes Bors tried to draw Alecto into a genuine conversation but she was noncommittal and only gave vague answers to his questions.

They knew the lady's habits, and in a few minutes she came out of a store and approached them, and when she was near Bors put his arm tightly around her waist and clamped his right hand over her mouth. Alecto jabbed a hypodermic needle into her left buttock, and during the brief struggle Alecto poured whiskey over her and put the half-empty bottle into one of her hands. Their victim grew weak and quiet, and instinctively held onto the neck of the bottle.

An elderly lady appeared.

"A little too much to drink," Bors chuckled. They hustled their mark into their van and drove off.

They parked back in the mountains where they had left their paraphernalia, and they dragged their *drunk* up the hill and out of sight into the trees.   Alecto gave her another shot, and this time their captive passed out completely.   Then they removed her clothes and tied her to a tree with a synthetic rope and a Gordian-like knot that would require much time to untie.

Alecto threw the clothes far away.   "Nice body, eh Bors?"

"I can only imagine that she looks a lot like you.   I hope she isn't eaten by bears."

"Wouldn't you like to know?   I'm better, and I'm too tough to be bear meat."

Alecto produced a can of bear repellent and sprayed it about liberally, then she threw the can close to the unfortunate nude.

"She'll be here for quite a while," Alecto murmured dispassionately.

Alecto had disabled John Langtree's motion detectors and video cameras.   That was one of her many specialties.

When Langtree came out to see what was wrong the jig was up.   Bors and Alecto, in Halloween face masks, gave him the needle, then hauled him to a part of the rail fence beneath a large tree.

"I'll cut off his clothes; you get the tar," Alecto ordered.

"It's actually roof coating that I thinned down to make the painting easier."

"Um."

She climbed the tree with the end of a rope and a pulley, then she descended and tied the rope around Langtree's chest.

Langtree was tall and extremely thin for his height, with almost no body hair. He had a full head of hair, and his facial features were like those of a hawk. He was uncommonly pale.

Bors returned. "Let the tarring begin."

They hoisted Langtree to a standing position and Alecto started painting, and Bors noticed that she spent extra time on his privates. Then Bors applied the feathers. Job complete, they swung Langtree onto the rail. Bors tied his ankles together so that, hands free, he would still have to work a long time to get loose. A long, uncomfortable time. Then all they had to do was wait until he revived and was able to maintain his balance so they could untie the rope from his chest. They would hang a *Mark II* sign on his neck, and would take photos.

Bors motioned Alecto to the shade of a nearby tree and they sat down to wait.

Bors leaned back against the trunk of the tree with his fingers clasped behind his head. "Ahh, it's beautiful here isn't it?"

"Would you like to live here? When they retire you?"

"I don't know. Would you?"

"I don't know either. That seems like so far off, and a lot can happen to us in the meantime."

"My relatives were all Norwegians so you'd think they would have come here to the mountains, but they went to the dry high prairie of the northeastern part of the state. I guess, despite my miserable childhood, I'm still a flatlander."

"Miserable childhood? What happened?"

"Oh, never mind. I'm not a crybaby and I only mentioned it in passing in regard to my still feeling like a flatlander."

She had seldom asked him about anything personal.

On their way back to New York Bors looked longingly northward as they passed through the prairie of northeastern Montana. His childhood home--the ruins of it--were only about seventy-five miles to the north, not far as distances up there went, and he would have detoured if he had been alone. Memories, some good, many disturbing, and a few terrible, but they were the only childhood memories he had, so he had to live with them for the rest of his life and make the best of them. He was not at all a revisionist, as many people are, and no way could he twist reality--especially past reality--into anything better. He was a total realist, unable to re-jigger reality. Not a overly optimistic realist either.

"You keep looking over there," Alecto observed, indicating north. "What are you thinking?"

Bors remained silent as he decided how to answer.

"That's where I grew up, on a farm up that way," he pointed with his thumb. "Not so far from Canada."

"Not a nice *Little House on the Prairie* childhood you said?"

Bors hesitated. "No. Quite the opposite. I'll tell you about it sometime when I've had a few drinks."

"You don't drink anymore."

"If I hang around you much longer I'll probably start again," he laughed, looking at her and half expecting to be pummeled, but she smiled back at him and he was taken by the genuineness of her smile.

Chapter Five

Paranoia

As they left Central Park, Alecto nudged Bors with her elbow. "Back there, to your right, under the tree. The big, seedy-looking guy with the umbrella."

"Another of your paranoid----?"

She grabbed his upper arm and squeezed, hard, with her incredible strength. "John Drake."

"The FBI man assigned to us?"

"Yes."

Bors stopped and stood on one leg, pretending to see if something was stuck to his shoe. Even from a hundred yards away he could see that Drake was well past middle age, and soft. Big, pale, and flabby.

"He was a lion once, I'm told," Alecto said. "Now he's an old lion, and the feeling is that the FBI higher ups assigned him to glorified patrol duty in order to get him out of their way.

"The feeling?"

"Rhamnusia told me. Still, Drake--old lion or not--will bite your head off if you stick it in his mouth."

"Um."

Alecto stopped. "I thought I saw Zabov back there. Back where you were waving your sword around that time."

Her eyes were wider than normal, and Bors saw she was spooked and her behavior unnerved him. He had begun to think she had a sixth sense, but the hell of it was that he could never be sure if her instincts were right or if she was going off into one of her paranoiac episodes . He instinctively put his hand into his pocket and felt the handle of his sword.

"I didn't tell you all of it," Alecto said. "All about Zabov and his methods. Remember, I told you about his zip gun? Not like shotgun-shell pipes the youth gangs in the '50s used to carry, but a small metal tube with a CO_2-powered dart gun built into the handle of his umbrella, and it's even worse than the----"

"Poisoned darts?"

"Yeah, but what makes them so terrible is that they have barbs all along, like fish hooks, and the darts keep working their way in deeper."

"Holy crap!"

"That's not all. After a few minutes there's a tiny, time-delayed charge which pushes out the back like a rocket engine, forcing it in even deeper."

Bors felt his knees weaken. "How do you know all that?"

"They did an autopsy on one of our people. A plug in the back end of the dart dissolves, the charge----"

"All right! I get it!"

"You asked. No matter how we feel about each other, we have to work together," Alecto said, and for the first time she was almost pleading.

"Actually I feel good working with you," Bors said. "I thought we've moved past that. I like you, and if you have any other concerns now's the time to----"

But again Alecto was staring off into the distance: a distance apparently of her mind. This time she didn't say anything, though her lips moved ever so delicately. They walked, and after a while Bors pulled her into the shade of a building."

"You alright?"

"Yes. Merely a slight lapse. Forget it."

"I must say, you have a way about you that's tough to understand," Bors said.

"I've been at this for a long time. Well actually only a few years, but in this line of work that's a long time and it can wear on you."

"I always thought that whatever doesn't kill you makes you stronger."

"Bull. I wouldn't have thought you were open to spouting such humbuggery." Her voice dripped with disappointment.

"I'm not. I'm merely trying to lighten our load."

"Well hold your tongue; it isn't working."

They walked for several more blocks without talking, then Alecto stopped and backed against the brick front of a jewelry store, next to the display window. Strauss & Brick Jewelry. Inside, a man with pince-nez glasses and a dark-blue business suit was dusting around the diamond wedding rings. Apparently he felt obligated to play the part of a jeweler, Bors thought. Maybe the man was Strauss himself. Or Brick. Probably not, but everybody has to play their part in life.

"We're doing a Mark IV," Alecto purred, almost growled. She was apparently regaining her equilibrium and she sounded not like a kitten, but like a tomcat. "This *jeweler* is one of our victim's main contacts."

Bors' back muscles tightened.

"And you're the designated fiend. That's why I had you bring your sword."

"So that's why you've been so----"

"Yeah."

"Who?" Bors croaked.

"Korean drug dealer. He's been in this country for ten years. Deals in everything. Runs a mob called *Kud*, which is the Korean personification of darkness and evil."

"What's his name?"

"Shinn. That's his last name. In Korean, last names come first."

"I know. What else about him?"

"Nothing. What's the difference?" Alecto asked. "Were you planning on asking about his wife and kids, and how the Korean soccer team is doing?"

Bors tried to relax the cramp in his gut. Thank goodness he didn't have to actually kill the guy. He had only killed one person, and that had been hand-to-hand self defense in a bar in Montana, back in his drinking days. An equally-drunk cowboy had pulled a foot-and-a-half long Bowie knife on him, and had wound up with it sticking out of his own chest. Bors had felt no remorse whatsoever, and he still didn't. There are some black-and-whites in life. Withal, his stomach hurt.

"And all you want me to do it is wave my katana around?"

"If it were up to me we would go all the way, but they only want you scare the crap out of him."

"How did *they* know about my sword in the first place?"

"Ragnarök sees all and knows all," Alecto said.

"Apparently. Christ."

Bors wished he had a real, one-piece katana. He had always guessed that this kind of assignment would come, and he had prepared by practicing on hams. His regular katana had done the job, going through the bone like it was nothing. The telescoping katana had gone only halfway through, and though the result wasn't pretty, the second ham was just as dead as the first one. Well, he wasn't supposed to kill Shinn anyway, but a real katana would make a better impression.

"If it makes you feel any better, this Shinn is the worst of the worst."

"Thanks. Clichés like that make me feel much better."

"I thought you wanted action. You've been crabbing for weeks about not doing anything. Won't you feel satisfaction about giving this asshole----?"

"All the same wish I had my regular katana. Maybe I could put it in a cello case and----"

"No time. Jesus mother of God, Bors, where are your balls? Whichever you use just touch him up good. It's a Mark IV, remember?"

"Terrific."

The jeweler in the window was eyeing them with either curiosity or suspicion.

Alecto continued. "He's studying us. He's our pathway to Shinn. Pretend like we're having an argument." She threw up her hands and waved them. "If anybody deserves Mark IV, it's Shinn. His organization is small compared to some, but he's the most ruthless. He maims, tortures, rapes, and kills; and I'm told he delights in it. Tough, too. The report I got said he took his Mark III without as much as a wince. They did about everything to him they could without killing him--including breaking both of his legs--and it was almost like he kept asking for more. How do you figure?"

"Yeah. Still----"

"You didn't join Ragnarök just to twist arms and give people black eyes did you? You knew from the start that we meant business. We're idealists working for a better world, and this is the only way to do it. You like cliches? Here's another one: fight fire with fire. Want another? If you can't stand the heat, get out of the kitchen. Or how about----?"

"All right! Quit preaching!" Alecto had taken on the musky smell that Bors now knew came when she was nervous.

She softened just perceptibly. "I know we'll face Shinn again and it'll be daunting, but we'll have to have faith in each other, as though my hands will be on the katana along with yours. We have to be . . . , what . . . , I can't think of the word."

"Soulmates."

"I guess. You have a peculiar, old-fashioned vocabulary, Bors, but yes. Soulmates, who share an intimacy beyond any physical bond. I'll be with you, always. You must trust me."

Bors was taken by surprise. "I do trust you," he said, "but you're so up and down with me. Let's not bring it up again. Maybe you'll level off eventually. I hope you're not bipolar."

"Try to calm down."

They walked for a long time, turning corners this way and that, and going in and out of stores; and all the time they did so Bors remained perplexed at Alecto's soulmate comment. And about the efficacy of dealing with Shinn.

As they came out onto the street from a drugstore, Bors knew the answer, but he had to ask. "But again, what good will it do to maim Shinn? You just said he withstood a severe Mark III."

Alecto answered immediately, like she had been expecting the question. "And again, you can ask that of any assignment we get. What good does it do? The answer is, it's a start.   Ragnarök is still fairly new and we must start somewhere, so we choose carefully.   We impart a message on all those who think they're above the law; who don't give a damn about the law.   But really, it isn't about the law, it's about morality.   We enforce human morality, and try to advance civilization."

"Our morality."

"No, common-good morality.   There's common-good morality, and there's immorality."   Alecto walked faster, weaving through the lunch-hour crowd.   Snaking through.   "You have to work harder at being a pragmatist, Bors.   If you try hard enough you can see things in black and white.   Stop all of the oriental *something for nothing*--seeing things as wholes--bullshit."

Bors stepped over a lump of dog shit. "Who are our goons this time?   The same two who delivered Lord Edmund?   And, for God's sake, the same place?"

"A bluff.   They won't suspect that we'll go to the same place.   And, no, not the same two.   A different two.   Shinn killed the first two when they tried to pick him up this time."

Alecto slowed as they approached the tenement, and Bors saw her eyes flicker from side to side behind her sunglasses while she held her head still.   She was looking for Zabov.

She shrugged one shoulder. "And what's the difference who the pickup men are? The less we know the----"

"Yeah, yeah, the less we know, the less we can tell." A fire truck wailed in the distance, and Bors started. He hated fire trucks, but he didn't know why. He reached into his bottomless pocket and felt his sword handle again.

"That sword is like a barometer," Alecto said. She was holding her breath and talking through clenched teeth as she sometimes did. "The more you reach for it, the bigger the storm. Or are you playing with yourself again?"

The fire truck noise faded and Bors tried to collect himself. Alecto's nervousness wasn't helping. She was usually edgy, but not this edgy. He noticed her right hand cross in front of her and feel her automatic through the thin cotton of her jacket.

"Now you're doing it," Bors winked.

"They'll leave him tied up in the same room as before," Alecto whispered. She had leaned close and her breath was sour. "You go in and see if he's there, and I'll keep walking, then I'll disappear and double back to make sure no one follows you in."

"How about you going in first?" Bors tried to joke.

"Coward."

"All right, but don't dawdle."

"I don't feel good about this," Alecto whispered. "Let's do it fast."

"You never feel good about anything," Bors said. "But neither do I."

He watched as Alecto continued down the sidewalk, then he lit one of her cigarettes to give himself a chance to look around before entering the building. He didn't smoke, but he made himself inhale deeply and blow a large cloud of smoke out through both his mouth and his nostrils. Most television and movie actors these days were obviously nonsmokers; they didn't inhale. Unwilling to make the necessary sacrifices for their trade.

When Bors glanced back in Alecto's direction she was gone. He took out the key Alecto had given him and tried to look casual as he entered the tenement. He closed the door behind him, locked it, turned, and wished he had time to let his eyes adjust to the darkness. He waited for only a few seconds, leaning back against the door, then he felt his way down the hall toward the glow of a the small stained-glass window at the far end. Shinn would be in the fourth room on the right. Bors reached out and ran his fingertips along the wall as he walked, across the open doorway of the first room, along the plaster again, then past the second doorway. His eyes were working better. Not good, but better. If he could have waited for fifteen minutes, he would have felt better.

Bors came to door three, stopped, and sensed the emptiness. He took a deep breath and continued. Then he paused and looked down at the glow coming from under door four. He put his hand on his katana and waited for Alecto. He could hear nothing except his own slow, deep breath, then his nervousness disappeared, and he didn't care. He would do it fast, but not because of any anxiety or misgiving. Simply because one should do things like this fast and efficiently.

The ever-present rat-shit smell-- complimented by mouse shit--was worse than usual. It reminded Bors of the outbuildings back on the farm, though there weren't many rats in northeastern Montana. A few stray Norway rats once in a while, but most of the rats were human. A hell of a lot of mice however, and he had become a connoisseur of *mouse dirt*--as his mother had called it--from cleaning sheds and granaries. Should have caught hantavirus, but nobody had even heard of it back then. One of the hazards of farming. The many hazards; it was the most dangerous occupation in the country. Either that or coal mining; it seemed like the two alternated for the top spot, depending on which survey you read.

Sure, there were worse, Bors supposed. Being a demolitions expert, or a mountaineer, or something like that. But what he was doing had to be right at the top. Dangerous for him and Alecto, and for the muscle men. Muscle was easy to find, but there weren't many like himself and Alecto.

Where the hell was Alecto? Bors leaned his right shoulder against the wall and wondered at how he could have been transformed so quickly--from uneasy to eager--in the short time since he had entered the building? A metamorphosis that had as its basis his obsessive-compulsive nature. He wondered not at his nature, but at how precipitously the change had enveloped him.

Then, down the hall, Bors heard the front door shut, and he would take some smug satisfaction in seeing Alecto when she couldn't see him. He listened for her footsteps, but she was quiet, and he saw her before he heard her.

"Here," Bors whispered, and she stopped and tensed, focusing on him vaguely.

"Everything okay?" she whispered back.

"Yeah."

"Sure you're alright?"

"Yes." And in her face he saw the reflection of his eager mood.

Bors stood straight, brushed a cobweb from his hair, took out his katana, and schucked it out. He nodded, and Alecto went first. She opened the door carefully and quietly.

Shinn sat tied to a large chair, and the chair was nailed to the floor. Bors hoped it was Shinn; there was a black hood over the man's head. If it wasn't Shinn, whoever it was was in for a big a surprise. There was an old-fashioned coal-oil lantern in one of the far corners. Next to the lantern was a small black, lacquered, wooden box with the lid open and a padlock hanging from the clasp. The box was empty. What was it for? A hand, or some other body part?

Alecto moved to the other far corner and stood rigidly with her arms down and her hands folded in front of her crotch, like she was praying, but her eyes were open, glowing in the lantern light.

Shinn, who had twitched ever so slightly when they entered, sat still. Bors wondered how they had ever gotten him there. Persistence, he guessed.

The lantern flickered. Suddenly Bors moved behind Shinn, extended his katana to his right side, and swung. Shinn's head rolled across the floor toward the black box, and blood pumped straight up from his neck. Bors flashed back at the smell of blood, and recalled when he used to help butcher cows on the farm; and now, how the blood smelled like cow

blood. It had been easier than with the ham.
He must have hit between the vertebrae,
because the cut was clean.

Alecto floated silently across the room
and lifted the hood by its drawstrings, pulling
them tight. She had on latex gloves. She
delicately dropped the head into the black box,
took off her gloves, and closed the lid. She
locked the padlock and threw the small key into
the garbage in the corner where she had been
standing. Then she stood, turned, and regarded
Bors.

He stood. He was strong now.

Alecto remained silent, not looking at
Shinn, whose body had stopped convulsing.

Bors glanced at the blood on his katana,
then around the room for something to wipe it
with. There was nothing, so he wiped it on
Shinn's shirt; one side on his right upper arm;
the other side on the other arm. Bors collapsed
his sword and put it back in its sheath.

"Fuck!" Alecto barked. "You did a Mark
V!"

"I couldn't help it. Besides, what was the
box for?"

"A hand, testicles, something. Not his
head for chrissake!"

She vomited delicately, went to the
lantern and blew it out, then crossed to the door.

"Aren't you taking the box?" Bors asked.

"Our helpers will make the delivery."

"To Kud?"

She nodded. "You're going to have some explaining to do."

Bors kept his jaw clenched. He didn't need censure; not when he was flying on wings of righteousness. Maybe when he came down, but not now, and not from her. He looked back at what was left of Shinn, and it didn't matter that there would be a replacement by tomorrow. What mattered was now. The present.

"The body?" Bors asked. "What are they going to do with that?"

"Who the hell cares?" Alecto walked away, down the hall.

Chapter Six

Disinclined partners

Bors and Alecto--again more or less disinclined partners--sat across from Rhamnusia in a booth in a busy sandwich shop in upper Manhattan. More of an upscale restaurant than a sandwich shop, it was new. The owner had tried, somewhat successfully, to imitate 1950s decor. A row of red booths lined the windowed street side, and opposite the windows was the obligatory red counter with chrome trim. In front of the counter were twenty red, chrome-legged stools. Bors had counted them. He wasn't the counting type of compulsive, but he had counted them. The main area of the restaurant was filled with small, round tables-- also red--and there was a large Rock-Ola Bubbler jukebox against the far wall. It wasn't playing, but it was bubbling.

Bors noted that Alecto was in one of her moods. Her aloof moods came infrequently now, but when they did she was glacial, like when he had first met her. He had never been put off by a woman before, except when he had tried too hard, of course, and he had learned not to try too hard. But, though he could never be sure, this time Bors felt that in the main Alecto's disinclination wasn't directed at him.

Ebony-haired Rhamnusia, on the other hand, was open. While Bors' confidence had failed him in regard to Alecto, he was in his comfort zone with Rhamnusia. He was sure he was still reading her correctly.

"Mayo," Rhamnusia said, holding up her plain, sliced-beef and cheese sandwich. "I don't like mayonnaise, but I can't stop eating it."

She shook her head and smiled, and Bors dutifully smiled back. Alecto sipped her tea and looked vaguely out the window at a stalled taxi. So far it had been all small talk, except for Alecto, who had said nothing at all to them, only to the waitress.

"First," Rhamnusia's face darkened and she lowered her voice, "Mr. Bors, don't ever fail to follow orders again. If you do, you yourself might be headless. You, as punishment, have been given a Mark I. The higher-ups mete out the same punishment to us as to our, eh, victims, but sometimes there is no intermediate. The next step could be Mark V."

Bors saw his face blanch in the mirror behind her. "Mother of----"

"Not by my doing," Rhamnusia continued. "I want you to know that. I could have--at great personal risk--refused to pass on the order, but the order would have been carried out one way or another, and your head might have been in a box before sundown the next day. And I would have been in deep doo-doo as well."

A tough-looking mobster type--dark haired, with a twisted mouth--walked past their booth, and Bors cringed slightly within. He could have been just a regular dufus, but the way he walked--with confidence and looking at no one--had made Bors edgy.

"Ragnarök maintains control of us in the same way they control their outside targets. Remember that."

"How could I forget?" Bors rumbled. "Off with his head."

"Not always. They have a perverse way of fitting the punishment to the misconduct. Say you emasculated someone without orders. You could expect the same for yourself."

They sat quietly for several minutes and Bors felt like a pouting child. "You once said that joining Ragnarök is like becoming a 14th-century nun," he maundered. "In my case like joining a monastery."

They were quiet again for quite a while.

Then Rhamnusia's dark complexion darkened even more, and her voice was almost inaudible. "I'm sure you have heard over the

years of the rumored corruption of Maryland
Senator Desmond Pennington?"

"Rumored?" Alecto rumbled. "He's the
biggest crook in congress. Opposes campaign
reform. Champion of tax breaks for the
wealthy. Uses government and religion as
tools of repression. He has ties to the----"

"Yes, we could go on all day,"
Rhamnusia cut in, looking around
apprehensively, but no one was listening. "The
epitome of corruption. So base as to be the
embodiment of philosophical and religious
imposition. An ideological con man. One of
the morally depraved and corrupt politicians,
industrialists, millionaires, and Washington
insiders who are part of the private and political
power structure who formed Scorpion."

"We *could* go on all day," Alecto spoke
sarcastically, "but why go after Pennington?
Why not target Scorpion's kingpin, Demetrius
Eppers?"

Rhamnusia leaned back and smiled
resignedly. "How would I know?" She put
both hands--palms down with fingers spread--
on the table as if she were getting ready to play
the piano. "I can only assume that Z wants to
reach Eppers through Pennington."

"Eppers is the root," Alecto said through
the rising noise level. "He should be our
immediate concern. He's the one we're looking

over our shoulder for every day. He and Zabov."

Zabov. Bors had worked against him back in his CIA days. He had only seen him twice, from a distance, but he knew Zabov's reputation, and he had seen firsthand his work in the form of dead CIA agents. Not just killed, but destroyed. With Zabov, you either won big, or you lost big, and so far no one had won. There had been one draw.

Bors breathed deeply. "A United States senator? You can't just go after a U.S. senator like that. Start bumping off members of our elected democracy. That's going too far."

Rhamnusia shrugged at them. "You two. You always question. Always heeing and hawing." She slowly shook her head, and the Rock-Ola began playing *Blue Suede Shoes*; not the original by Carl Perkins, but the knock-off by Elvis. "Number one, we didn't *just start*. Two, mediocre politicians are elected by, at best, mediocre voters; and I must say calling the average voter mediocre is like gilding a skunk. And number three Bors, you can't be so dull that you don't know our governments--federal, state, local--from the top down are working under great disadvantages. Handicaps in the form of corruption, rules, outmoded regulations and laws, a now-peculiar constitution that, like The Ten Commandments--or the Bible itself--is in large part irrelevant in our age. How can any government fight the ills of the country and the world with one hand behind its back? It's a new world, so get real. Oh, yes, number four. When criminals commit their crimes, if they don't outright kill or maim people they more than likely put them in some distress, and sometimes that distress kills them indirectly."

Rhamnusia turned to Alecto and they lowered at each other, but they both kept quiet, and Bors wondered at the dissonance between them.

Then, "Have you heard the joke about the three men shipwrecked on a deserted Island?" Rhamnusia asked, still staring at Alecto. "After months of nothing to do but listen to each other's jokes, they started repeating them. When they had heard the same jokes dozens of times they decided it would be easier if they developed a code. They numbered their jokes. The first guy would say *twenty-three*, and the others would laugh. Then the second one would say *four*, and the other two would laugh, and so on." Rhamnusia narrowed her eyes and stared icily at Alecto. "We could use numbers. For example, every time you disagree with Z on an assignment, just say *one*. Whenever you want to imply that I know more than I'm telling you, say *two*. When you want to show disdain for me, that would be *three*. Contempt for Bors could be *four*."

Bors was surprised at Rhamnusia's toughness. He had not previously seen it in her. And he was surprised when Alecto not only didn't flare up and say *four*, but she shrank slightly.

"Whatever we think of each other," Rhamnusia continued coldly to Alecto, "our feelings shouldn't interfere with our work. And you should be even more careful in your estimation of Bors. And one more thing." Her voice rasped like a steel file. "When you fail, I fail, and I seldom fail."

"Have I ever failed?" Alecto asked.

"We could ask Griffith. Unfortunately Griffith isn't here."

Griffith had been killed by Zabov. Beyond that, Bors knew nothing.

"It wasn't my fault." Alecto sank deeper into the cushions of the booth.

"Number thirteen. You've said it so many times, we shall call it *thirteen*."

Alecto hung her head. The noontime crowd began to leave and the waitresses--in their starched, white blouses; long pink skirts; and ponytails--began clearing the tables. The Rock-Ola finished *Blueberry Hill* by Fats Domino, then it went silent. A well-dressed man with a mop came out to do the red-and-white checked floor, and Bors assumed the man was the owner, or the manager. Nobody liked to do the dirty work. Bors knew he himself was an exception: he had his ups and downs, but in general he liked dirty work. When he was in a black mood. Otherwise he was indifferent, even reluctant.

The restaurant became quiet, then two people in the kitchen started talking and laughing through the red bat-wing doors, and Bors heard one of them--a young lady--say, ". . . kiss my sweet ass."

Rhamnusia looked at her coffee cup and started tapping it with the long nail of her index finger. Alecto sat with her hands folded on the table, still downcast, still dispirited. Bors finished his glass of water, and waited.

"Ha, ha, ha," came a young, nasal laugh from in back.

Bors waited. It wasn't his struggle.

"Mark II to Senator Desmond Pennington," Rhamnusia said after the well-dressed man had mopped his way to the far side of the dining area. She said it quietly, but she didn't whisper. "I don't know for certain, but I get the feeling that this is a test for you two, after the head-lopping, so don't screw it up."

When Rhamnusia was gone Bors stayed with Alecto, who was still subdued. "What happened to Griffith?" he asked, popping it on her suddenly.

She kept her head down.

Bors felt he had the advantage, and though his feeling for her had softened he pressed on.

"Look here, I have a right to know."

She lowered her head even more.

"Griffith and I were on an assignment." She spoke so softly that Bors had to lean forward to hear. "He was new--as you are--and we were to give a Mark II to the president of a large corporation who, with a few of his accountants and other cronies, were bleeding the corporation white. Selling stock and getting big bonuses, while the employees and stockholders were going down the tubes. We----"

"How did Z know the company was in trouble?"

"I don't know. How would I? You insist on asking questions than neither I nor any at my level know. Don't you get it by now? I just do what I'm told."

"Sorry. So you and Griffith were to do a Mark II. Then what?"

"Senator Pennington must have found out and told Demetrius Eppers at Scorpion, and they sent their hitman, Zabov, to intercept us. We were walking down 27th Street and Griffith took a poison dart in the back. Zabov's favorite weapon. Street gangs didn't use poison and why would they have been after him? I don't know what poison Zabov used-- no one in Ragnarök knows--but they suspected it was a combination of sea wasp jellyfish venom and something else. Whatever it was, you're dead in minutes. There I was looking down at Griffith, watching him die while Zabov faded into the crowd." Alecto began to cry silently.

"Then what?"

"There was nothing I could do of course. I had to fade into the crowd like Zabov. I couldn't be there when the police came, so as he was writhing in agony on the sidewalk--in too much pain to talk--I walked away. His eyes followed me. He knew he was dying, but his eyes said he didn't want to die alone, and I walked away and left him. Left him to die like a mongrel dog." Alecto put her elbows on the table and covered her face with her hands, and tears oozed through her fingers, but she cried quietly. "He has many weapons; Zabov. One of his favorites is a radio-controlled model airplane rigged with poison or with a bomb. He sits on a rooftop, or looking out a window, and when you come by he hits you like a kamikaze pilot. Boom, and that's it. He uses drones too. I could go on and on about his devices and methods."

Bors didn't know what to say.

"Worse, he knows who I am," Alecto moaned from behind her hands. "He knows what I look like, and I have to watch for him every minute, and it's driving me mad. You sometimes think I'm cockeyed, seeing things which aren't there, but I have reason to be."

"How did he find out? About you and Griffith?"

"I don't know. He couldn't have known anything about me, so it must have been Griffith, but now that Griffith's dead there's no way of finding out. Maybe they--Scorpion-- have infiltrated us. A mole somewhere higher up." Alecto's shoulders started to tremble.

"Tell me about Demetrius Eppers," Bors said.

Alecto remained silent and still.

Bors reached across the table and lightly touched her forearm. "Eppers?" he asked softly.

Alecto flinched and sat up straight. She wiped her face with her napkin. "Eppers is more than the leader of Scorpion; he is the essence of Scorpion. In Ragnarök we have Z, and I once told you that I'm pretty sure Z is at least three people. I've heard as many as five. In Scorpion it's different. Eppers is in complete control. My guess is that Pennington and his malefactors have a perpetual relationship with Eppers."

"Alright, Eppers and his people know you, but you know him. That counts for a lot." Bors looked around. The mopper had gone to the back room, leaving only a tired-looking blond waitress behind the counter, and an elderly, balding, heavyset man in a dark blue suit sitting on a stool with his buttocks hanging down on each side. The man was eating pie. "Describe Eppers to me."

"Shouldn't we go----?"

"Go where? What's the difference? Him?" Bors nodded toward the man on the stool. "Don't get jumpy. Tell me about Eppers."

"He's tall, and dark, and bald . . . . Severe looking, and he's always dressed in expensive, black suits; and he wears diamond jewelry. Cuff links, rings, lapel pins, tie tack; all diamond and sterling."

"Tie tacks went out years ago."

"And he carries a black cane with a silver scorpion on the handle."

"Silver scorpion? Oh, for gosh sake!" Bors threw his hands up in resignation. "I feel like I'm one of the characters in a not-so-good spy novel. This is absurd!"

"So you may think," Alecto muttered, "but I can assure you that--absurd as he may appear--Eppers is anything but."

Bors let his arms fall to the table, palms down. "He always dresses the same? Isn't he afraid of retribution? How does he stay healthy?"

"He's always protected by his toughs."

"They can't cover him completely, and certainly not from long-distance hits."

"He's as sinister and dangerous as they come, but I didn't say he's all that bright." She stood. "If you ever see Eppers close up--and I hope to hell you don't--take a look at his tie tack."

"Don't tell me. A scorpion?"

Alecto nodded, and left, and as she did Bors reached out and squeezed her hand.

Bors went to his hotel--the Crowne Plaza Manhattan on Broadway and 48th--took an unopened bottle of Lauder's Scotch Whiskey from his suitcase, and poured three shots into a glass. He went to the bed, kicked off his shoes without untying them, propped both pillows against the headboard, and slumped down. He took a drink and shuddered slightly as it ran down his throat and puddled in his stomach.

He didn't like whiskey but he liked the effect. Once he had liked the effect too much, and now he had to strictly limit himself. He didn't fit the mold in which most alcoholics had been formed; he could still drink and control his urgings. Only three shots at most. Four and he would be gone. And if three, only once or twice a year, if that.

Ragnarök put its operatives in decent places. They could afford it; usually the Mark II targets made monetary *contributions*.

The room--spacious, with a recliner and a writing desk--was done in golden brown, and it featured a Degas reproduction on each wall. The reproduction above the television set was *Blue Dancers*, and Bors leaned his head back and stared at it until the dancers started to move. He seldom watched television; only to keep up on the news. He read a lot, and when he could he entertained women. He wished he could entertain Alecto now. He didn't know where she was staying. A special caution for their current operation in case one of them was kidnapped and made to talk. And they would talk. Bors had never heard of anyone who wouldn't talk, though he guessed if there was such a person it would be Zabov.

Bors shifted uncomfortably, took the Beretta out of his back pocket, and laid it on the lamp table beside him. He thought carrying a pistol was farcical, but Ragnarök insisted, so now he carried the Beretta. The old Colt 1908 .25 his father had given him would have been good enough. A piddling weapon, according to Alecto, but sufficient at short range.

The window drapes were drawn and Bors shut off the light above the bed so that the only illumination was from the light above the bathroom sink. He was like his father who had liked the dark. His father had been a farmer, whose greatest luxury had been to sit inside, sheltered from the sun, dust, and insects. Bors preferred darkness because it made him feel secure.

Bors felt the emptiness that always came from being alone on a queen-sized bed. One of Degas' dancers emerged from the picture and floated toward him, and as she wafted closer Bors saw that it was Alecto, and she was smiling. He had seldom seen her smile real smiles before; mostly bitter smiles. Knowing that she would disappear if he kept staring, he closed his eyes and kept the vision. Keeping her was difficult, but he did keep her, and he even managed to make her more distinct and vivid, and when he had done that--when he was confident that she would not dissipate--he felt for his glass, and, eyes still closed, slugged down what was left of his three shots. He relaxed and let the Scotch work, savoring

Alecto as she held out her arms to him. She
was wearing a white, loose-flowing, sleeveless
gown that turned translucent as she drew closer.
Bors reached for her, but his hands went
through her, and she began to cry, and he cried
along with her.

Bors looked at the whiskey bottle,
wishing he could have just one more; the one
that would put him over the edge. He had
worked so hard at not trying with Alecto that it
had become the same as trying too hard. He
knew it, and she knew it, and the worst of it
was, he knew what he didn't want to know
about her. God-dammit anyway, she was a
sapphist.

Bors awoke with what felt like an electric
shock. There had been a knock on the door,
and now there was another; three in rapid
succession, a pause, then one more. It meant
nothing to him so he padded barefoot to the
peephole. It was Alecto.

She entered, and with only a slight glance
at him she went to the bed, removed her outer
clothing, and lay down. Bors felt the whiskey
bubble in his stomach and he became
lightheaded. He hesitated, and Alecto
beckoned.

They held each other all night, and once
they both cried.

89

In the morning, when Bors woke up, she was gone.

Chapter Seven

Months later

Bors sat in a plush recliner in his New York city apartment that Ragnarök had provided. They liked to move him around every several months for his own safety. As usual he was bored--for some reason he smiled to himself--and such extreme boredom always reminded him of the old portrayal of war: long periods of tedium interrupted by sheer terror.

He imagined he was standing on the knoll immediately behind the old house his grandparents had built when they had homesteaded in northeastern Montana in the early 1900s. His goddamn knoll where he had often come for solace as a child. Now the farm was abandoned, the house and outbuildings run down; and the revenants were no more, either long dead or long gone in some other physical or spiritual way. There was only nothingness.

He had to sort out things that could comprise his life now. His Mark I for the decapitation, Alecto, and everything. Rhamnusia had made things very clear, and first he had a big decision to make. He had been threatened with Mark V for Christ's sake, and even without that there was no leaving Ragnarök and staying alive. What a way to move up the ranks.

The room was dark but in his mind's eye the Montana evening sun blinded him if he looked westward, so he didn't look westward, and even if he had been able to, there would have been nothing to see; nothing but a horizon thirty miles away, and fields, drought, dust, shimmering heat, and an occasional fox, deer, antelope, tractors, trucks, ... The only break in the summer monotony was an occasional rain or thunderstorm, but they were never enough. Life had been difficult ever since the early homesteaders had arrived in the early 1900s, and those pioneers and their offspring had been leaving ever since. Now the farms were fewer and much larger, and far more expensive to own and operate; and the technology was much more complex.

To the east was an old guy named Harald Nordraak, a fifth-generation Norwegian, and his wife Marie. He didn't know them; he had left the area years ago, and anyway grudges went way back. His parents and grandparents had never gotten along with the Nordraaks. Something to do with Harald's grandfather Lars being a member of the American communist party back in the '20s and '30s, and that the Nordraaks had always been shitasses. Or at least somewhat egotistical and hard to get along with. And he had heard that Harald, though better than his relatives, was kind of odd. He was a writer, and one of his books was nonfiction about world conditions or some such. The title was *Rat*-something or other. A bit of a hermit too. How would he have heard that; he hadn't been up there for many years?

Hotter than the Devil's dick. Bors had never been able to tolerate heat. There was no wind, and to the south, about a quarter of a mile away, a dust devil whirled through an empty field, picking up weeds and wheat straw; and far off to the west a vehicle, probably a truck, left a trail of dust a mile long. It could have just as well been 1932.

Well if he did get into more trouble with Ragnarök he would have no choice but to run. They never kicked anybody out. He guessed he would go back up there to the old farm and build a fortress of some kind, with escape tunnels, thick walls, safe rooms, poison gas safeguards, and so on. He had the money to do so. Ill-gotten gains that had come along with his activities with Ragnarök. And if things got too hot he could light out onto the prairie and hole up in old abandoned buildings, gulches, ... He began to think he had brain fever. The kind of brain fever the English got in the 1800s, which usually meant intense mental strain, madness, or worse due to inflammation of the brain.

The sun fell to the horizon, and the heat remained intense. It would be a hot, sleepless night.

Withal, he was devoted to his work with Ragnarök. He could make amends. He had always been a contrarian, but he was not beyond redemption. Most of all he had to remember that he now had purpose and he was more content than he had ever been.

Birds began their evening songs. He didn't know much about prairie birds, but he knew their songs, and he knew they weren't singing children's storybook songs, ditties or anything like that; they were warning other birds away, trying to attract mates, just to make noise, or for no reason at all. Life isn't a childlike, religious, poetic, or a fairy-tale affair. It's essence is realism. Some egghead academics try to define *realism*, but in doing so they fall into the common trap of defining the obvious.

Then what about Alecto? It was time to be realistic about her. She was a lesbian, and that was that. Maybe she was. He had been attracted to her from the moment he had first seen her, and he had been in denial from that

time on. Damn, damn, damn, it had always
been part of his nature to pick losing horses,
either to ride, or to bet on at the track. Most of
the time he had the perspicacity to look down
on himself and see his weaknesses, but not
enough sense to do anything about them. He
was weak. He had always been weak; not
physically, rather in some internal way that he
had never been able to overcome. He knew his
conviction wasn't reasonable, but that was the
way he was.

Alecto. He had to give her up. But
couldn't give her up because he had never had
her. What then?

An owl hooted from some distant part of
the old shelterbelt. Must have lost his way.
Or her way, to be politically correct, which he
hated to do. He always tried to be politically
incorrect. Anyway, not many owls came to
this part of the prairie. He had always been
fond of owls because of their perceived
sagacity. Ha. But mostly for----

Then he would. He would give her up
but see if she would be his friend. He almost
gagged at the thought, but he would do it
because he had to. And maybe she would be
his best friend. His only friend. He had no
friends. Never had. He had always been
incapable of having friends. Friendship was
overrated, except for some wives, and he had

never been married. Had never so much as thought seriously about it. Perhaps Alecto would marry him as a friend, but they could sleep apart.

Bors blinked and revived himself, leaned forward in the recliner, and held his head in both hands, returning to reality. God. His visions slowly evaporated.

He had always considered himself slightly mentally afflicted, but he had seen it as an asset; a manifestation of high intelligence, unusual creativity, and so on, but now he hoped his condition wasn't becoming a detriment. Possibly it always had been. Sometimes he thought he should have chosen a normal occupation, like farming, beekeeping, or making fancy, improved yo-yos. As it was, there was probably no occupation more unusual--bizarre--than his, if one could call intimidation, torture, and occasional killing an occupation. Further, what the hell did it matter what he and his cohorts called it? Justice? An effort to save all of humanity from worldwide self destruction as per the Doomsday Clock? Opposing ultimate moral corruption? Or whatever others in Ragnarök thought they were doing, though he didn't know what they thought because they never met each other, and because he didn't give a tinker's damn what motivated them.

Somewhat to the contrary one of his
ultimate goals, he had just in that moment
realized, was to meet some of the Ragnarök
heads. Find out what they were really like and
if they were as elevated and brilliant as they
would have their underlings believe. Going
face-to-face with any of them was, all the same,
as probable as winning some stupendous
national lottery.

Well, well, nothing to do but abide. Stiff
upper lip and all that. Stay calm and . . . .

Chapter Eight

Full immersion

They were in a room somewhere. As usual two thugs had delivered their *angel of virtue*. Their victim in need of remediation.

The room was, for a change, clean, modern, and well lighted, with the scent of lilac. The only unusual aspects were that there were no windows, no wall hangings, there was no furniture, and only one door. Most unusual was the rolled-up carpet on the floor.

The thugs handed Bors and Alecto rubber masks which they put on.

One of men grabbed the carpet edge and pulled hard, and out rolled a pale, pudgy, egg-bald man who appeared to have been drugged. He was bound with a hemp rope, round and round. He moaned and twitched slightly, and one of the helpers slapped him on his right cheek. He groaned and opened his eyes half way, and the helper slapped him on the other cheek.

"Senator Pennington," said Alecto. "How nice of you to join us again."

Pennington opened his eyes all the way and struggled to focus on her.

"May I offer you a drink?" Alecto continued. "Oh, dear me, I believe our liquor bar is empty. Please forgive me. Wait, it seems we have no liquor bar, and anyway, you seem to be tied up at the moment. Sorry, that's such an old line."

One of the helpers went to the kitchenette, unwrapped a package, turned on the gas stove and put something on one of the burners. At first Bors couldn't tell what it was so he moved a few steps to his left. It was a small branding iron with a Mark III on the business end. He had branded cattle in his younger days in Montana, but he had never branded a cow on the forehead.

"You are a stubborn one Mr. Pennington." Alecto was playing it for all it was worth. "I should have thought you were more intelligent, but power corrupts, and apparently you just can't let go. And it seems to me you aren't very intelligent after all. Dear me, now it has come to this: a Mark III."

Pennington had recovered his senses and he tried to sit up, but could only wiggle. "I wouldn't advise you to do anything rash," he said. "I have told Demetrius Eppers at Scorpion that you might try something, and what happens to me will happen to you, but worse." He drooled slightly as he spoke. "To you, only worse." He tried to leer menacingly, but it emerged as fear.

Alecto grimaced slightly. "My goodness, you are shaking me to my core. Trouble is, when you say *only worse*, it doesn't get much worse than Mark III, and if I get worse than that I'm in big trouble. Well, it does get worse, but though Eppers knows me, I know him. Please convey my regards to him and remind him of that. Anyway, don't you realize you have further incriminated yourself as regards Eppers? We already knew about your relationship with him, but now we have videoed your confession," she motioned to a camera on the wall, "and the whole world will know what you are: a slightly clever con man. You--and others--have been able to fool the general public, but there are those of higher intellect who will not be fooled; those whom you cannot hoodwink, and who, until now, have not had the means to combat you. Now we have those means, and people like you are to realize that your cleverness is insufficient. Our work will take time, but we will prevail. I hope you will smile for the camera."

"Wha, what are you going to do?"

"I guess you have deduced that today we are not here to bring about your demise."

Pennington seemed to relax slightly.
Bors assumed he had not seen the branding
iron.

"Relax Mr. Pennington, it won't be as bad
as you might imagine. Still, we do have to
make an impression on you. A real
impression. One that will be hard for you to
forget."

Then Pennington saw the hot iron and he
turned pallid and began to drool again, and one
eye blinked.

"Now wait a minute," he cried, "if you're
going to do what I think you are; that would be
inhumane!"

Alecto laughed. "Throughout much of
human history there have been those honest
souls who think, work, and regard life as to be
improved. On the other hand there have
always been those who, instead of trying to
improve our miserable human conditions
through honorable means, gravitate toward
dishonesty. They don't understand that if they
had spent their time and efforts honestly they
could most likely have achieved the same gains,
but improbity comes naturally to them.
Cleverness is not intelligence my dear Mr.
Pennington."

Bors had always been uncomfortable with
the way in which Alecto toyed cat and mouse

with their victims.   Why not get down to
business?

Alecto glanced at the helper by the stove.
Pennington looked toward the stove, and though
it was impossible for him to see what the helper
was doing, he didn't like what he couldn't see.
He began to sweat and his face turned red.

"Look here," Pennington whined, "I think
we can work this out to our mutual satisfaction.
There's no need to . . . , to go about, about
whatever it is you are preparing to do.   I can
assure you that----"

"Oh, you have assured us before," Alecto
said acidly.   "No, I am afraid there is no
turning back.   No indeed, your clinging to
power and corruption has led you to this, and
you must face some consequences; and perhaps
you will undergo a radical change of attitude.
Perhaps not.   Those of your ilk are usually
intransigent until the last, but one can only hope
you are above your deplorable peers."

She looked again at the stove, then at
Bors, and as more often than he wished, he felt
the sickness in his stomach.   Branded cattle
was one thing, but this was another.   He
wished he had brought along some whiskey,
and he might even have given some to
Pennington.

The helper at the stove turned and nodded
at Bors and handed him the iron.   Pennington

screamed and his eyes bulged out to the point of popping.

The other helper knelt behind Pennington with his head held tightly between his knees. He took a rag from a back pocket, knotted it, and forced the knot into Pennington's mouth. Then he took out another rag; a blindfold. When that was done he clasped his hands under the unfortunate's chin. "Ready," he said, "and be careful with the iron." Pennington's face looked like it had been bleached.

Bors took the iron and straddled Pennington on his knees. His hands trembled ever so slightly and he knew Alecto was enjoying it all. He felt his target, the forehead, and he knew he was stalling. Suddenly he pressed the Mark III iron down and Pennington screamed through his gag and the scream was much louder than Bors had expected, and the helper--though huge and strong--struggled to hold on. Smoke arose and it was not the familiar smell of burnt hair and cow flesh; but something worse, and nauseating. After several minutes Pennington's screams subsided into groans, then he grew mostly silent except for what could only have been taken as intermittent sobs.

Alecto interrupted the sobs. "Take him away, and give him my best regards."

After it was all over and Bors and Alecto were outside, a strange thought came: Bors actually knew once and forever that he did not want to be on the bad side of Ragnarök, walking around with a Roman numeral on his forehead--or worse--even if he lived, which he more than likely wouldn't.   And then another thought surfaced: he wouldn't like to be on Alecto's shitlist either.

Alecto had instructed the assistants to strip Pennington naked, tie his hands behind his back, take him somewhere far down the street, and let him go.   They were to take a few photos of him for the media, and to be sure to remove the gag so he could sing to his heart's content. Good publicity.

The helpers later reported that the last they had seen of Senator Pennington he had been running down the street like a lunatic escaping an insane asylum.

Chapter Nine

Second thoughts

Bors walked down some street in New York City. He didn't know which street, but it didn't matter because he had a bigger headache: he was being followed by someone he didn't know, and no matter what he did or where he turned there was his tail. In stores, out the back, here, there, wherever, behind him at exactly the same distance was the apparition. Every trick he knew had failed.

The man in the long, gray, hooded coat may not have even been a man, but that didn't matter. Whatever it was was extremely dangerous; that Bors knew intuitively. Vile and murderous.

It began to rain, lightly, and the day was turning to night. Bors entered some tall building and ran to the elevator. He was alone, and he pushed one of the buttons. It turned out to be five. He exited and found himself in a hall of apartments. Crap. Stupid. Now what? He started down a stairway but came face to face with the apparition. He ran

*back to the elevator but again there was the
specter, and as Bors backed away his knees
gave out and he fell to the floor.*

The Night-hag slowly faded and Bors
came to soaked in sweat, and shaking. He had
been seeing the same phantasm in different
forms for weeks. There were always
inconsistencies; time warps, total irrelevancies--
the usual stuff--but the follower always loomed,
nightmarish, and curiously, it always had a
large gold-colored medal hung from its neck
with a red, white, and blue strap.

Bors reached for the cigarettes on his
nightstand but he had quit smoking years ago
and there were none. He needed a drink, but
he had pretty much quit drinking too, so he
flopped back in bed and tried to meditate on
something tranquil and soothing, and even that
failed, so he lay until the shaking stopped of its
own accord, as it always did, but that took a
long time. He tried to concentrate on Alecto
and that helped some, but he wished she were
there, beside him, holding him. He was so bad
off he would have taken his chances with her.

As his usual last resort he turned his
thoughts to Montana. Not to his boyhood--but
northeastern Montana in general--its good
qualities like solitude, safety, open prairie, plain
people . . . . When he blotted out his childhood

it evoked a feeling of perfect peace and contentment, more so as he had no more relatives or friends there. It was a waking dream that he had embellished over many years and had perfected along the way. It wasn't as good as having Alecto there. Or at least someone like her, or like Rhamnusia.

The best times in that part of Montana were when it rained. Rain was the blood of life there, and even those who grew up there and left were conditioned to like rain. A part of their childhood that never left them. So, Bors made it rain, and he laid back on his pillow and luxuriated in the drops splatting on his face, and on the fresh, clean smell. Then there was thunder and lightning and he was transported.

Alas, Bors could only embrace his dream for a limited time.

His motel room was okay. Nice in fact, but living in motels was getting darned tiresome, and the worst part was that he would most likely live out the rest of his life in them. He would do his Ragnarök job--constant danger and all--but the worst part was knowing there was no end. No pot of gold at the end of the rainbow; only forced retirement without knowing what that retirement would entail. Peace and opulence, or constant danger, nervousness, and outright fear? He felt like a small child longing for comfort, but there was

no one to whom to appeal. Alecto? Even
Rhamnusia? But now there was no one, and
there might well never be anyone. He felt like
crying but he tried to avoid that, even when he
was alone. But he had never before been so
alone.

He sat back up in bed and there he was,
studying wallpaper again. He knew about
every motel wallpaper pattern there was. This
one was flowers, but he didn't know what kind;
small, red ones. A line from an old county-
western song came to mind: *Counting flowers
on the wall, ...* And another he thought was
from the same song: *Playing solitaire with a
deck of fifty-one, ...* His life was a mess.

His head buzzed; then he realized it was a
big, part-blue fly and he tried to grab it but of
course it got away. His father had told him
that back in the heyday of boxing in the early
part of the 1920s and '30s some of the boxers
would sit in bars and exercise their reflexes by
attempting to catch flies. With only two
fingers and their thumb. He later wondered
how sitting in bars helped their reflexes or any
other of their skills.

But goddamn he wished he were in
Montana, and free. The paradox was that when
he was active with Ragnarök he was on top of
the world. Like war, but in reverse: long

periods of fear punctuated by short episodes of ecstasy?

What in blue blazes did the gold medal represent? Nothing good, even if it did resemble an Olympic award. Usually when he had dreams--good, bad, or mediocre--he could figure them out, but not this medal thing. The person in the hooded coat was obvious, but not the medal. Some sort of good versus evil oracle? How does one interpret such visions, or does one, or should one? And is it even possible to do so; delve into the impossible structure and workings of the brain? Where is the borderline separating sanity and madness? And who decides? Furthermore, it's probably not a distinct borderline at all; most definitely not. What is sanity? What is madness? Age-old questions. All vexing. All----

Bors reached for his phone to call Alecto, but stopped himself. She would either hang up, put him off, or worse, try to help him but come to the conclusion he was mad, in which case she would be lost to him personally. And no matter what, she would despise him. As best he could tell she could not tolerate weakness, except for her own weaknesses, of which he was not fully conscious.

Bors got up and made himself two strong cups of coffee, and thus fortified he called Alecto.

Chapter Ten

Admonishment

"Adviser, lobbyist, strategist, researcher, and so on, are his euphemistic self descriptions. Plotter, schemer, dirty trickster, conspirator, snake, rat, and treasonist are more accurate, realistic portrayals."

The Ragnarök representative was describing political malefactor C. W. B. Quiff. "Have you heard of him?"

"Never," Bors replied. Something big must be coming, as he had been driven in the back of a blacked-out van to some city or large town near wherever they had switched vans. He had been blindfolded, but they hadn't plugged his ears.

The Ragnarök man was short and pudgy with a large, round, bald head, and he had told Bors to call him *Porky*.

"Where are we?" Bors asked.

"Do you think we would blindfold you, drive all over, change vehicles and all, and then tell you where you are? Your file says nothing about you being simple-minded."

"Not *where are we*, but where are we sitting?"

"Never mind."

"I've been at this for some time now but this beats all when you can't even trust me!"

"Nevertheless."

They were in a dark room that looked like an inner chamber of an ancient Chinese temple. The only light was from candles, and there were chimes continually sounding in the background, and thick cedar incense wafted through. A large statue of Buddha rested on an ornate marble base along the wall behind Bors, opposite the door where they had entered: the old fat Buddha which most people think of, and Porky resembled him. Large and small enclaves indented the walls all around. More Buddhist stuff, but Bors ignored it. He had left the Buddhist path; hocus pocus wasn't his strength.

Bors and Porky sat across from each other at a small ornamented table.

"I'm not a nervous type," Bors began. "Not when facing physical danger, but this is making me nervous. Isn't it about time you tell me what's up?"

Someone came from behind him and threw a fat brown envelope on the table. Bors eyed Porky.

Porky waved the envelope deliverer away with the back of his hand.

"Open it."

Bors did so.

"Read it. Take your time."

Bors read. Then, "Mother of----"

"Read it again."

After he had read the half-dozen papers again Bors' forehead started to sweat and he surreptitiously wiped it by putting his elbows on the table and holding his hands to his head.

"Are you alright?"

Bors sat back. "Yes. But Mark IV? A strong Mark IV? That's bitter medicine. Why don't we just kill him?"

A large gong sounded once behind a curtain and Bors was lifted an inch or two from his chair."

"Calm yourself."

"I am calm. You should see me when I'm----"

"I don't know, but I assume that would be too good for him. Are you losing your nerve?"

"No, but I can't help wondering why he deserves this."

"Why? Well such I do know. It's because his kind of evil is too much for humanity--at least in our country--to absorb. If you will, compare him to a common criminal who steals, connives, robs, kills, ... That's

pretty bad, certainly, but those like Quiff are far
worse. Far more insidious, and they inflict
immeasurably more harm on humanity. Why?
Simply because it's their nature. No use going
into a bunch of psychobabble about them, but in
their unique way they can be as evil as the
Hitlers and Stalins of the world, and the
overriding problem is the vast majority of
people don't see--don't recognize--their impact.
You ask why? Why the average citizens of this
world don't know their impact? Because they
are too obtuse. Simply put, they are too damn
dumb."

"But will it," Bors patted the envelope,
"do any good?"

"I'm amazed you should ask. What the
blue blazes do you think you have been doing
since you joined our group, slapping
malefactor's hands with a ruler? I've been told
you're not weak-kneed, that's why I chose you."

Bors flushed.

Porky went on. "There are all kinds of
villains, but the ones who believe they can hide
behind insidious political and other government
groups are in many regards the most monstrous
and contemptible. Or who conceal themselves
and their abhorrent connivances behind big
business, trusts, monopolies, fame, fortune, and
likewise. They are far worse than simple
transgressors. But listen here, I'm getting

sucked into a discussion about the efficacy or moral propriety of this. Maybe when we've been at it for five or ten more years we'll be bumped up the ladder, but right now we're more likely to be bumped off than bumped up." He tried to smile but his plump countenance did not lend itself to smiles. "So, I'm not here to get into a long-winded discussion."

"When am I to----?"

"We. When do we pull it off? There will be four of us. After we do the job we'll never see each other again. We'll contact you in about a week, and a few days after that we'll hit him."

Bors looked at a statuette in one of the enclaves; another Buddhist representation. He neither knew nor cared whether Porky was a Buddhist, but he thought that if one were to be an adherent of some largely mystical belief that would be the one. But only if one left out the Zen stuff.

Porky stood, took up a club, and hit a large gong, and Bors jumped again.

After the assignment had been completed Bors returned to Alecto, but he had been sworn--warned--to breath nothing to her or to anyone else. She was curious, but he knew she understood. He also knew what even she would have never understood about it: the

savagery with which they had *admonished* C.
W. B. Quiff. He pushed it from his mind as he
always did with unpleasant memories, yet it
wasn't that simple.

It was like a recent dream he had had--a
rather unpleasant one--of meeting an old, retired
movie star and having a bitter conversation with
him. But in the morning no matter how hard
he tried he couldn't remember the name of the
star or what any of his movies had been. The
dream was locked in his mind, but could
probably only be recalled through hypnosis or
some such. He wasn't given to Freudian
psychology, but there was something to it.

The next day he told his dream to Alecto
and she had little to say. Self analysis was not
one of her strong points either; even less than
his. Her only response was that she hoped his
repressions of reality didn't come back to bite
him in the butt some day. That was her
succinct way. Alas, Bors regarded repressions
as good, whether of dreams or of reality.

Bors was tense, but when he tried to take
Alecto's hand, only as a comfort, she pulled it
back. Not roughly or angrily, and that alone
was of some small comfort. And she had
looked at him with what he thought was
compassion. It was always hard to tell. Then
she moved away. Everything was puzzling.
Here they were, partners who had had a rough

start with each other, but who nevertheless still lived together. Go figure.

Bors sat sullenly on one end of the sofa, and Alecto sat on the other. He was certainly tense but that wasn't all. One of his shortcomings was his propensity to get caught up in self analysis. Bogged down, and what good did it do? It seemed like whatever insight he arrived at never helped, and usually it put him in a foul mood. Then why do it? Because of his obsessiveness. What could he do, just tell himself to stop? Go to a psychiatrist? Start drinking? Smoke pot? Immerse himself in his *work*? He was already immersed.

So he concentrated on nothing. Ha! That always worked, and while he concentrated on nothing he also concentrated on the toes of his stockings. But he was interrupted.

Alecto came back and sat with her arm around his shoulders, kissed him on the cheek, slid sideways, and put her head in his lap. Cautiously he put his hand on her shoulder, and they were still and quiet for a very long time.

Chapter Eleven

Scorpion

Bors, if he had regained more consciousness, would have heard a low buzzing sound, but he was not fully conscious, and that he knew. The next thing he was aware of, in some feeble way, was a sensation of floating, as if on a firm cloud, or on calm water. The cloud, or water, began to rock him slowly and gently, then faster, then roughly and very fast. He couldn't see anything, as if his eyelids were glued shut, and he felt around for something to hang onto, but there was nothing. A hand grasped one of his hands and there was immense relief even though the rocking became violent and he was still unable to open his eyes. Someone spoke to him in a mild, comforting way, but he couldn't understand her. The voice sounded familiar.

Bors tried to go into his Buddhist mode, but it didn't work, and he remembered that recently he had decided it and all other mystical cognitive crutches were nothing more than mental bullshit.

After a few minutes, hours, or days, Bors recognized the voice, and he was able to open his eyes. Alecto was holding his right hand and speaking to him in a strange language. He wanted to ask her to speak English, but he could only guggle. He felt on both sides, and he seemed to be lying on a bed

Alecto was sitting on a chair close to him, and what struck him was her bearing: for the first time ever she had an almost loving look. Always before she had reminded him of Aello, a harpy: a bird-like creature with either a beautiful face or the face of an ugly old woman, who carried out punishments for crimes; who took people to the Underworld to torture them. Alecto had never shown the ugly face, but at her worst she had, to him, been virtually ugly. But now----

"Can you speak now?" she asked. To Bors' surprise she leaned forward and kissed him, first on his forehead, then gently on his lips, then she brushed back his hair with her hand.

"What . . . , what happened?"

"It's a long story."

"Scorpion?"

"Yes. But I rescued you."

Another surprise. Normally it would have been some smart reply like, *"Lucky for you I saved your ass, but you can thank me later."*

"I----"

"You were drugged. You're in a hospital. The doctor said if you woke up and if you knew who you were you might, um, would be alright. Who are you?"

It could have been one of her mean jokes, but it wasn't. It was a simple caring, pleading question.

"I'm what's left of a wretched character, but I can't remember who."

"But who *are* you?" Alecto asked again.

"I'm Uther Pendragon Montgomery."

"Yes, good, but----"

"Easy," someone said. Bors assumed he was a doctor. "Nudge him gently."

Alecto again. "And who else?"

Bors faltered and put his hand to his face. "Wait, I've almost got it. Give a moment. Starts with a B. Wait a minute."

"Take your time."

"I have little trick I use to remember things. Once I get the first letter, if it's a consonant I run through the vowels, and I can usually get the word. B, a. Nope. B, e. No. B, i. No. B, o. B, o something. Then I go through the consonants again. Wait. Bors! I'm Bors!"

Alecto sobbed, only once. "Rest, now that I know you'll be okay. I knew you were alright as soon as you started on your cockamamie consonant and vowel thing. The doctor will give you something to make you feel better, and in a day or two I'll tell you the whole story. But for now I will only say you are alright, and that I will be with you."

She kissed him again, and turned off the light beside the bed.

"I don't need any----" But he felt the jab of a needle in his arm. As he drifted off, his best solace was Alecto. Before, when they had pledged to be soulmates, it had been forced, but now it was real, and he knew he loved her more than before, and in a better way. It was a stronger bond than he had ever known, and it would be until he breathed his last.

Two days later Bors could sit up in bed, and the next day in a chair. Alecto was always there.

On the sixth day they sat in plush armchairs face to face and close.

"You're *home*," Alecto said. She was tense, but not as before, and she smiled more genuinely, and he smiled back at her in the same way, though he dreaded what she was about to tell. He remembered nothing of his attack. Almost nothing; just a vague mental image of Zabov, and he was by no means sure of that.

Bors looked around and saw he was in a bedroom decorated with strange wallpaper and 1930s-style art objects.

"You are strong again," Alecto said. "I have always appreciated that, but you should know I would have stuck by you forever no matter what."

Bors didn't feel very strong, and he worked at holding back tears.

"You know we are in New York City don't you?" she continued.

"Yes. Well I guess so."

"And you already suspect Scorpion?" One eye developed a tic so slight that Bors almost missed it. She had never done that before.

"Yes."

She looked down at her folded hands, then back up as if steeling herself.

"Some Scorpion gorillas, perhaps led by Zabov himself but I'm not sure, snatched you right off the street. I know, because I was following you, but there was nothing I could do right then. They threw you into a pink van and took off. I immediately informed Ragnarök, and shit hit the . . . , well luckily they had been tracking the Scorpion boys here in town--as you know there are no women in Scorpion--and while our people didn't know where their headquarters are, or even if there is a permanent head of the beast, they knew where some of the tentacles were. We were dispatched in groups, but I had a hunch--don't ask--and I pretended like I had lost communication. I went to where I thought they had taken you, but it took a while. And god, I was far from sure."

She took a bottle of Maker's Mark Kentucky whiskey from an end table and poured herself a double shot. "None for you." She emptied the glass with three gulps.

She went on. "But there was the pink van! In front of an old 1950s house, with a tough leaning against the side of it pretending to nonchalantly smoke a cigar."

"How did you know where to go?" Bors gurgled.

"Later." Alecto said.

A visiting nurse came and took his temperature and pulse, then left.

Alecto continued, "I had on my old-lady clothes and makeup so I circled around to the back, but same thing."

"Jeez!"

Alecto held up her hand. "It's just getting good," she beamed. "I had stuff with me. You know, *stuff*. A small grenade with special fragments that would only travel a few feet, my rocket pistol, an old Beretta same as yours, and so on. The usual, everyday things that women carry." She laughed at her joke.

"Yeah," Bors winced.

"Well the guy in the back looked pretty rough, but dumber than the one in the front, so it wasn't going to get any better, and knowing them they weren't going to mess around with what they had in mind for you. As you know I'm basically a coward," she paused to let her wit soak in, "so I got ready for hell to break loose. I'd zap the one in back with my rocket pistol. We can play that game too."

"But he'd shoot you before the poison took effect!"

"Not if I could distract him for several seconds; at least that's how long they told me it would take, and anyway the pain is excruciating. And they said most people are stunned when they get hit. They are only prepared to be shot with a bullet, even if they've never been shot with one before."

"*They?* How the devil would *they* know? How many of them have been shot with your rocket?"

"None that I know of, but they have tested them on animals and----"

"Animals?!"

"And human volunteers, and on some who didn't volunteer."

Bors leaned back. "Lord give me strength. So what happened?"

"After I zapped the stiff I sneaked into the house like a cat. You know how cat-like I can be."

She seemed to be increasingly relishing her witticisms.

"I crept to a front window and rocketed the Neanderthal in front. He never knew what hit him, and didn't make a sound. I was actually almost enjoying myself. I had seen two other thugs in a room with you, but no sign of Zabov. You were strapped to a table, and one of them said he wanted to wait for you to wake up so you could "enjoy the operation.""

"Operation?"

"Literally. They had removed your pants and shorts, and there was a scalpel and----"

"Jeesus! What then?"

Bors resisted feeling between his legs.

Alecto suddenly turned pale. "I rolled the grenade into the room, figuring that if you got hit, too bad, it was our only chance. I assumed you would prefer death to what they were about to do to you."

"You assumed right."

"I ducked behind two walls when it went off and I heard screaming. I popped back into the doorway and both men were rolling around on the floor, but when they saw me they reached for their guns."

She paused, gasping for breath.

"Well?"

"I shot them. It was extremely gratifying."

There was a knock and Alecto jumped up and landed facing the door, gun in hand, all in one smooth move.

"Yes?"

"Pizza."

She moved to a special peep-hole that offered a wide view of the hall. Then she went to the massive outer door that had a peep-hole built like a horizontal periscope so the viewer couldn't be shot in the eye.

When the delivery girl had left she brought the pizza to Bors.

"Anchovy," she smiled.

Bors was in no mood for pizza. "Get on with it."

"Oh, it felt so good that I shot each one of them twice more even though they were both dead. Then I untied you and hauled you out." She was regaining her sense of humor. "You had come *within a hair's breadth* of losing your facial hair for the rest of you life. Get it, *a hair's breadth*?"

Bors sagged back in his chair and simply stared at her, bewildered and on the verge of either anger or gratitude. He leaned toward gratitude. He groaned.

"Ha," Alecto said.   It wasn't a laugh.

"Why did it take me so long to wake up?"

"I dunno.   The drugs of course, and perhaps a concussion from the grenade."

"I owe you my life, and----"

"And your privates?"   She was milking it for all it was worth.

Bors sagged his chin to his chest and closed his eyes, and for a long time neither of them moved or spoke.

"You are courageous," he said.

She cleared her throat, evidently thinking. "I would say *motivated* if I were to say anything at all."

"Alright, *courageous and motivated*."

"I love you," Alecto sighed.

Bors lifted his head.   "I love you as well. With a different, special kind of love.   You know that."   His eyes were moist.

Chapter Twelve

Alecto melts

Bors woke up in bed with his right arm around Alecto's waist. At first he was troubled, until she opened her eyes halfway and smiled. Even so he quickly withdrew his arm.

"Don't worry," she whispered, "we're making up the rules as we go. Our first rule is that we can touch."

"In what way?"

"Any way we want."

Bors was speechless. What the hell was going on?

"The second rule is no sexual intercourse unless we both agree. You know, the old *me too* thing, but of course I trust you without that. And no more of that phony hitting on me like when we first met. You seemed to think you were a teenager."

"I agree."

"You----? Oh, of course," she said, "I should have seen that coming. If you weren't busy trying to save the world you could have been a comedian."

"I'm not joking. I agree."

Alecto. *Unceasing pursuit.* Now,
looking back, it had become clear that he had
been infatuated with her since he had first seen
her, when she was at her bitchiest. He had
been smitten by much more than her unusual
form of beauty. Bors rolled onto his back.
What the hell had happened? From the time
they had been forced to work as a pair she had
disliked him. But had she really disliked him?
If not she sure had been hard to read. But
forget it; water under the Bridge of Bumfuzzle.

A cuckoo clock cuckooed eight times
with the bird bouncing up and down each time.
It looked like an old Swiss clock, but maybe it
was new and made to look old. It matched the
wallpaper. They were still where he had woke
up after being rescued, and Alecto had told him
it was on the far outskirts of the city. It had
been specially built as a safe house with thick
concrete walls and a bunker for a basement, but
the outside looked like the surrounding houses,
though somewhat shabbier.

How could one characterize Alecto? She
seemed to fit no single category. Bors' head
ached and the ceiling undulated, and he closed
his eyes. She was still enigmatic. His best
guess was that she had crafted her own mold,
and he would do his best to discover what that
mold had been. No, that wasn't it; her

condition--her composition--was genetic. Yet could she have experienced some grand enlightenment, or a traumatic, life-changing event? He had never come across anyone remotely like her.

Well he would have to restrain himself and see what developed, though self-restraint wasn't one of his best characteristics. A fly landed on his nose.

"Do I get to make some of the rules?" he asked.

"Of course, but keep in mind that I made the first one."

"You made two."

"There was one before those two, didn't I tell you?"

"What was it?"

"That there would be rules." She chortled softly.

Bors was beginning to relax and he almost giggled. "Do I get breakfast in bed?"

"Yes, but that's all you're going to get in this bed."

"You said I could make rules too."

"Of course, but I have veto power."

"Says who?"

"I do."

"Who are you to declare you have veto power?"

"I am. I'm the declarer of veto power."

"Well I am the Regent of Rules. The Duke of Decrees. The----"

"And I am the Queen of Consent. Furthermore, I outrank you."

"How's that?"

"I joined Ragnarök before you did," and she turned and went into the kitchen area.

Coincidentally there was a large picture of a queen on the wall opposite the bed. Someone more knowledgeable could have known who it was, but Bors thought it might have been someone from the 15th century. And as usual he recognized his limitations as to art; plants; flowers, unless they were prairie flowers; sculptures; most forms of abstractionism; . . . . He was like Sherlock Holmes whose knowledge was strictly limited to his detective work.

Bors tried to make the large portrait resemble Alecto, but he couldn't. The figure was not alluring in the same way, or else he was losing his powers of creative cogitation.

The rest of bedroom was garish, with cheap old-fashioned wall plaques and pictures of other historic figures and events. One caught his eye though, a painting of somebody being led to a guillotine. Surprisingly, the victim appeared to be joyful.

Bors re-arranged his pillows and flopped back. Nothing about Ragnarök made much

sense anymore except for their basic philosophy
and tenets. Their methods and everything on
an everyday plane verged on the bizarre. The
most bizarre of all was the enthusiasm with
which the members carried out their
assignments. He himself was devoted, but not
as fanatic. *Fanatic* was not the word--it was
too harsh--*extraordinarily enthusiastic* was
more like it. Okay, but about the time he had
lost control and sliced off the guy's head? One
can't get more enthusiastic than that; or could
he even call it enthusiasm? *Barbaric* would be
more accurate. He had resorted to savagery for
the sake of savagery, to a far greater degree
than anyone else in the organization had done,
as far as he knew, and he had tried to justify it
as a personal lapse, knowing all the time while
there was still to be no mincing around, there
was never to be brutality beyond what was
necessary. Beyond what was required to fight
moral depravity with moral fire. The moral
fire was necessary because legal, or ethical, or
whatever, most efforts could never suffice.
Could never prevail over both the secular and
the nonsecular evil that pervades much of
humanity.

He hoped his decapitation incident would
not induce the upper-level bosses to make an
expert of him in what they might perceive as a
special skill. In the abstract he believed in

tough remedies, but his everyday activities were far from abstract.

Enough.   Bors shut his eyes and tried to alleviate his bedevilment by concentrating on Alecto.   She thought she had won; that she had conquered him, in a wonderful way, but it was the other way around.   God he loved her.

Chapter Thirteen

A month later: Decapitation

"You lopped off a guy's head!"
Rhamnusia growled at Bors.

They--Bors, Alecto, Rhamnusia, and a
tall, skinny, goofy-looking character--were in a
greasy-spoon restaurant somewhere. Bors
hadn't even noticed the name of the restaurant;
furthermore he didn't even know where it was,
though he hadn't been blindfolded, and Alecto
had driven him there. He tended to ignore
things that were not relevant to his singular
objective. In other words he didn't give a hoot
where he was.

"I lost my temper. Who's he?" He
pointed to the goof.

"Call him John." Rhamnusia controlled
herself.

"I mean, who the hell is he?"

"Never mind," she answered calmly.
"Relax, he's okay."

"Relax? I nearly had my private parts
cut off and would have been singing soprano for

the rest of my life," he shot a glance at Alecto, "and you want me to relax!"

"Don't worry, most changes like that occur only when the, eh, operation is performed on young boys. Besides, control yourself, your voice is rising. Are you sure they didn't succeed in----?"

"You mean to tell me----?"

Alecto kicked him under the table, and he slumped forward with his head on his chest. They were all quiet while the waitress put menus on the table.

The place was every small, plain, restaurant, and it was cleaner than many. They ordered; all except Bors. He wanted only water. He knew, childish as it was, that he was making a point, and he knew that they knew.

"Well, then," Rhamnusia started again, "don't be so harsh with me. We're here for a good reason. We are looking to move a team up the ladder, and you two are just who we need. But there is the *head* issue, and as far as that goes Alecto isn't, um, blemish free either."

Alecto threw her a dour look.

Bors thought, *Here we go; they're going to make me the head head-chopper.*

"We can easily overlook her errant, ah, missteps in view of her mostly-admirable work. Most recently she did ignore our calls and instead went looking for you. Turned out for the best, but she has to improve her self control. I had quite a time smoothing things over.

Rhamnusia continued to focus on Bors.

"Now as to the head lopping, I put my own head on the--so to say--*chopping block* on your behalf, and lord knows why they didn't put you, and me as well, out to pasture. We all know what *out to pasture* means----"

"We know what it means," Bors said with contrived politeness.

"You owe me, Bors, a profound and sincere apology, and when you are through groveling I wish you would try to explain it as best you can, before--if--we get to what John and I came here for."

Alecto took Bors' hand under the table and held it.

"I know it wasn't right. And that sort of thing isn't me. Whenever we have a job to do I'm the squeamish one, not Alecto. It wasn't that. It's hard to explain, but I'll try. I have always been a vigilante type, and an ultimate realist. You don't have to waste time defining what realism is; if you're a realist you just know. I sometimes lack patience, and when I do I have a compulsion to skip intermediate thoughts or actions and get to the point, or to the thing. The deed. I'm action-driven."

Bors looked out the front window and thought for a moment.

"I was new at this. Not really an excuse as much as a reason. I realize I lost it. All I can say is, if I tried to make elaborate, long-drawn excuses I would probably be unsound, or on the verge of eccentricity. And I am not either. Or I would be a chronic bullshitter, and I am not that."

Nobody said anything for a while, until the pause became uncomfortable.

"Anyhow, being promoted *up the ladder* isn't uppermost in my mind. I'm satisfied in doing what I do now, and, um, working with Alecto is, is----"

Bors detected something in Rhamnusia's countenance. A knowing look; probably to do with his and Alecto's liaison. And something else.

They all sat looking at Bors again for longer than was comfortable.

"Besides, if I were to be kicked out of," he lowered his voice to a whisper, "Ragnarök, I know what my fate would be. I understand I wouldn't be around long enough to tell any tales." He managed a stiff smile. "Good thing for me I'm not a blabber."

They finished, eating and the silence was overwhelming for Bors, and probably for Alecto. He didn't care about the others.

At last, "Good enough for me," Rhamnusia said. Will you excuse us for a moment; John and I need to go outside for a bit?"

"Um," Bors replied. They were about to make him their assassin. He watched them leave, and through a window saw them sit on a bench under a tree in front of the restaurant. Rhamnusia said something and John waved his hands in front of her, then they settled down and talked.

Bors and Alecto looked at each other

"What's happening?" Alecto asked.

"Nothing much. Only how our lives are going to change in a big way. If I know them-- and I admit I don't really--they're going to promote us."

"I think you convinced them."

"I was totally sincere."

Alecto blanched slightly. "That's good isn't it? That you convinced them?"

"Dunno." He leaned close and whispered. "I'm afraid that, because of my head incident, they intend to make me their chief executioner."

She gasped. "That's absurd! How did you come up with that----?"

"Think about it. It's not as strange as you assume. We, they, do assassinate people, and our superiors might as well appoint someone who's a professional. But----"

"You're not a professional!" Alecto whispered loudly, and several diners turned and stared at her. She lowered her voice. "You're just a dope who made a mistake. Put any normal person in your position and they may have done the same thing."

"First, I never thought of myself as a dope; second, I'm not a normal person; and third, few people would have been in my position."

"Thank you! Okay, you're not a dope, but your other two observations support my point: you were put in an untenable situation and you were not responsible."

Bors glanced idly around. The restaurant could have been from 1957: record player, red-and-white checkered tablecloth, plain wooden chairs, milkshake machine, ... Like in old movies. He clasped his hands on the table and twiddled his thumbs.

At last Rhamnusia and *John* returned and sat down.

"We agree, but we'll have to consult with some higher-ups," said Rhamnusia. "But as they usually do what I recommend, I'll tell you more about Ragnarök and its overall and sometimes evolving philosophy. Principles. And rules."

"We have known all that for a long time," Bors said.

Alecto stiffened, and Bors waited for the ax--or the sword--to fall, but Rhamnusia kept quiet, ignoring them. Then she went on.

"First let me refresh your memory of our Codex.

One, enforce natural moral laws.

Two, fight intellectual corruption.

Three, oppose philosophical and religious meddling in people's lives.

"As the world degenerates because of the threat of nuclear war, climate change, overpopulation, and so on--and due to human fecklessness--world governments are unable to manage most such problems. The governors are usually not intelligent enough--whether dictators, oligarchs, democratically elected-- and even if they were able, they often don't have the authority to do so. They are abiding by the laws and rules of their respective countries; even dictators who always face opposition. They can't prevail over those who don't play by the rules, so to speak. There have been ideas of how enlightened people could work to improve things, like Ayn Rand's books, but such works have been largely impractical drivel. An elderly writer up in Montana wrote a nonfiction book titled *Rat-tail Curves*, an odd title to be sure, wherein he traced our present world miseries from prehistoric times on up until now, and he offered some suggestions on how to save the world. The suggestions were based on working through normal, legal means, thus even if people followed them, they would in all likelihood fail. As a footnote, many intelligent people don't believe democracies as they exist are viable. Far too often we are governed by the dim-witted and the corrupt, when we should be led by the most intelligent. Democracies are upside down."

A few people entered and took tables, and Rhamnusia leaned forward and lowered her voice.

"Common sense and the ability to remove the shackles of past thinking would tell any even half-way reasonable and quick person that it's not possible to--as I said--*play by the rules* and get anything done, even if those doing the playing know what to do. Most of humanity don't even recognize or agree on what the problems are, much less have the foggiest idea of how to deal with them. You have to fight fire with fire. I ask you, how the hell else can you combat evil on an equal footing? Give up? You can't! And for a change why not have an organization doing just that? It's been done before, but only halfheartedly and ineptly. Seems like it's human nature to have malevolent groups, and if you dismiss religion as flimflam, or worse, there are few who organize *good* groups to oppose the malevolent entities, and even fewer, who in noble cause, engage the malevolents on an equal footing."

Silence.

"Any questions?"

Alecto opened her half-open eyes.

"You've been through all of this before."

"Yes. This is just positive reinforcement. Okay?"

"Okay. I'm just tired. Worn out from saving what's-his-name here."

Rhamnusia tried to stifle a laugh, but Bors only grunted. A bee landed on Alecto's nose, but she refused to brush it away.

Bors felt his heart skip now and then for several minutes, then he settled down. "That's it?"

"Yes, only we have some special, important jobs for you two."

"You mean we're still together?" Bors asked.

"Yes. Goodness knows why."

"Any head-chopping?"

Rhamnusia started. "Any what?"

"You know, decapitations?" Bors answered

"Decapi---- What? What are you asking? You think that's funny?"

"No, I, I wasn't joking. I just don't want to be the Ragnarök assassin!

"What? And lower your voice when you say the *R* word. Assassin? Who said anything about that? Have you lost your marbles? Get the hell out of here!"

Chapter Fourteen

Reflection

Dereck Bors had taken time off to reflect. His life, his personality, . . . , everything about himself. In his younger days he had never been one for soul searching, but he guessed everyone above idiot level did it, and now was his time.

His mother had been okay but not overly bright. His father, Milo, was a different story: a smart-enough, hard-working farmer who had resembled Abraham Lincoln but in a handsome way. In public he had been well regarded, but at home he had become a different person due to his mental illness; some form of neurosis that had made him bitter and psychologically abusive most of the time.

Bors fiddled with an unlit cigar, licking it. He had never told anyone in Ragnarök, or anyone else except Alecto, that he was somewhat obsessive compulsive, and possibly much too pragmatic. On the good side he would be inclined to enforce human politeness and decency, and on the bad side he was usually on the verge of enforcing human morality overzealously. Head-lopping. Well, that was extreme, at any rate some perceptive wag would probably characterize him as a headhunter or something, and he admitted to himself that he had polar extremes, and throughout he sometimes felt his Ragnarök activities weren't as rewarding as he had thought they would be. It seemed that only when he was physically active did he feel good, but the familiar feeling of guilt always surfaced afterward.

Bors was in such a near fugue--a condition which enveloped him several times a year, depending on his stress--that he scarcely knew where he was. He was sitting on a park bench somewhere. It seemed like he was always on a park bench, but where else could he go?

Alecto had been raped some years ago. Her disclosure had come to Bors as a shock even though she had provided few details, and it had certainly given a vital insight into her lingering, damaged subconscious. Now he and Rhamnusia were the only ones who knew. Maybe some at a higher level also knew, but----

Alecto had then told Bors of some of the killings she had committed. She had lashed back by killing, and she admitted she had been too enthusiastic about it. She further confessed to initially not knowing why she had such a compulsion. She had wept in his arms, like a small child.

And Bors realized that Alecto had killed people. It was not all a figment of her poor, wounded imagination. She was hurt in not a few ways; still and all there was a noble strength that had always shone. Lord what a mess he was in as regards her, and he would be from then through it all unto the end.

Alecto had never loved anyone before him, and now she loved him. He knew life would have been ever so much easier without her, but unbearable and incomplete. She was uncomplicated, but she was----

A midget walked by and Bors knew he was reentering the real world. The guy was middle aged and handsome, with a handlebar mustache and fine dress clothes. Bors knew it was now proper to call such people *little people*, but to hell with it, there were much, much *bigger* problems in the world than honing niceties. But wait, had he not just reflected on his penchant for enforcing human politeness and decency? What the devil?

The small guy smiled at him as he passed and Bors smiled back. Must be tough for him.

It was cloudy and hard to tell what time it was. Around three in the afternoon Bors guessed. He never carried a watch; for some weird reason he couldn't stand watches. Or clocks. Seemed like time was either passing too quickly or too slowly. Maybe he was Einstein's doppelganger. Ha! He was no Einstein.

Damned if another small person, a lady, didn't come along, and she looked like she should have had a rolling pin in her hand. She obviously had business with the fellow who had just passed, and it wasn't going to be pleasant. She was hard looking and she might have been able to give more than she received to a normal-sized person. There was a slight froth on her lips.

When Alecto had told Bors about her rape he had been cold on the outside, melting on the inside; and for an instant she had taken him as altogether stone cold, until he had begun to sob, upon which she had melted into his arms. He asked no questions as he held her for a long, long time. And when she looked up at him and tried to tell him more he had put his fingers to her lips.

It was obvious that he was an epitome of contradictions: cold on the outside, soft on the inside; capable of murder for a just and practical cause, yet nagged by guilt for doing so; clear-headed when it came to reality, but totally unconcerned and uncaring when it came to irreality, repudiating all phantasy except his own. He was illogical--even ridiculous--in his inconsistency, but he couldn't change. Absolutely not. Another quirk was his impatience with dumbbells and those who disagreed with him, but forbearing when he had to be. Oh, mercy. He was as much a wretch as was Alecto.

The little guy came running back from whence he had gone, sweat dripping from his face and fear in his eyes, and presently appeared the hard-boiled little lady waving her imaginary rolling pin and shouting at him; something about being out late at night with other women. Bors covered his mouth with his hand to hide his smile. The lady was lagging and flagging, but still cursing as she tried to catch up.

Bors knew he was pissing and moaning too much, but at least it was to himself. More than once he had wished he could return to the old farmstead out on the Montana prairie and just rot. Too melodramatic; maybe not rot, but simply exist. See the wild crocuses come up in the spring; watch the thunderstorms appear in the west, smell the freshness of the rain, sit in front of a fireplace when it was twenty below outside and snowing, ... He knew Alecto would like it.

People held grudges for generations, but maybe that had all changed, and in any case they wouldn't recognize his professional name; his and Alecto's. It would likely take years for them to become part of the community, even though there wasn't much of a community left. They probably wouldn't ever fully fit in, but what the heck, it would be peaceful.

Cart before the horse though. Bors still liked--rather, had faith in--the work he was doing. He had to keep the faith, and with Alecto's support he would.

The small guy came running again, and by now his handlebar mustache was sweat-soaked and drooping, and he was staggering slightly as he passed. And sure enough there came his wife or whoever she was. She had apparently thrown down the imaginary rolling pin and was now trying to sic a small, black dog on him, though the dog had little enthusiasm and looked more worn than their quarry. The whole affair was a pathetic living cartoon.

Chapter Fifteen

Dr. Munch

Bors had never imagined the day when he would come crawling to a psychiatrist, but now he had crawled.

The room was straight out of many of those depicted in old--very old--paintings, with Victorian dark wood walls, plaster ceiling, plank floor, 19th century decor, and of all things a black chaise lounge. Perhaps the setting--the ambiance--was meant to enhance the therapy. He hoped it would work on him.

The doctor, furthermore, was from the 1800s, minus the pince-nez spectacles. Above-average height, dark, lean, balding, pale, and severe, with a thin aquiline nose. And he was jittery to the extent that his fingers never stopped twitching. He and Bors shook hands and Bors caught himself hoping the doctor wasn't an alcoholic.

"Please Mr. Capewell, be seated here at the table so we can become better acquainted." He indicated a large, ornate, dark-oak table with straight, padded chairs. "Now what seems to be your concern?"

Bors immediately sensed that while Dr. Munch appeared to be a decent sort, he had to work at liking him. And *seems to be* the problem rubbed him wrong.

"Well, as I told your receptionist, I'm in a high-stress job which involves activities which are of a confidential nature, and which require me to do things that could make me an anathema to some--even many--average people. Oh, nothing illegal or evil I can assure you."

A suspicious look had come to Dr. Munch's face. "I hope to establish a rapport with you, and that would be difficult or impossible if you withhold anything from me. You realize that, as with lawyers and medical doctors, I am bound to keep everything you tell me confidential."

"Yes, of course," Bors replied, but he knew it was bullshit. Push came to shove Dr. Munch would sing like a canary in a cage full of birdseed.

They talked, and Dr. Munch mostly listened and asked short, direct questions. When Bors had said everything he thought was relevant the grilling began, and it lasted for most of a half hour.

"Now Mr. Capewell, I want to read out loud a list of words, and after each one please

tell me what first flashes into your mind.
Okay?"

"Alright."

"Then here we go. Fear."

Bors hesitated. "Pain."

"Thank you, but a little faster. Love."

"Alecto."

Dr. Munch raised his eyebrows and
paused for and instant. "Dreams."

"Gruesome."

"Duty.

"Obey."

"Peace."

"Montana." Except for the memories of
his father. The doctor again gave him another
curious look.

"Red."

"Blood"

"Flower."

"Beautiful."

"Country."

Bors stiffened. "Corrupt."

"Well," Dr. Munch said. Then he
continued.

"Clouds."

"Heaven."

"Dog."

"Bite."

"Police."

"Overwhelmed."

After he had finished with his word list the doctor asked Bors to lie on the chaise lounge and relax. Bors, feeling kind of silly, did so but the relaxing didn't come. The doctor noticed, and gave him some time, while turning on some calming classical music. Bors knew no more about classical music than he did about art and things like that, but it was soothing.

"Now Mr. Capewell, let me ask you about some of your dreams. If you close your eyes it may help. Can you remember your most recent dream?" He took up a notepad and a pencil.

"Certainly." Bors closed his eyes. "I was standing on a cloud, looking down on the whole of humanity. Strangely I could see all around the world, even the opposite side." He stopped and lay silent for a time.

"Remain relaxed. What did you see?"

"Um, well, it wasn't pretty. I saw all of the misery of the--pardon me for the banality-- *human condition*. Hunger, crime, stupidity, vice, ... It was all before me, and I felt powerless to ameliorate it. It was unbearable." Bors choked off his description.

"Um." Dr. Munch studied his notes, and he seemed to be struggling. "Well, then, let's move on to some other recent dreams. Can you think of another one?"

"A few weeks ago I dreamed of being kidnapped by a group of thugs."

"Go on."

"They tied me up and blindfolded me, and put me into a vehicle, and it took a long time to get to wherever we were going; maybe an hour. When they stopped they pulled me out and removed the blindfold, and we were in a small, open area in some woods. They led me to a deep pit and asked me if I had any last words. Before I could answer they pushed me in. I remember I wasn't at all worried about dying, but as I struggled to keep from drowning I discovered that I was up to my neck in shit, and I knew it was human shit. I then became terrified and started to struggle, but the more I struggled the deeper----"

Dr. Munch coughed delicately into his handkerchief as if he were stalling.

"You were drowning in, in human feces? I must say. That. I have never." He fiddled with his pad and pencil. Bors opened his eyes and Dr. Munch was obviously aghast.

"Have you had pleasant dreams?"

After a short pause Bors' face brightened. "Yes. I was a child on the plains of northeastern Montana, and I was about twelve years old. We lived on a farm. I was an only child, and I was free and carefree as I have seldom been since in real life. Free to roam the prairie and the wheat fields, free to do anything I wanted to do, free to appreciate the fine summer days, the thunderstorms, the wild flowers, . . . , free, free, free."

"What about your parents?

"My mother was the epitome of goodness. Kind, caring, understanding, but not very smart. Good looking though. Almost beautiful." He stopped.

"And your father?"

"Well, here comes the best part. He died. Got caught up in a wheat combine and was ground to pieces."

Dr. Munch's hands shook violently and his pad and pencil fell into his lap. Bors saw his face lose what little color it had.

"You mean to say you----?"

"Why yes, of course. But don't think me despicable. My life until he died had been hellish. And aren't we all responsible for carrying out justice in this miserable world, even if sometimes we have to resort to going outside of the law now and then?"

"You mean you pushed him in?"

"Huh? Oh, no! Surely not. But many were the times I would have liked to." Bors attempted a smile, but he knew it was a grimace.

"Mr. Capewell, now that we are off to a good start I will need to study your, hem, case, please make an appointment with my receptionist for a week from now."

As Bors stood to leave he knew he had blown it by coming. He wasn't as bad as all that.

Bors--Mr. Capewell--made an appointment, but he didn't keep it. There was no help for him with headshrinkers, and after his last performance he worried that Dr. Munch would break his confidentiality rules if he returned to for another session.

Maybe he could turn over a new leaf on his own. Buddhism had been a solace to him once; perhaps again. Leave out the reincarnation and it made some sense as a path to a more peaceful life, and heaven knows he longed for peace. Heaven? Gracious, he would never sink that low on the phantasmagorical scale, and if there were no such scale some practical philosopher, atheist, or other profound and realistic thinker should develop one as a monumental gift to humankind.

Chapter Sixteen

On and on . . . .

Doldrums. Both Bors and Alecto were action people. Alecto was in many respects more cerebral, but Bors thought himself ahead of her in some ways, especially in his grasp of reality. And he was ahead of her in practicality.

Alecto, on the other hand, was more creative; more imaginative, and thus was her compliment to him and his stodginess. Like him she had her limitations, and the main one was her pseudo-religious belief: the old *I don't know much about religion, but I do think there must be something* notion which many people cling to when they can't face the real world, but when at the same time they can't swallow the balderdash of religion, or when they don't possess the intellectual wherewithal to figure out things for themselves.

Bors put down his magical folding sword that he had been cleaning and polishing. He and Alecto remained holed up in the safe house, and Alecto was still in the bedroom sleeping.

They slept together, but he was playing it slowly and carefully.

They had found out, online, about a Mark I which had been publicized regarding a dishonest industrialist in Germany, and the warning--which could only have come from Ragnarök--was the first they had heard about more worldwide activity. Obviously Ragnarök was starting a publicity campaign. Or a propaganda campaign.

They had also been informed that they were to bless a venal judge with a Mark II, but the details and severity of the Mark II were yet to come.

When the assignment was finalized they were told only the judge's last name, Denzer, and to use their discretion on any severity, and that he suffered from coulrophobia: fear of clowns. Acute coulrophobia.

When the day of retribution arrived Bors and Alecto were to meet their Mark in, of all places, the abandoned warehouse where he had been taken, blindfolded, when he had first met Rhamnusia at his Ragnarök initiation. Two helpers had delivered Denzer--bound, gagged, and blindfolded--to a small side room.

Bors and Alecto stopped outside the room and put down their bags. They each had clown clothes, makeup, wigs, . . . , and to add to their menacing performance they inserted voice modifiers into their mouths that would give their speech ominous, almost buzzing sounds.

"This seems ridiculous," Alecto buzzed.

"Not if you have an excruciating phobia," Bors buzzed grimly.

Alecto regarded him thoughtfully. "You don't have clown phobia do you?"

"No. What? Why in the world would you ask that?"

"I don't know. It seems you have so many eccentricities that you must have phobias. No phobias at all?"

"Only one. I have extreme fear of anyone who asks too many personal questions."

"Sorry."

They finished by preparing each other's makeup.

"Are we going to lay a little pain on him?" Bors asked quietly.

"We'll see. If we can get him to mess his pants that would be enough."

Two thugs came out and walked down the hall to wait. They all looked the same, and they never spoke unless asked a direct question.

"Guess we'd better get this over with," Bors said. "Sometimes I'm not in the mood. Not sympathy, just tired of all of humankind, and I wonder how anyone or any association

can make much of a dent in worldwide
malevolence and stupidity."

"I know the feeling. But as we are each
in a grim mood that should add to our
fiendishness. Here we go."

Denzer had been placed on an old
wooden chair in the center of the room. The
room was otherwise empty, and the walls and
floor were covered with dust and cobwebs. It
was nearly dark, with only a small black light
overhead.

Bors stood several paces in front of
Denzer while Alecto ripped the duct tape from
his eyes.

"Aeeee!" Denzer screeched through his
gag as his eyelids snapped back over his
eyeballs. "Owww! Oh, god!"

They waited for him to regain his vision,
and that took a long time. Alecto pulled out
his gag and threw it in a corner, then she stood
in front of him beside Bors. Their victim's
outcries gradually subsided into moans and
sobs, and finally he opened his eyes. It took a
few more minutes for him to focus.

"Ahhh! Ohhhh! What in the name of
heaven? Who, who are you?? Where am I?
Oh lord, save me!"

"Shut the fuck up," Alecto droned in her
mechanical voice.

"Why am I here?" The judge tried to stand, but the chair was nailed to the floor, and in any case he was tied like a cocoon.

Alecto stepped forward and zapped him with and old-fashioned electric cattle prod on his bare belly which was hanging out from under his shirt. He screamed and Bors thought he was having a stroke.

"Quiet!" Alecto said, and she leaned down with her clown face close to his.

Bors couldn't see how that would quiet him, but it did, except for some low gurgling.

"You see," she droned, "we are here to help you. Help you to see the errors of your ways."

Denzer, who had squeezed his eyes shut, opened them, and they widened with terror.

"This is your Mark II. You have been corrupt, and you will now change."

"I haven't been----"

She waved the prod menacingly. "We talk; you listen. One more outburst and you will wish for death."

Denzer clamped his mouth shut and sat shaking.

"We have the goods on you: bribes, kickbacks, all of the usual corruptions that too many of those in high positions but of low-level intelligence succumb to. Hard evidence that we could show you, but why bother? You already know. There can be no denial, and any further attempt to do so would be a personal affront to us, and we don't like to be affronted. Believe me, we do not."

She leaned down so that her clown face was close to Denzer's face and wagged her finger in front of him as a school teacher would at an unruly child. Bors thought that Denzer was having a heart attack.

"Here's what will happen," Alecto resumed. "You will resign your position. Furthermore you will change for the better. No more professional or personal corruption. You will change your ways as an atheist or a common villain does when he or she finds the Lord. Believe me, you do not want to be visited by us again. That's as simple and plain as I can put it. If you agree, don't speak, just nod."

Denzer blubbered slightly, and nodded.

"Very well. My friend Giggles," she pointed to Bors, "and I would hate to bestow on you a Mark III, believe you me. Sometimes fat, sedentary people like you don't survive the Mark IIs, much less the IIIs, etcetera. But we know you, and we have faith in you. We know you can change for the better. No more bribery, collusion, and all of that. You will be a model citizen, and who can tell, perhaps you will devote the rest of your life to charitable work of some kind or another? I feel it in my bones that you will make us proud."

Bors smelled urine.

Alecto blew a noisemaker in Denzer's face, then she pulled out a bulb horn and tooted it loudly in his ear. He fainted.

As they left Alecto said, "Pissed his pants and passed out. I guess that was enough."

"We could go back and----"

"Naw, he might have a heart attack or a stroke or whatnot."

"Would that be so bad?"

She took off her mask and looked at him quizzically.

He removed his buzzer and removed his mask. "What?"

They walked down the hall.

"We'll get a lot of publicity out of him. I suspect there will be far fewer corrupt officials after this."

Chapter Seventeen

Later
The further decline of humanity

Bors and Alecto sat side by side on a bench in Town Square Park in Hattiesburg, Mississippi. They were on a mandatory vacation, and it had been up to them whether to go together. It was Sunday and the only sounds were church bells and chirping birds; and the chatter of some heathens who were not in church but who nonetheless looked happy enough. It was peaceful.

Bors, not by nature scholarly, had nevertheless begun to wax philosophical about a nonfiction book he had read. The one by the old goat up in Montana close to where he had grown up, titled *Rat-tail Curves*. It was a literary work.

Bors was reading part of the book to Alecto, and he couldn't tell whether she was interested or not.

He read on.

There are courses of
action that could offer some hope
of secular salvation. Harald
revisited his conviction that only
the world's most intelligent
people can improve the world,
and possibly save humanity from
its own annihilation. Built on
that premise there has to be a
starting point; a platform on
which to build. The best and
only platforms from which to
choose are western democracies,
despite their democracyness.

Alecto seemed to be listening, but she
was a captive audience and it was hard to tell.
"The Harald in the book--the main
character--is the author," Bors said. "This next
part is in italics to indicate the main character's
alter ego."

*Despite their being
democracies?*
*Yes, capitalistic
democracies. And I will
interject here that capitalism has
become a contradiction. Here
we are crowing about capitalism,
while many of us insist on*

fulfilling everyone's every want and need, making everyone equal, penalizing success, ... Socialism to the point of absurdity and impracticablness.

Well, and all, I can't repeat it to you enough: the most important function of a government is to look after the well-being of its citizens and any other residents, and that of the world in general, and how the hell can that be done when every booby in most such countries is allowed and encouraged to vote? Talk about a paradox!

What? Are you advocating for the overthrow of the country?

No.

Then what?

Hang in there.

People must have been getting out of church; there were more of them strolling around in the park and they looked like they had just had their batteries charged. Alecto stood and straightened her long, white, lace dress, then she sat down again. Bors had never seen her wear a dress before, leastways such a fancy one.

"I didn't know you read such literary books," Alecto said.

"They're only literary to those who are somewhat dull."

"What do you mean?"

"Too dull to read them."

She frowned at him.

"I fear I have bored you to death," Bors said. "*Bored* to death."

"Not at all," Alecto winked at him. "I'm not a dullard."

He ignored her. "I have heard that this author is too advanced for a great many readers. Most of them are into bodice rippers and such pulp. But he appeals to me, and in fact I believe every word he has written. I consider his work to be my everyday bible, but he has missed an important point: that you can't fight stupidity and moral and ethical depravity entirely through normal, legal means."

"Does that make us heroes; you and me?"

"I've never thought of us that way. Let me continue. Don't worry, I won't start reading again. As you must know, most new and revolutionary devices or concepts that have benefited humankind have been met with fear or scorn by the general populations. When the Doomsday Clock strikes two minutes to twelve the world masses of people don't know it, are indifferent, or are too goddamned dumb to do anything about it even if they wanted to."

Alecto responded, "Or they're smarter than the eggheads who think they have all of the answers because they instinctively know there is nothing that can be done."

"Horseshit. They're just dopey. Look at what we're doing."

A hefty late-middle-age lady approached them and laid a New Testament on the bench between them and smiled warmly. "What a lovely day," she said.

"Let's go back to the motel," Alecto said.

Chapter Eighteen

What passes for relaxation

In the morning Bors and Alecto were
back on the same park bench in Hattiesburg. It
was good to *get out of the office* for a while.

The park was busy with both locals and
tourists; mostly tourists it seemed. It was easy
to tell them apart. Families, teenagers, old
couples, and single people; many single elderly
men. It was like going back to the '50s, Bors
supposed, when, as *they* say, life was simpler.
Dogs too, most on leashes, but a few running
loose and shitting on the grass. There was a
large, stray, fearless black tomcat boldly eyeing
the dogs with evil intent.

Bors clasped his hands behind his head
and relaxed, and Alecto placed her hand on his
knee and tried to do the same, but he knew she
was working at it. She was no more of a
natural relaxer than he was. Far from it. A
cardinal landed in a nearby tree and Bors
watched it. Cardinals had been the mascot of
his Montana football and basketball teams,

though there hadn't been a cardinal within a thousand miles.

Bors stiffened, and Alecto felt it.

"Don't look around," Bors said. "Good thing we're wearing sunglasses."

"What?"

"I think we're being watched. Followed. If you want to see who I'm talking about, just move your eyes, not your head. There's a guy about fifty yards away, ahead and a little to the left, standing there trying not to look our way."

"I don't see him. Only an old lady."

"That's him. I've been observing him, and he doesn't make a very good old lady. I feel like Sherlock Holmes and I'm trying to deduce as much as I can about him. He walks like a man, therefore he is a man. He's young and inexperienced or he wouldn't be so obviously tracking us. He's anxious, twitching and always glancing around. And a few other things."

"He's not the only one who's twitchy."

"Take it easy. He's not going to try anything on us here in public; and certainly not with that cop nearby. He's no Barney Fife."

There was a policeman near them: young, athletic, and bright looking.

"How in the world did you pick him out?" Alecto asked.

"The cop?"

"Don't trifle with me."

"He was sitting over across from us pretending to read a newspaper, and he was using the old trick of punching a hole in the paper through which to see us. That's another reason he's new: no one nowadays does that."

The cardinal ruffled its feathers as if it too were anxious. It seemed to Bors that birds in general were always nervous, and probably with good reason; everything was stacked against them. The only exceptions were owls.

"Oh Christ," Alecto moaned. That wasn't like her. "Are we destined to live the rest of our lives like this? Will we have to get plastic surgery and walk around in disguises until our final days?"

Bors couldn't help smiling. "Good grief, aren't you being a little melodramatic? And I'm not going to let you ruin your angelic face. You're my angel. What's the matter, can't you stand beauty?"

"Better to look like a hag than to wind up dead!"

"No it isn't. Anyway I'll protect you."

"Like you protected yourself when you about got neutered?"

Bors turned to her, lowered his glasses, and scowled. "Thank you ever so much." He lifted his glasses and turned away. "We'll work it out. We're going to have words with

Rhamnusia about this, that's for sure. They send us on R&R, and we find ourselves worse off than if we had stayed where we were. What kind of tinpot operation is Ragnarök running?" He had whispered *Ragnarök*, and he took Alecto's hand. It was stiff and cold like that of a two-day-old corpse. "I swear by the Almighty that I will take care of you, even if it means my own life."

"You idiot," Alecto monotoned. "And there's no Almighty."

"I'd like to knock the guy off right now. You got your rocket gun with you?"

"No, and don't be silly. The poison is fast, but not that fast, and the rocket range isn't that far. The cop or some other do-gooder would tackle you before you put away the gun, even if you had shot it through your straw hat. Don't try to be a hero."

"I'm not trying to be a hero, I just can't stand it when someone tries to do us in. It riles me up."

"I doubt if he's going to try to do us in."

"Why not?" Bors eyed the cardinal. "Why would they go to all of this trouble-- sending some jerk all the way down here--just to spy on us?"

"Um."

"And even if you are, unofficially, the senior partner, we're going to take out this old lady before this vacation of ours is over.   I'm feeling a definite dislike of this guy."

"Now listen to me Mr. Bors, what if this guy is FBI?   Eh?   Knocking off an FBI agent? That's not what we do, even if he is following us."

"Shush."   Bors looked slowly around. "Well----"

"Well nothing.   Sometimes you fly off the handle.   Who's being melodramatic now?"

They sat quietly for a while.

"Couldn't we at least knock him on the head and----"

"No!"   Alecto jumped to her feet and stood in front of him.   And that's that!"

Bors felt his face redden.   He reached for her hand and guided her back to the bench, and put his arm around her shoulders, and again they were quiet.

Finally Bors smiled at her.   "But no plastic surgery for you."

In spite of herself Alecto giggled.

Two days later Bors got up early in the morning and went in search of their mystery man.   He found him behind their motel smoking a cigarette, and knocked him cold with the leather sap that he always took with him. Then he woke Alecto and hurried her, half-asleep and confused, out to the taxi he had called.

Later, on the airplane, he confessed, and he was surprised by Alecto's nonchalance. "I guess I have to allow you a little leeway," she said.

Chapter Nineteen

Bors' *heavenly* dream

When Bors opened his eyes he didn't know what had happened, where he was, or for all that, who he was. All he knew was that it hadn't been a regular dream, and the reason he knew was that it had been a pleasant experience, whereas most of his dreams were bad. And, with regular dreams he was self aware when he awoke.

Alecto was beside him in bed, still asleep, and then he remembered who he was, and that they had rented a room in a cheap-but-clean motel somewhere; but he couldn't yet recall what town they were in. He had never heard of anyone forgetting who they were unless it was due to an injury, or to permanent senility. Well, there was that drunk up in Montana who woke up----

The *dream* had been about, of all things, Heaven. Or leastwise a Utopia. And that in itself was almost as strange as forgetting who he was. A wonderful mental state to which he wished he could return, but then--as Alecto rolled toward him in her sleep and threw her arm over his face--a wave of horror enveloped him: what was wrong? Was he showing the first symptom of some severe mental illness? A brain tumor or something? Heredity? His old second uncle Howetson had gone mad, and while Bors was aware of few details he recalled some the the family lore, and it sounded like he might be following the same path. Uncle Howetson had wound up running around naked crowing like a rooster, in between periods of catalepsy, and in his final years the catalepsy had prevailed and he had starved to death after his feeding tube had been disconnected.

Alecto opened one eye and seemed confused, then she laughed and grabbed his privates. He pushed away her hand.

"What's the matter, too much last night?" she giggled.

Bors tried to speak, but he hadn't fully recovered, and she knew something was wrong.

"Are you sick?" she asked.

"It was a dream," he whispered. "A strange dream." He was trembling.

Alecto got up in bed and knelt over him, feeling his forehead, then she took his wrist and felt his pulse. "What, . . . , what happened?"

Bors sat up, and as he did so he felt how weak and shaky he was.

Alecto took his face in her hands. "For God's sake, what's wrong?" She was frantic.

"I woke up, and as I was admiring your angelic face something happened, and the next thing I knew I woke up again from some kind of trance."

"Trance?"

"Yeah. Well I guess it was a dream, but what a dream!"

"Holy cow."

Bors worked up a weak smile. "The dream, or whatever, was unusual, even for me. It was actually a pleasant, blissful state; kind of like having died and gone to Heaven, or Valhalla, or----"

"But you don't believe in any of that Heaven bunk!"

"I know, but that's where I was, or someplace much like it."

"And if your dream was so heavenly, why are you so agitated?" Alecto relaxed somewhat and propped her pillow up beside him, regarding him. "Settle down and tell me about it."

Bors drew in a deep breath and exhaled slowly, and his tremors subsided. "Agitated? You'd be agitated too if you didn't believe in all religious nonsense." He tried, and failed, to suppress a smile, and he gathered himself.

"I was in Heaven, or somewhere like it.
Not the familiar *up in the sky* Heaven as in most
religious myths, but more like the Garden of
Eden myth.   It was like a tropical paradise, but
with no insects, poisonous reptiles, or anything,
and no dangerous wild beasts.   I was
completely calm like I had never been before;
perhaps nirvana."

"Take it easy."

He stopped at the thought of nirvana.

"Go on," Alecto urged.

"I had the feeling that I wanted to stay
there forever, and then you approached, and
there were three of you.   Don't laugh."

"Do I look like I'm laughing?   I'm sure as
hell not laughing."   She put her head on his
chest.   "Don't worry, we'll manage this."

"There were three of you, all seraphic----"

"All what?"

"Angelic.   One of you wore a golden
crown, the second *you* wore a silver crown
adorned with pearls, and the third *you* had on a
bronze crown studded with gems: diamonds,
rubies, ...   You all came toward me, but you
weren't walking, you were floating.   As you
grew nearer I could see your beatific smiles,
and then I knew for sure I would try to stay
there forever--in the realm of light I was in--for
after all what could be better than staying there

alone than staying there throughout eternity with you?"

"But with three of me?"   Alecto tried to stifle a giggle.

Her giggle did more to assuage his fear than had her words.

"The more of you the better," he smirked. "As all three of you drew close your crowns disappeared and you merged into one, and it was then that I knew I could manage."   He smiled at his quip.

"What next? Alecto asked.

"I don't remember much, except, as I said, I didn't want to leave.   We cavorted around in Eden.   But then everything began to fade as if in a heavy fog, and I seemed to rise and drift away.   You were calling to me to stay, and I flailed around attempting to descend, but it was no use."

"And?"

Bors felt himself tense again.   "I was half conscious and I didn't know where I was, or even who I was.   I knew nothing until I looked over at you again."

Alecto kissed him on his cheek.   "Don't worry, we'll get you straightened out even if you have to go back and see Dr. Munch."

"Oh, no, not that quack!   He made me feel worse."

"Well someone.   Anyway maybe it was an isolated occurrence; your dreamy-weamy."

"I sure hope so.   An old second uncle of mine got kind of like that, and he wound up in a nuthouse.   Uncle Howetson.   Come to think of it some of my other relatives were pretty goofy too.   Grandpa Fetlock----"

Alecto put her index finger over his lips. "Shush.   It's over now.   I have excellent instincts, and I know it's over.   It was just a temporary lapse.   Actually, it was certainly just a dream.   In any case we will carry on together, in each other's strength, in each other's love, and in each other's humor.   That's what carries us through a lot of our trials: our humor.   Even your sarcastic, sometimes bitter, sense of humor."

"And your common-sense humor."

"Have you heard the one," Bors began, "about the three owls who went into a bar?"

"Oh, lord.   No."

"Well these three old owls went into a bar and----"

"How did they get in?"

"I don't know.   Somebody left the door open.   Anyway they bellied up to the bar and each ordered two straight shots of whiskey. Then----"

"How could they pick up the shot glasses?"

"Good grief I don't know!   Probably *beak-us--because*--they did it with their beaks. Well, the first owl . . . ."

"Were they guy or girl owls?"

"Males.   After they each drank their first shot . . . ."

Chapter Twenty

Job security

Bors and Alecto were up a notch in the Ragnarök hierarchy but they didn't know what that meant. Not money--they had plenty of that and not much to spend it on, and little opportunity to do so--not prestige because other than their superiors there was no one to impress; not job satisfaction because they either had that or not, and if not they shouldn't have joined in the first place. Job security, since they were members--inmates--for life.

Bors hated New York City and everything about it and many of the people in it. It was a city of scum and he wished they could be based it some small, idyllic town in North Carolina, Vermont, or Montana.

He, Alecto, and Rhamnusia were in the rear of a small coffee shop staring at the cups and donuts on the table. The place was busy, which was the way Rhamnusia liked it: being lost in a group. And they could tell she had something big.

Bors toyed with his cup and Alecto studied the corny signs on the walls: *Coffee is the Stuff (Staff) of Life*, and so on. Bors shifted in his chair as a curious thought popped to mind: the signs probably appealed to a large majority of voters. What a way to run a country. Most of the fellow coffee drinkers looked like typical voters.

He wished Rhamnusia would get to it. Thus far she had sat silently with her eyes on the wall opposite her, and that wasn't a good sign. He didn't know her well, but he knew tension when he saw it.

"It has come down to us that we are to take out Zabov," she said.

Bors started and looked at Alecto, who always took satisfaction in her calm demeanor. Except this time she had been startled too. They each tried to speak, but neither could. Rhamnusia, who usually had a slight sense of humor and smiled whenever popping some assignment on them, showed no emotion. Her countenance was bland; as vacant as a featureless white mask. A death mask.

Bors' hand wanted to shake as he took a gulp of coffee.

"Mother of pearl," he said, "we aren't even certain of what he looks like. He may have undergone surgery, and he is a master of disguise. How in the world----?"

Rhamnusia held up her hand. "Don't worry, we have new photos of him."

"Don't worry?" Alecto quavered. Quavering wasn't in her nature. "Now I see why you have *promoted* us; we're expendable."

"Not at all. You two have your faults, but for this you are the best. You know you are."

Rhamnusia turned to a shade of gray as they studied her for signs of acerbity.

A nondescript young waiter poured more coffee for them. His main feature was his pimply complexion, otherwise he was a typical young guy.

Bors put down his cup and squinted sideways at Alecto, and his only thought was how lucky he was to have her working alongside him. She had saved him once and she could possibly save him again, and she was capable of saving him from himself. He would do his utmost to look after her too, and, well, crap. Alecto looked back at him, and he reaffirmed what he had known from the day they had first met: rough as she had been he had seen her soft spots, and he would give his life for her. His miserable life, which wasn't worth much. Well, it was still a good thing she had him. He was better than----

"What does he look like then, where is he, and are you particular about what we do with him?" Alecto asked.

Rhamnusia breathed in and out slowly and deeply. "First off you should understand how much I regret dumping this on you. I----"

"Thanks, but we know what's coming," Alecto interrupted with a hint of sarcasm.

"You don't," Rhamnusia countered. "Not the degree. Obviously those higher on the totem pole know more."

Alecto shrank ever so slightly.

Rhamnusia went on. "I'll give you a packet with all of the info when we leave here. Don't lose it. Study the contents carefully. And there are photos. I must tell you that however he looks like in your mind's eye, he doesn't look like that in real life. Not the *Rocky and Bullwinkle* character Boris Badenov, or like----"

"*Rocky and Bullwinkle?*" Bors croaked.

"Nor does he resemble any of the James Bond villains, or the villains in most of the banal commercial television shows. He is as nondescript as a man can be, and that is one of his assets. He looks like the kindly neighbor on the block."

"Crap," Alecto grumbled. "But I guess what's the difference if he's usually in disguise anyway?"

"It's not all bad. Besides the photos we have artistic renderings of him in his disguises. One of his flaws is that his repertoire is limited to about a half dozen facades. He's been so successful that he's getting lazy."

"Where is he?" Bors asked.

"Somewhere here in town. We'll----"

"Somewhere here in the city? Well that's a big help!"

Rhamnusia glared at him. "If you will let me finish. Dear me. We'll let you know when we narrow down his location, and we'll find him. You'll will know everything from exactly where he is to what time of day and night he takes a leak."

A twinge of enthusiasm came to Alecto's eyes. "What do we do with him?"

"Whatever you want, but do it quickly."

Bors looked up at another inane coffee sign: *The Brew for You, and You for the Brew!* God!

Rhamnusia resumed. "It will take us a few weeks to prepare, and in the meantime we'll have several easy jobs for you."

"We could use some rest," Alecto said.

"Those easy jobs *are* your rest."

"Oh for----" Alecto fell forward with her face on the table.

Bors sat still. Rhamnusia had meant it as a joke, but Alecto, who had never really liked her anyway, probably unconsciously had turned it into cruel tartness.

"She only meant it as----"

Rhamnusia held up her hand, and he caught the *thank you* in her eyes.

Bors took Alecto by the hair on the back of her head and playfully pulled her back upright.

A few minutes later Bors and Alecto walked hand-in-hand away from the coffee shop.

"Oh, my" Alecto sighed. "I have no religious faith at all, but it must be comforting for those who do."

"A while back I thought the same thing. I tell you what, I'll start a new religion--people have been doing it for millennia--but I'll make my religion more reasonable and believable, like no more angels, no goofy miracles, and all that. Given enough time, and if we're desperate enough, we might even start to believe in it. Might even attract some followers who we could start fleecing."

"What will you call this new religion?"

"Oh I don't know, I hadn't thought of it till now. Let me see. The Knights of Salvation. Yeah, The Knights of Salvation. Even better, The Knights of the Golden Fleece.

Many religions sanction fleecing of their flocks."

"I sometimes wonder about you."

"Good.   Keeps you on your toes.   You know, it has to do with our work.   It gives my life meaning."

Chapter Twenty-one

Heart and soul

Bors woke up and Alecto was on top of him, although she was still sleeping. He thought he had been in Paradise, but reality was pretty good too.

Afterward fatigue overcame him and he fell back asleep.

When he awoke again Alecto was alongside him with one hand between his legs. She was studying his face and smiling wickedly but charmingly. Bors had recovered his stamina enough to have an erection.

"Good morning you animal," she said.

"Ohhh, am I in heaven?"

"Yes you are, and I am the Angel of Aphrodisiac."

"More like the Angel of Exhaustion. You're the animal."

"Thank you."

He looked about and remembered they were in a safe house again. It had been pitch dark when they had arrived and he didn't know where they were.

They sat up in bed.

"We are entitled to some rest and relaxation," Alecto said.

"Some rest and relaxation. Apparently you have changed the rules."

She smiled but didn't answer.

"Now do I get to make another rule?" he asked.

"Yes. What?"

"That you take it a little easier on me. In bed." He winked at her. "By the way, where is this place?

Alecto hesitated. "They think the fewer who know the better. Like if someone threatens to cut off your balls again you would talk. That would be harder on me than on----"

"Huh. We've been through that witticism before."

"We'll find out when we leave here. Once we go into action it's us or them and of no use to keep secrets."

Bors didn't quite follow her logic but it didn't matter. He studied the bedroom. Not much to study; just the same old wallpaper and so on.

"Is this place gas-proof?"

"Yes, and it would take a hellacious bomb to do any significant damage. We're safe unless they lay a nuclear bomb on us."

"You did that last night. I'm lucky to be alive."

Instead of smiling Alecto winced, and Bors didn't follow that either, and he realized again how complicated she was.

After a moment of quiet Alecto turned even more grave.

"This is also our place of planning and preparation," she began. "We are not likely to be put up against anyone as dangerous as Zabov again, and if we fail we'll probably die."

Bors stared at the ceiling.

"We'll get to that in a few days, after our rest and relaxation," Alecto went on. "Our greatest challenge so far. On another subject, I can tell you that Ragnarök will be expanding even more to other countries, and working overseas may be more dangerous to us than confronting Zabov."

"How come you always know more than I do?"

"You persist in asking. I've been at it longer, and while I like confronting the bad guys I don't go off unhinged and lop off heads on the spur of the moment."

Bors stifled his urge to argue about his misstep or about her fantasy of killing bad guys.

They got up, dressed and went into the front room.

"Do you know any foreign languages?" Alecto asked.

"Norwegian."

"A lot of good that'll do you. Not much world crime hatched in Norway." Having recovered her good humor she giggled.

"Dritt," Bors growled. "*Shit* in Norwegian. Tull. *Bullshit.* I happen to know it's getting rough over there too. There are few refuges these days."

"I still don't think it will be Norway. They'll give you a crash course in some language, and though you won't pass for a native speaker, you'll leastwise be able to get by when they----"

"Alright! Can't we talk about something more pleasant?"

"Certainly. What would you like to talk about? What would you like for breakfast? Anything you want, but cook it yourself."

Bors focused on an old lithograph on the wall behind Alecto's head. It was of a riotous celebration involving beer drinking and debauchery, probably in Belgium or Holland in the 18th century. Beer steins, bare breasted women, ...

"Marry me," Bors said, rather than asked, out of the blue. He had surprised even himself.

Alecto looked like she had been slapped across her face, and she shrank back against the wall hard enough to knock down a picture. There she stood, frozen and expressionless, then she melted and slid to the floor and slumped forward with both hands over her face, weeping quietly.

Bors went blank and fell backward several steps. He felt like every part of him had turned to stone, and when he had recovered some composure he was unable to tell whether she was glad, or whether he had committed some terrible misstep. He moved toward her, but she waved him back. He went to the table and sat down.

After some time Alecto got to her feet, wiped her face with the backs of her hands, and smoothed her hair. She sat across from him and looked at him pathetically.

"You take the cake. You join Ragnarök, from which there is no escape for either of us, we get embroiled in what many would consider to be vile endeavors, we're both eccentrics--to put it politely--we both have suspect pasts, ... And of all things, you ask me to marry you! Wouldn't that be great? No little gingerbread house with a picket fence, no nice neighbors, no children. None of that."

She exhaled one final, long sob and reached across the table for his hand.

"I know you meant it with love, but sometimes you are such a dope."

Bors wiped his face with both hands. "It just came out. I don't know what----"

"Do you expect me to be flattered?"

"No, I----"

"Well I am. But Christ!"

They held hands across the table, and for a long while that was all they could do. Nothing more would suffice and he knew that Alecto felt the same; and as she was in some ways more cerebral than he, she likely felt their rapport more intensely.

When their communion was over Bors emboldened himself and, against his better judgment tried again.

"Still, regards my question--which I now assume is unspeakable--don't you think that someday----?"

"What question?"

"The, um *M* word."

"Married?" she asked.

"Yeah. If someday we're finished with Ragnarök----"

"We'll never be completely free, you know that. Only in Ragnarök's version of retirement, and by then, even if we survived, we'd be too old. You aren't thinking of bailing out are you? That would be----"

"No. But like the guy in an old, old song *. . . you can't go to jail for what you're thinking, . . . ,* I can't help wondering."

Alecto withdrew her hands and put them to her temples. "You're giving me a headache."

Bors waited. Then, "But just suppose. For my sake. For our sake."

Chapter Twenty-two

Zabov

Bors and Alecto were in Denver where they had bestowed a Mark I on a foreign news reporter. They were then free for a few days.

As they walked idly down a side street in a downtown area they pondered their upcoming Zabov assignment, and the possibility that after Zabov they would be sent abroad.

"I look forward to the Zabov thing, but I'm not enthusiastic about going to another country," Bors reflected. "Unless it's Norway, and I must admit that my view of Norwegians is based on the bumpkins who emigrated from *the old country* around the time my grandparents did. Back then they limited themselves mostly to drinking, wife beating, philandering, and things like that. I hesitate to think what Norway is like now."

"Probably still better than here. I can't wait to get my hands on Zabov," Alecto said.

"How about when we get sent to China?"

"I don't care. The main thing there is, you don't look Chinese."

Bors grinned. "No, but more than you do. Still, a little eye surgery and a light tan, and you----"

Alecto smiled. "Same for you." She picked up an aluminum can and threw it into a nearby trash bin. "And as you are getting more full of baloney all the time, I don't think they will have to give you an artificial tan. We'd best start eating at more Chinese restaurants; my Mandarin is a bit rusty. How about you?"

"So is my Cantonese."

"More likely we will go to Europe."

"I have always liked western Europe."

"I didn't know you had been there."

Bors smirked. "I haven't."

"Dear lord. Behave yourself."

"Good thing I'm going with you; I'm just a hayseed from Montana."

"You certainly are."

They walked quietly until they came to a low stone wall in front of a house that was for sale, and they sat perched on the wall. A couple of young boys went by on their bicycles. They were about ten years old, and both were already bordering on obese.

Bors considered for a while, then, "I have two questions for you."

Alecto looked at him with her eyebrows raised.

"When we first met," Bors started, "what was it about me that you couldn't stand?"

Alecto, who almost never blushed, blushed lightly. "Well, I, um, didn't think I was so hard on you."

"You were. I was starting to think there really was something fundamentally wrong with me. Or with you. Truth is, I suspected you were a lesbian."

"A lesbian! What the----?"

"Well I had never been treated that way by women, and in fact they have usually clung to me; and you treated me like I was a leper, or like I was always wearing dirty underwear."

"Sorry, I didn't think I was that unkind."

"You were."

"And I'm not a lesbian. Nothing against them, but I'm straight."

"Oh, dear me, are you sure?"

They sat watching the two boys pass by the other way. Bors felt a tic in his right eyelid as he regretted his bitter comment.

Alecto merely patted his knee and watched the boys fade into the distance, and Bors could not begin to imagine what she was thinking. She had on her melancholy look.

"The partner I had, Griffith, looked a lot like you," Alecto said. She turned her head and looked away toward the house across the street. "Griffith."

She had told him about Griffith long ago.
He waited, but she remained silent. "And?"

"I don't like to talk about him."

"Alright, sorry, but you brought him up."

"I didn't mean to; it just came out."

"At least tell me if you loved him. Don't
you think I'm worthy of that?"

Alecto turned--full body--to him.

"I'm so ashamed. Certainly you are
worthy. You are the most worthy person I
have ever known." She sobbed softly. "Love?
Oh, no, if fact I didn't like him much, but I cried
for a long time."

"Oh."

"Besides, remember, he was gay."

"Right."

"That had nothing to do with my feeling
toward him. I simply didn't care much for him,
and I didn't know why. I still don't. I
sometimes think it was me more than him. I
guess he was an okay guy."

Bors knew when to keep quiet, and this
was one of those times. They were both still.

Then, "Do you have another question?"
Alecto asked.

"Oh I just wanted to know if under
different circumstances you would marry me?"

Alecto stiffened and slid off the wall, and
she scowled at Bors so fiercely that he thought
she was going to beat him with her fists. But

she turned away and started crying. He wanted
to come to her, but he held back for a while.
When her crying had subsided to soft
blubbering he came behind her and took her in
his arms. At first she tried to get away, but
then she stopped struggling and twisted around
to face him.

"You nitwit," she said. "That again.
You know we can't, yet you keep bringing it up.
What if one of us got killed, or----"

Bors tightened his arms around her.
"This time I was only kidding."

"The devil you were, and I'm glad you
weren't because kidding would have been
worse." She cried again.

"Come and sit on the fence again," Bors
said as he moved her back. "I have one more
idea, and no, don't look at me like that, I just
want you to think about it. You don't have to
agree or even answer me."

When they were settled Bors said,
"Consider this: when our Ragnarök days are
over, let's revisit this."

Alecto stared mournfully at him. "If we
both live."

"Well, yes."

"Wonderful. We'll spend the next ten or
twenty years worrying about which of us gets
killed first."

"It would be something to look forward to. I mean, at the end of our Ragnarök time. We wouldn't be very old really, and until then we'll consider ourselves married. How's that?"

A 1957 Chevy passed by and an old geezer looked at them.

She looked blankly at him. "Piffle."

Bors continued, "Also, we could bail out of Ragnarök early."

"Hogwash! Are you getting senile; you've been through that before too. You know nobody has ever succeeded in doing it."

"I have heard of one."

"Who told you?"

"I can't remember. But if it's possible then we can do it. I have a place up in Montana, and I've thought it all through. Eh-eh, don't interrupt. Listen, all I am asking is for you to think about it."

She looked at him doubtfully. "Alright."

"See, we have something to look forward to already."

"I don't know what to think of you."

"Well figure something out. I can't abide not being thought about."

Alecto didn't smile, but she didn't frown or grimace either. "Let's go back to the motel, I'm horny and so are you."

"I am?"

"You are when I say you are."

Chapter Twenty-three

Never more

Bors was aware of Rhamnusia holding his hand and speaking to him, then nothing.

Again Bors felt someone holding his hand. He was in bed, and he was unable to open his eyes.

"Welcome back." Rhamnusia was beside him. She stroked his cheeks, one after the other, and kissed him on his forehead.

"What happened?" Bors whispered. "Where----?"

"You're safe. Try to open your eyes."

"Unh, I can't."

She gently massaged his eyelids with her fingertips. "Now try."

He opened his eyes but nothing came into focus; only a blurred face hovering over him. "I don't feel good. Where are we? Alecto?"

"She's, she's away.   I'm here to take care of you.   Don't worry."   She took both of his hands and squeezed them.

Bors woke up again and looked around.
Rhamnusia was still by his bedside and there was someone standing behind her.   "This is Dr. Magnus," she said.   "You've been out for weeks."
"Comatose," said Dr. Magnus.   "We've been feeding you through throat tubes and intravenously."   He sounded gruff.
"My throat's sore," Bors said.
"Here, drink some water."   Rhamnusia lifted his head and held a glass to his lips. After he had drunk the glass dry Rhamnusia eased his head back onto the pillow.
"Alecto?" he asked again.
"She had a bad time too.   But don't worry about that now.   You know she would want you to recover."
"Recover?   What happened to me?   I can't----"   As he fell asleep he heard Rhamnusia ask the doctor, "What's going to----?"
"It'll take time."   He lowered his voice to a loud whisper, "Don't tell him about Alecto until we feel he's ready."
"Ready?   He'll never be ready!"
"Nevertheless."

Over the next few days Bors felt himself grow stronger, but whenever he asked about Alecto, Rhamnusia was evasive. One day he exploded.

"God dammit, I have to know about Alecto! What happened to her? Tell me!"

Rhamnusia stepped back from the bed, shocked. "Please, I'll tell you. I promise. Wait until the doctor gets here, and I will tell you everything. I swear."

"When?"

"Soon. Any time now."

"Your silence is killing me," Bors said, but he quieted himself. He concentrated on the ceiling: large red and black checkered squares, and his head began to swim so he closed his eyes.

A young, chubby, large-breasted nurse with a cheerful demeanor came in and felt his forehead. If she lost twenty pounds she would be gorgeous, Bors considered, but he instantly wondered what had brought that to mind.

"If you don't beat all," she said, "it was touch and go there for a while, but look at you now. You're a vision!"

"A vision?"

"Quiet now."

She put a stethoscope to his chest and moved it around.

"Well, your heart is still there and your lungs sound good.   Still nothing wrong physically."

She left the room.

When Dr. Magnus arrived Bors sat up in bed for the first time.   "Alright, out with it. I'm through listening to your bullshit, and I want to know right now what happened to me and to Alecto.   Start talking, and don't hold anything back.   I can take it.   And when do I get out of here."

The doctor and Rhamnusia pulled chairs close to the bed and sat down.

Dr. Magnus began.   He seemed less gruff; even sympathetic.

"First," he studied Bors," you are not as strong as you think you are.   You've been comatose for weeks.   You suffered, as *they* say, a nervous breakdown.   I'm a psychiatrist, and there are technical terms for it, but nervous breakdown best describes your condition."

"So that's it," Bors said.   "I wondered what had happened to me.   But why did I break down?"

Rhamnusia looked at Dr. Magnus, and he nodded.   She turned back to Bors.   "You were told that Alecto is dead."

Bors felt his face freeze, and his heart started thumping and skipping beats. "Dead?" was all he could say.

Rhamnusia pulled her chair closer and took one of his shaking hands. He pulled his hand away.

"Why didn't you tell me?" he shrieked at her. "You should have told me! I had a right---"

Dr. Magnus broke in. "I told her not to. You weren't ready. If you insist on blaming someone, blame me."

Bors glared at Dr. Magnus, then Rhamnusia, and back at the doctor. "I could have handled it."

"You couldn't have," Dr. Magnus said firmly. "Being told was what caused you to go under in the first place."

"You mean I had no physical injury?"

"No. You were simply told the truth about Alecto."

"Ohhhh," Bors groaned. The room swirled about him and he could hardly breath.

Dr. Magnus went to a small leather bag, took out a syringe and a small vial, prepared it, returned to Bors, and gave him an injection. "This will help."

They all sat quietly, and Rhamnusia again took his hand, which was no longer shaking.

Dr. Magnus looked at his watch several times, and finally he said, "I think we can continue."

"Continue with what?" Bors asked.

"With everything." Dr. Magnus nodded to Rhamnusia again.

She started again, quietly. "Alecto was killed, and when we told you, well, you left us for weeks." She regarded Bors to get his reaction, but there was none.

After a few minutes Bors simply asked, "Who killed her?"

"Zabov." Rhamnusia began to cry.

"How?"

She looked again to Dr. Magnus, who replied, "We won't get into details yet, but it was a dreadful death."

Bors opened his mouth to speak, but Dr. Magnus held up his hand. "We'll hold back nothing from you, but I want to wait two days before giving you any further details. Do you agree to that?"

Bors nodded and pulled Rhamnusia to him. She fell on top of him with her head on his chest, and lay sobbing.

When the two days were up Dr. Magnus and Rhamnusia told of Alecto's death, and it was worse than Bors had expected. He turned stiff and silent for a long time. After a few minutes he asked, "May I see her body?"

"I'm sorry," Dr. Magnus replied, "but she has been cremated and buried. No relatives we could contact; nobody." He paused and looked down at his own clasped hands. "And I am obligated to tell you there really wasn't much left to see." He staggered to a chair and fell into it, and Rhamnusia collapsed to the floor.

When his head had cleared to where he was rational Bors was struck by an awareness-- actually a reconfirmation--that there was no afterlife. What a strange intellection, renewed by his recent horrible experience. He had never had any firm religious inclinations, but this was the clincher. He had died, in any spiritual sense that he might have clung to. If before he had felt the presence of a god; not now. Certainly not the foolish *gods* encountered by people in dreams, waking from dreams or from anesthetic, and all other such nonsense; and definitely not a real, comforting god who would have greeted him at the Pearly Gate. Now there was absolutely nothing; a nothingness he had never before experienced; a consummate void that could not be conveyed. Not even the part of Buddhism that was more of a philosophy of life than a religion. The purest nihility he had ever experienced. Mentally he was dead.

Rhamnusia had crawled to his bed and
flung herself over him, and he was grateful.
He loved her now, but as a child loves a mother.
There would never be another Alecto.

Chapter Twenty-four

Rhamnusia

Bors' recovery took a long time, and all through it all he planned his revenge on Zabov. Revenge of the most terrible kind, through Ragnarök or not, and whether he lost his own life or not. Until then he had felt young physically and mentally, despite his demanding, often onerous work for the group he had joined, on principle, for the salvation of humankind. And he now knew that whatever befell him from then on would fall on a different person; and immersing in Ragnarök work would nevermore be a complete solace. Maybe no solace at all. In the meantime, for however long it took, he had one mission, and Rhamnusia had promised to help. She had pulled some strings.

There were three muscle men this time. The task required three. When Bors and Rhamnusia entered the small room one of them was fiddling with a battery-operated drill and some large screws and washers.

Bors knew of Zabov's several plastic surgeries, the most recent of which had transformed him into a bland-looking, pudgy cartoon character. Except for his deadly eyes.

Zabov showed no fear. "Ah, Mr. Bors," he said. That was all.

Bors didn't look at him while he unrolled a large 3'x4' photo of Alecto and removed some tape from his pocket. He taped the photo to the back of a wooden dinner chair and faced it toward Zabov.

"Beautiful," Zabov said.

No amount of surgery could disguise Zabov's small size, nor his venom. When he had first learned of Zabov, Bors had naturally pictured a large, mean, Russian stereotype.

"I don't know what you have in mind for me," Zabov said, "but don't think I will ever show remorse. It's easy to make people talk, and perhaps even me, but you should realize that whatever I say under duress will not be true." He was sitting bound to a large chair.

Bors faced him. "*Duress?* Ha! You call it duress? Oh my, you have a way with words. Good gracious, you of all people should----"

"I prefer the delicate term," Zabov smiled.

"It's a pity that I'm not here to trade jibes and banter with you."

The walls of the room were of bare concrete except for one which had been lined with thick wooden beams. Rhamnusia had told Bors that the entire structure, a small nondescript home, was completely soundproof, including the concrete ceiling. No one could be heard from within, and no one without a jackhammer could escape.

Rhamnusia stood rigidly in one corner, and Bors looked at her for reassurance. She gave it, in some way which even he could not have described, for she moved not a muscle in face or body.

Bors nodded to the two men standing beside Zabov's chair. "Hang him up."

Zabov showed no emotion as they untied him and held him to the wall crucifixion style. The third man approached with a large screw and a flat washer in one hand and an electric drill in the other, and affixed Zabov's left hand to the wall. Zabov winced but uttered not a sound. Then up went the other hand, and the only sound was that of the drill. Blood trickled down.

Bors thought he would have taken more satisfaction, and he was surprised at his own benumbdness. "Now the feet."

Zabov's toes barely touched the floor and the goons crossed his feet and tied them, then drilled a larger screw through them between the ankles and toes. This time Zabov tried to stifle a groan. Just to make sure, the three men took up a wide leather belt and fixed it across Zabov's waist, screwing it to the wall on each side to ensure that he could not tear himself loose.

Bors moved the chair with Alecto's photo closer to Zabov. Zabov tried unsuccessfully to spit on it.

"The room is soundproof," Bors said, "and even if by some miracle you were to work yourself loose you could not escape. Nor could anyone without a code enter even if they knew where you were. The outside of this place is disguised as a modest older home, and the mail, utilities, garbage, and so on have all been canceled while the *family* is on vacation."

Zabov tried to spit on Bors.

"Eh, eh, none of that old sport. I must say, you're not a very good spitter. Oh, by the way, I am going to set a glass of water on the stand here beside the chair just in case you get thirsty." He did so. "Well tah, tah, and off we go. Give my regards to Satan when you get there."

Outside Bors first noticed the perspiration on Rhamnusia's face, then the weakness in his own legs. They both leaned back against the wall of the house as their accomplices finished locking up.

A young girl walked by bouncing a basketball, and she was followed by an old, slow beagle. The girl waved and they waved back.

"Good gracious," Rhamnusia huffed. "That was rough. I've been out of the muscle stuff for too long."

"I've been in it for too long," Bors countered. "I go from week to week, on again off again. Sometimes I'm zealous, other times I'm ready to give up."

They turned to each other and smiled. Their smiles were weak.

Chapter Twenty-five

Another episode

Bors first thought he was in the room with Zabov; then it dawned on him that he had had another of his *episodes*. A mild one, for his head didn't ache and it didn't take long for him to make out where he was. He was in bed in the dumpy motel room several miles outside of New York City where Ragnarök had put him up, and Rhamnusia was sitting beside him. Unlike any major blackout, this one had apparently only amounted to a short amnesia.

"Well as I seem to have needed a babysitter, thank you," he half mouthed, and she seemed to understand.

"Do you remember anything?" Rhamnusia asked quietly.

Bors thought for a few seconds. "Some."

She felt his forehead and the coolness of her hand felt good.

"I was in some kind of large, cavernous, foreboding place. I was cold, and the only illumination came from torches. I called out but there was no answer; only my echo, but it didn't sound like me. It was like someone was mimicking me. Ridiculing me. I was looking for someone--but as in dreams--when I tried to walk I could hardly move."

"Who were you looking for?"

"I'm not sure. Maybe you."

But he was sure. It was Alecto.

"Then?"

"Well you know, the usual: apprehension, vulnerability, confusion."

"What else?"

"That's about it."

He didn't know how long he had been out but he thought Rhamnusia had aged and had become permanently worried. She looked down.

"What?" Bors asked.

She raised her head and her look of reprimand withered him.

"I've saved your sorry ass more than once, Bors, and the least you can do is be straight with me."

He flinched. She had seldom been harsh with him, but this was different. She was severe. He put his hand over his eyes for several minutes.

"Alright. No more bullshit between us."

"From you, don't you mean? I've been straightforward with you!" she burst out.

Bors took his hand away from his eyes. "Alecto was in the dream. I'm sorry."

Rhamnusia sat still, looking at him an a strange way.

"Don't be sorry for something over which you have no control," she said. "I don't need, or want, guilt from you, but if we're going to, . . . , to get along, or whatever else may develop, don't lie or withhold things from me. Okay? I won't do that to you, and you have to be open with me."

"You're right. I guess I was still a little under----" He stopped, knowing how disingenuous he sounded. "Whatever happened to me, I was wrong to shut myself up like that. It won't happen again. I promise, and I never break my promises." He smiled.

She didn't respond to his smile, but she edged closer and held both of his hands in hers, and her face melted.

After a few minutes Bors asked, "How long was I in Dreamland?"

"About an hour. Do you do that often?"

"I don't *do* it; it comes over me. But no. Don't worry, it seldom happens, and never when I'm in action, so you can be sure I'll never let you down when it counts."

"And afterward?"

"That's when it occurs. And after it does all I need is a little rest. It comes less often now. Give me time. Can you live with that?"

"Certainly."

"Anything like that I should know about you?"

"No," she said. "As you have no doubt figured out I'm perfect."

"But if there is now's the time----"

"Later. You may think me perfect but I have my weaknesses."

"I didn't think you're perfect; I only . . . ."

A week later Bors and Rhamnusia lay in bed staring blankly at nothing. He felt guilty, and he wondered what she felt. Occasional footsteps in a nearby stairway were the only sounds. It wasn't supposed to have happened. Not that soon. Rhamnusia was exquisite, and moreover he had a rapport with her.

She took his hand. "We've done it now haven't we?"

Despite his misgiving he had to smile over at her. "Done it? Yes, we have certainly *done it*." And thus having voiced it, his guilt abated. "And I think we can both congratulate each other on----"

"Oh, please." Her eyes were moist. "It wasn't supposed to come to this."

"I believe it was. We mustn't let this cause us any regret whatsoever. We have a bond, you and I, and we're more than friends. You know that. Don't worry, we'll be discrete, and we'll carry on. You'll treat me with some disdain around others, as usual, but we'll both know."

Bors rolled toward her and kissed her full on her lips, long and passionately, and she returned his kiss with the same feeling, and he felt her melt in his arms; then they lay holding hands like school children.

Bors said, "We're here to relax, and I don't know about you, but I feel darned relaxed."

Rhamnusia had brought him to a small inn not far from Burlington, Vermont, to further convalesce after his relapse. It had been only a slight setback, but she had insisted.

Bors forced himself to get up, fully aware of his old bugaboo of trying too hard.

The inn--named Maple *Something or Other*--was clean and comfortable and Bors surprised himself by feeling relaxed and optimistic. He wanted to thank Rhamnusia for that, but such plain, overt talk was not his style and he knew she would see it as corny and insincere.

Nonetheless another purpose of their visit was for Rhamnusia to fill him in on a new development in the Ragnarök organization. At the suggestion of one of the lower agents apparently there would be a trial effort to not only punish the lowest and most nefarious of society, but to reward the best. If the concept worked it would be adopted by agents in other countries. Seldom had the high mucky-mucks asked for--much-less followed--suggestions from below, and Bors guessed the new proposal had registered with them despite their apparent--somewhat stodgy--mentality.

Bors was skeptical of the idea, but he hoped it would work. Rhamnusia had tried to shine her best light on the effort but it was apparent that she too had reservations. It wasn't yet clear what the rewards were to be, and that was probably the sticking point: rewarding people for doing what they should already be doing. What foolishness. Ragnarök was good at punishing people, but . . . .

Too bad that his *recovery* came mixed with Ragnarök bullshit.

Part II

Chapter Twenty-six

Forging on together

They walked down the street holding hands; Bors and Rhamnusia. They were still new to each other in their relationship, but he had always been able to sense women's----

"Denver, Colorado, my favorite city in the entire country," she burst out.

"I loathe it," Bors said.

"What? Why?"

"Don't know."

"I think you do know and it has something to do with our assignment."

He let go of her hand and stopped by a drugstore. "How could you know that? You think you're clairvoyant? You know nothing of what I'm thinking."

"Well pardon me all to hell. No need to get huffy."

Lightning flashed in the north and a split-second later thunder rolled in, and as Bors and Rhamnusia riveted their eyes on each other for a few seconds large raindrops began to pelt them.

Bors removed his jacket and put it over her. "I apologize. I'm not like that."

"I should hope not."

"May I give you an excuse?"

"As long as it's reasonable and you don't make a habit of it. Making excuses. I should say, doing things that call for excuses."

"I'm not big on excuses, and never have been. I can't tolerate those who routinely make them. As to that crack about you being clairvoyant, my only explanation--not even an excuse--is that I feel we are being downgraded--even denigrated--by being given petty jobs. Here we are to put a Mark II on some goofus who----"

"Goofus? You sound like you grew up in the 1940s or 1950s. I've noticed it since we first met."

"Could just as well have. Northeastern Montana a long time ago."

To his relief Rhamnusia was attempting to cover up a smile.

"Allow me to continue with my lame non-excuse, and don't smile."

She smiled.

"You can't reproach me for being hot under the collar," he continued, "and I have observed that you yourself have been a wee unsettled. Here we have a moron who----"

"Ha, ha, hah! Hee! Listen to you! Ha, hah----"

"Enjoy yourself," Bors huffed, but he couldn't muffle his own laugh.

"But this Mr. So-and-so must be small potatoes if all he----"

"Not Mr. Miss. Miss Hornpiper."

"You don't say. But allow me to get to my point; aren't we beneath ourselves to be fooling around with minnows? Why aren't we going for the sharks? And how are we to give her a Mark II all by ourselves out in the open?"

The rain had stopped and they walked on.

"Here's what little I know," Rhamnusia began. "The *minnow* is not so small. She was involved in a bank--or savings-and-loan or something--fraud whereby hundreds, maybe more, of people lost their savings."

"And all she gets is a Mark II?"

"Calm down. She's our path to the real culprit; the *shark*."

"Who's he?"

"Dunno. That's why we need her to talk."

"That's not much to go on, but how come it's always you they tell?"

"What's the difference? Is it your ego?"

"Ego schmeego, I simply get tired of being so low on the hierarchy."

They entered an ice cream shop, bought cones, and sat at a small, blue, old-style table in back.   In back, out of habit facing the front where they could see the entrance, and close to a back door.   Bors was unaware of their caution until Rhamnusia mumbled something.

"Hum?"

"Are we paranoid?" she asked.

"I hope so; I don't want to go to the Happy Hunting Ground before I have to."

"Happy----   Oh for----   You must be far older than you look to be speaking in that dialect."

"I'm twenty-three."

"I'm sixteen."

"I tell you what, I'll call it Elysian Plain, the ancient Greek paradise.   Wait, better yet I shall call it Valhalla.   I'm sure I have Viking ancestors there, wherever *there* is, and they are more than likely raiding some poor Italians or Frenchmen or such.   Then they grab the women by the hair and drag them back to their longboats and take them back to Norway where they have their way with them, and before they know it those women start liking their treatment, and furthermore they get together their own weapons and shields and go raiding with the men.   Well that's all fine and good till they start kidnapping men!   Then----"

"Oh for criminy sake!" Rhamnusia said.
"What am I going to do with you?"

"You could start by capturing me!
Taking me to----"

"I'm becoming nauseous, Pickle Dick."

They licked their ice cream cones for a
while.

"What are we going to do with the
minnow?" Bors asked.

"My idea, unless you have a better one, is
to nab her and take her to a motel where we can
encourage her to talk. I don't think it will be
too difficult, as they say she's pretty fragile; one
of those types is clever and devious of mind but
who doesn't function well in the real world; and
we are going to impose some of that reality on
her. It won't take much and I suspect she'll
warble like a canary."

She licked her cone.

"You have a better idea?" she asked.

"Nope."

A tough-looking elderly man dressed in a
black suit came in and glanced at them, and
Bors felt for his gun but the old fart sat down
with his back to them.

Rhamnusia, who had noticed the man too,
went on.

"The real culprit--the one she worked for-
-is a mystery so far, but we'll find out all we
need to know from the minnow. What we do

know, or suspect, is that he is either in law enforcement or a high-up money man of some sort."

The black-suit customer glanced at them, and Bors felt for his gun again, and this time he grasped the handle and flipped off the safety.

"The money man will get more than a Mark II, I'm sure of that, and you will likely get your wish for a higher-up assignment."

Three days later they had a *talk* with the canary, who warbled so long that they actually had cut her off.

Chapter Twenty-seven

Haskell?

Bors woke up and bumbled in the dark to the bathroom. He had had one of his infrequent good dreams, and he had wanted it to continue. Maybe he could go back to bed and revive it. The clock struck once; one o'clock, or some half hour, but he didn't care.

Back in bed he reviewed his dream. It had been about his childhood on the farm back in Montana, and despite his father's psychopathic abuse, some of his early years had been okay, mainly because his father--when he wasn't mistreating him--had pretty much left him alone.

So, even while knowing how silly he was being, he closed his eyes and concentrated on his dream. He lay for a long time but he couldn't sleep, so he got up much dismayed and padded barefoot to the kitchenette and prepared coffee, and as he waited he remembered how dreams occurred just before wakefulness.
Well, the whole thing was far-fetched anyway.

Bors was in an apartment in Baltimore and he was alone, waiting for a temporary partner to show up, and he sorely missed Rhamnusia who was off somewhere doing something. She had refused to tell him anything about it.

A guy named Haskell was to help him put the fear of Beelzebub into a presidential candidate. Candidate for president of the United States for chrissake, who was about as vile, loony, and moronic as they come. And totally corrupt.

There was a knock on the door and Bors, now clothed and alert, got up from his chair and stepped behind a wall within a few steps of the peep hole.

"Yes?"

"Mugwump," was the answer.

Bors opened the door and was face-to-face with a tall, thin man who appeared to be in his early thirties. "Haskell," the man said as they shook hands.

Bors was surprised at the power of his temporary partner's grip; he reminded him of Sherlock Holmes in both appearance and in deceptive strength. "Pleased to meet you," Bors said. He instantly liked Haskell, though he didn't know why; he didn't like many people, and almost never right away.

Bors closed the door and locked it, and offered Haskell the best armchair. "It's too bad we are sworn to so much secrecy," Bors started. "You look like the kind of guy I could talk to." He felt awkward.

Haskell studied him for a moment, then, "You know, I was just thinking the same about you. Strange isn't it? Things like that don't happen."

They slumped back in their chairs and stared at each other with no awkwardness.

After a minute Bors began. "I guess you aren't here to talk about the Baltimore weather or politics."

"Oh I don't mind."

"Tea? Coffee? I don't have much else."

"No, thanks."

Bors felt at ease. "What's up?" he asked.

"Strangely, nothing in particular. I've simply been sent by some of the upper-ups to get to know you. I assume they'll have me working with you, but I have no idea of what we'll be doing, or when. They just said we should talk about anything that's relative to Ragnarök; and that it's important we should try to form a professional bond, so I suppose we'll be seeing each other now and then. That's all I know."

"That's certainly more than I know," Bors smiled. "But nothing new there; I'm usually in

the dark about everything.   I guess they figure
the less I know the less I can reveal.   That old
thing."

"Don't you have a full-time partner?"

"Yeah.   Rhamnusia.   She's the order-
giver.   I don't mind."

Haskell sat stone-faced and silent for a
moment.   Then, "You two get along okay?"

"Yeah.   Any better and I'd be----   You
know."

"Well," Haskell went on, "nothing much
to know about me.   Farm kid from Kansas,
college, majored in accounting and went to
work for an agricultural chemical corporation.
Just about went nuts from boredom.   Became
obsessed with politics, then the obsession
turned to revulsion at the corruption and idiocy.
After ranting and railing online and so on for a
few years there came a young lady who seemed
to have all of the answers.   In short, she was
from Ragnarök, and I was off to the races."   He
grinned.

"Ha!   About the same with me," Bors
countered.   "I joined, and the gorgeous lady
who first worked with me convinced me I had
made the right choice."

"Rhamnusia?"

Bors could actually feel his face go white.
A sort of paralysis came over him for an instant.

"No.   Another.   But she died."

"Oh.   I am sorry."

Bors lifted his right hand from the arm of his chair.   "She was the best friend I have ever had."   He reached out with one leg and stepped on an ant.   "To be honest, the only true friend."

"And now?"

"Rhamnusia."   He stomped on the ant again to make sure.   "Nothing like Alecto, but a true friend.   It's queer how Ragnarök pairs us up like they do.   You'd think the personal attachments would be a liability.   Hmmm. Maybe they are, I don't know.   Or perhaps they're the glue that holds us together through the onerous work we do."

He had been looking down at his feet, but he abruptly stared up at Haskell.   "And you? A colleague?"

"I have several."

"Then why me?   Why more?"

"How the deuce would I know?   You should know better to to question----"

"Yeah, but I have never heard of anyone having more than one."

"Listen, I have never heard of it either, but I know enough not to ask too many questions.   I did once and I was knocked down a peg or two; and it wasn't pretty."   He laughed in a way that sounded odd to Bors.   "Anyhow, ask me anything else you want to know; I have no secrets."

"How often do you sleep with your partners?"

"Never. They're men."

"Whew! You won't be chasing me then!"

They both guffawed heartily, and Bors knew they would be fast friends.

Yet----

Chapter Twenty-eight

Same old thing

". . . the shark," Rhamnusia continued. "So back to Denver we go."

"I hope the minnow hasn't warned him," Bors said. He hadn't asked about her recent absence, and he hadn't bothered to tell her anything about Haskell.

"Not likely after we made her foul her pants. Anyway she's been *relocated*."

"Relocated? I didn't know that."

"Oh, did I forget to tell you? Sorry."

"You forgot? Horseshit. Why do you----?"

Rhamnusia regarded him with her unique expression. Humor, mostly, but something else he hadn't been able to figure out. He hoped it was lust.

"I didn't want to burden you," she said, "because I know how fragile you are."

"Yeah, well if you weren't so gorgeous I'd kick your----"

"Poo, poo!"

"Where did they take her?"

"All I know is it's someplace where she can't communicate with anyone, and after we bless the money man--his name is Oswald--with a Mark II they'll let her go."

"First name or last?" Bors asked. "Oswald?"

"Um? Oh, last."

Bors got up from the sofa and went to the window. Rhamnusia had found a nice, clean mom and pop motel outside of some small town far from New York City.

"Isn't a Mark II kind of mild for someone who has ruined people's lives?" Bors asked.

"Of course we do have some leeway, and if you agree I'm inclined to lean more toward a Mark III."

"I agree."

"And once in a while we get lucky, like when we know our mark has a severe phobia. In Oswald's case he suffers form Belonephobia."

"Belone----?"

"Fear of pins and needles," Rhamnusia smiled. "That'll make our job much easier. He won't just be nervous; he'll be *on pins and needles*. I've arranged to have an acupuncturist help us, and by the time she's through with him and we turn him out onto the street naked he'll look like a porcupine."

"Lord," Bors groaned. "How many needles?"

"Oh I don't know. Fifty or a hundred."

"That'd make me see the errors of my ways."

"Really? I didn't know you ever made errors. You're old-fashioned, and thus are as pure as the driven snow."

"And if you keep on with the time-worn adages you'll put me into a funk."

"See, there you go again. *Funk.* You sound like you've just arrived from the sticks of Montana in the 1960s."

"*Sticks?* That's not much better. Really, how old are you anyway?" he asked.

She put on her demure mask. "You'll never know."

"I'll seduce you, and right in the middle I'll ask you, and you'll tell me."

"You're so full of----"

"You will. That trick never fails." He could play the game too and he had on his court jester face.

But his jester face failed. Rhamnusia had assumed a doleful, disgusted mask and while he didn't know what line he had crossed, he realized then that she was not as secure as he had assumed, and perhaps not as secure as she herself had thought. From then on he would

treat her with extra consideration. She was
paradoxical; so hard, and so soft.

"Come on," Bors said, "let's go for a
walk. Motels, hotels, safe houses, I'm getting
claustrophobic." He didn't know what mask to
put on for claustrophobia.

She hesitated for a second, then took his
hand and got up from the sofa. She wobbled to
the door and he had to go back to the closet for
her straw summer hat.

It was a nice day for walking; sunny, no
wind, mild. Bors tried to take Rhamnusia's
hand but she shook him off. After a few
blocks he tried again and she gave in. She then
turned and smiled at him.

He said, "I don't know what I did to upset
you, but----"

"It wasn't you. Well, it was kind of a
crude joke, but that wasn't it. Usually I'm calm
but I have these lapses that have nothing to do
with anyone, and certainly not with you, Mr.
Bors."

"Can you tell me about it?"

"I would, if I knew myself. All I can say
is that once in a while I take things the wrong
way, and it's no one's fault but mine; and maybe
not even mine because it's like a lot of other
personal quirks people have; that are probably
innate. I don't know. I hope you'll make
allowances."

"Of course I will."   He squeezed her hand.

They walked on and Bors started over. "Have you ever wondered why Ragnarök often teams men and women together?"

"No. It seems obvious to me that there are far more men than women, and since women are the weaker sex it wouldn't be practical to team women together."

"That's kind of sexist isn't it?"

"No. Just realistic."

"Okay. Here's another one. How many of the women take up with the men they are with?"

"Take up? Spit it out. Have personal relationships with?"

"Yeah."

"I don't know."

Bors pondered.   "I've been curious about what Ragnarök thinks about such things."

"I assume they don't care, since as far as I know they haven't been handing out chastity belts to the women."

"If they had, would I have the key to yours?"

"Yes you would, if I could steal one from Ragnarök."

An owl hooted far away and Bors stopped.

"What?" Rhamnusia asked.

"What, what?" Bors responded.

"Why did you stop?"

He looked around. "Stop? Oh, yeah. I don't know. I must have daydreaming."

"About chastity belts?"

"Ha. I guess so."

When they got back to the motel they sat at the kitchenette table to plan the upcoming Mark II.

"Same old thing," Rhamnusia said, "there are a couple of muscle men, and an acupuncturist, out there right now finding a place to do the job, and checking out Oswald; his home, his movements, and all that. I don't think there will be any problems."

"I'm ready," Bors said, but he couldn't bring himself to tell her that he was getting burned out. As for her, at times she was transparent and at other times opaque, and as regards their recent work she was opaque, and he was afraid to ask questions.

He had to ask one question; one that surely wouldn't agitate her. "Wouldn't it be nice if they picked us to hand out some of those so-called rewards?"

"Who?"

"Ragnarök. Their carrot-and-stick plan. Reward people as well as punish them. I'm cynical though; I'll bet it's just a recruiting plan to turn them into snitches."

"It so happened that they gave up on their harebrained plan."

Chapter Twenty-nine

Charity, Montana

"I'm going to take you on a little tour," Bors said, "along the Montana Hi-Line--a very picturesque, if barren, drive--and east to my old home and the farm where I grew up. You're in for a real treat."

He and Rhamnusia were driving north out of Denver in the 1993 GMC van they had been provided.

"Whatever you say," she answered, "I'm ready for a break."

"Why this roundabout route?" Bors asked. "Because it's unique, and one has to experience it all in order to appreciate it. This way you'll appreciate the vast area more."

When they got to Great Falls, Montana, Bors stopped and bought a tent, two sleeping bags, a camp stove, and all of the other things they would need. Rhamnusia was perplexed but she kept quiet as he loaded the equipment into the back of the van.

"There," he said, "got everything. The sleeping bags can be used individually or they can be zipped together. That's up to you."

"Actually, it's up to you."

"Hmm?"

"Depending on whether or not you misbehave."

"Umm? I think you're trying to bend me over, but assume you want me to misbehave."

Next Bors slipped into a liquor store and bought a large bottle of Kentucky bourbon whiskey.

As they drove out of town Rhamnusia couldn't hold her peace. "You don't drink!"

"No, but you do, and I figure if I can get you piffed I can have my way with you."

"First of all that would be rape, and second you don't have to go to all that trouble you know."

"Rape? Not at all. I'll have you sign a consent form before I ply you with drink."

She regarded him with a sour look that lasted for a half minute.

"I know you're extraordinarily intelligent," she said, "but often genius comes at a price, and that price is all too often insanity. Right now you're being crude, and you think you're funny. You must be a genius."

Her excoriation stung.

After they had driven a mile or two he began his apology.

"As you know I'm a depressive, and though I don't know if I'm as smart as you think, depression is sometimes called the genius disease because intelligent people are more able to comprehend human misery and the causes. Certainly most people comprehend misery, that's obvious, but knowing the higher-level causes--and being powerless to do anything about them--is terribly depressing. Sometimes I'm criticized for it."

Bors glanced at her, and she seemed bewildered.

"Why do you think I'm in Ragnarök?" he asked. "For my health? Because I'm vile and evil and I enjoy hurting and killing people? For the thrill of it?" His anger built. "I know all too well I can be abrasive, even crude, but you know what? In spite of trying as hard as I can not to boil over, sometimes I do. My frustration builds and then I either have to find some escape--like heavy exercise, getting away from it all for a while, or simply being with you--or I'm prone to a melt down. I never know what kind of meltdown or when. But listen to me. Since I've become close to you I've noticed a big difference in myself. It's all because of you."

Her face reddened.

"You are not only my life, you're my lifeline, and don't think I'm head over heels in love with you as a way of saving my life, that came as a special blessing."

"I'm----"

He stopped her. "There's more. Don't, even when I'm at my best, think I'm such a prize. If you ever do. Please remember, those like me, though they do their best to be *normal*, are technically mentally ill, and occasionally they have lapses. I'm not trying to use my condition as an excuse; only pointing out that on rare occasions I'm not altogether in control of myself."

"I know that." She leaned over against him. "I was----"

"One final thing--and I swear it's not to lay guilt on you--I would do the same for you, and more if I could, even if it meant my life."

"Oh, god," Rhamnusia blubbered, "I've been a fool." Her head fell onto his lap.

Bors put his fingers in her hair and rubbed her head soothingly, and he wished there was something to phrenology so he could fathom her inner workings. She could be so mysterious.

They continued along the highway as one, stopping at motels whenever they felt like it; the camping equipment was for later. Havre, Malta, Glasgow, and small, dying towns between; but it was a peaceful drive. They they could see for miles, usually in every direction, and often there was nothing to see other than wheat fields, range, and rugged openness. Widespread farms and ranches, occasionally a pickup or a horse and rider in the distance, and now and then a farm vehicle or a tourist on the highway, but not many. Bors felt his muscles loosen, and whenever Rhamnusia released her seat belt and leaned on him he felt her tension fade too.

Bors waved his hand across the windshield. "This was all homesteaded in the late 1800s and early 1900s, but for different reasons the people have been leaving ever since. Drought, pestilence, poor farming methods, The Great Depression, and changing times in general. Farms and ranches have become fewer and larger. It's a tough life."

"Survival of the fittest?" Rhamnusia asked.

"In a popular way. I see it as a good place to live if you're not farming."

"Huh?"

"At times--when I become fed up with what we're doing, and with life in general--I might just want to get away from it all, and this would be one of the best places to do that. It's called Big Sky Country, from a book titled *The Big Sky* years ago."

Rhamnusia's voice hardened ever so slightly. "Here, where it's hotter than blue blazes in the summers, dry, windy, lonely; and anywhere from twenty to forty degrees below zero or colder in the winters? That's your idea of a good place to *get away from it all*? Are you batty?"

"There's an old saying up here: *Twenty below zero keeps out the riff-raff.*"

Rhamnusia winced. "What about the summers?"

"The dime-sized mosquitoes take care of that," Bors chuckled."

She sagged back in her seat and if not for her seat belt he thought she would have slid to the floorboards.

"Cheer up," he chirped, "the cold snaps don't last long, and----"

"Yeah, I know a bit about the north, and even if the thirty and fifty below only lasts a few weeks, and it gets back up to minus ten and twenty below, whoopee!"

"And with a little mosquito repellent the summers are not too----"

"I give up!" Rhamnusia threw up her hands in surrender. "Only don't regale me with any more. I know you have a kind heart. Have mercy."

Bors usually knew when to keep his mouth shut. He kept quiet as he slowed for an antelope in the ditch. You couldn't hit an antelope if you tried. Deer acted like they were trying to get hit, but not antelope, though they were the goofier-looking of the two. Besides, deer came out in the evenings and went around trying to commit suicide at night, while----

"Did you see that antelope?"

"A blind person could have seen him."

They arrived in Charity--the town near which Bors had grown up--in late afternoon, and as they drove through what remained of it. Bors thought he heard an ever-so-slight gasp from Rhamnusia. A dirty, dusty main street with still some early 1900s buildings surrounded by mostly dilapidated houses, a few residents walking around, several dogs, a cat, two beat-up pickups, ... They drove eastward up the street and Bors waved at an elderly man who was coming out of the Silver Slipper Bar and the man waved back and weaved his way to one of the pickups.

"You know him guy?" Rhamnusia asked.

"Of course not. Up here you wave at everyone. Not a kiddie wave, but a reserved thumb and two-finger, or some such, greeting. Never a one-finger salute though. There are protocols and attitudes."

"Attitudes? Like what?"

"Like if your people didn't homestead here you're always an outsider."

"Really?"

They passed two closed churches. Only one, the Lutheran church, was still in business, but business was slow.

"What a dismal, desolate place," Rhamnusia observed.

"What do you mean?"

"In general. Everything."

"Like?"

"I don't know where to begin. What about that old coot who just came out of the bar? How does he get by with his drunk driving?"

"There probably isn't a cop within twenty miles or more. It would be a waste of their time to doodle around here, and no doubt everyone knows to give that geezer a wide berth. The worst that could happen would be that he would drive in the ditch and sleep it off, or someone would find him and take him home. Guys like that at least have enough sense not to drive on the highways.

"What about if someone has a heart attack or stroke or something?"

"There's a good medical facility south of here where we turned north, and there's still a volunteer ambulance service."

"You could be dead by the time you got there!"

"The lesson is to never have a heart attack or a stroke," Bors laughed.

"Someday I'm going to----"

"Let me just say, this place can be hellish, but it can be heavenly in every way: peaceful, safe, beautiful----"

"Safe during blizzards? Safe when----?"

"You have to know the area like I do."

"And the isolation? From people. Loneliness."

Bors paused to consider his answer. Not for himself, but as to how it would be received by Rhamnusia.

He resorted to a question. "Wouldn't that be one of the prime attractions?"

They pulled into the old homestead and even Bors was nonplussed. The old two-story farmhouse was beyond dilapidation, the barn had fallen sideways, and the other outbuildings were in similar stages of decay. The trees were mostly dead except for one old cottonwood, and the caraganas, and they were really only large shrubs. You couldn't kill them if you tried. Someone had left an old 1930s Chevrolet pickup there and it was rusted all over. A fox darted out of a hole and ran away and sparrows twittered in and out of the broken windows of the house.

Bors swallowed hard and looked at Rhamnusia, expecting the worst, but she was impassive.

Bors had to say something. "I haven't been here since I left when I was young."

"How old were you?"

"Around fourteen or fifteen. I went south with a custom combiner. We started out in Texas and worked our way north."

"Pretty young."

"I was big for my age, and mature. And desperate." He looked away and winced.

"And your mother?"

"I loved her, but I always held it against her for not standing up for herself and me against my father, all the while knowing she couldn't have. And she wasn't very bright."

"She could have left him."

"Times were different then."

"Was she attractive?"

"Yes."

"Then she could have left him."

"No. As I said, she wasn't smart enough, and anyway whoever took her up would have had to have left the area, and that wouldn't have been likely. If they had stayed my father would have wreaked terrible vengeance on her and on whomever she had taken up with; would possibly have killed them both."

"Dear lord.   What became of her?"

"I heard she died fifteen years ago."

"You never----?   Didn't you hear from her, or from anyone who knew her?"

"No, and I didn't want to."

"You----?"

Bors put his arm around her shoulders and they stood looking at the house.   "You have to understand, I was so damaged that I was almost inhuman.   It took me years to recover. Partially recover I should say.   You never fully come back from something like that.   The best you can do is to persevere, get on with life, and lay off feeling sorry for yourself.   Hang on like grim death."

Rhamnusia tightened her grip.   "Then I will feel sorry for you."

"No need to."

"Nevertheless.

They were like statues, rigid and silent.

After a spiritual eternity Bors spoke. "Someday I'll ask around and find out what happened to her, and I'll visit her grave."

They carried their camping equipment to a flat spot in the shade of the cottonwood, and Bors started to set up the tent while Rhamnusia blew up the air mattress.   When they were through, Bors saw that she was zipping together sleeping bags.

They had folding chairs and Bors made a table of old boards and rocks.

"There," he said, bowing and sweeping his arm, "your palace awaits, Madame."

Rhamnusia sat down. "What now?"

"What now? We relax!"

"I'm not good at relaxing."

"Exactly! We're here to practice relaxing."

"I don't think one can practice----"

"Tut-tut. As the old '60s saying went, *Don't knock it till you've tried it!*" Bors said.

"So to start with, and as you said you wanted a cup of coffee, I shall light the stove and make some."

"I didn't say I want----"

"Want coffee? Yes you did. You said it with your eyes."

"I give up. You are a caution, you know that?"

"Whatever you say."

They stayed for a week, then it was time to move on. Bors had relaxed for the first time in months, and from what he could tell Rhamnusia had unwound too.

Chapter Thirty

Flights of imagination

They were nearing the Black Hills of South Dakota.

"What is reality?" Bors asked suddenly.

"What? What is reality?" Rhamnusia asked. "Why do you bring that up now, of all times, and how would I know. I'm a simple farm girl from Indiana. What the hell is reality? You know, being with you is a continual adventure, which in itself would be enough without any of our Ragnarök escapades. Reality indeed."

"Whoa, calm down. It's just a rhetorical question."

"It sounds like hot air."

"Then what is the essence of hot air?" He turned from the interstate into Rapid City, where they were to pull off another *job*.

"Jesus Christ, I'd rather talk about reality."

"Really? I think about it sometimes. The nature of reality. Don't you?"

"No."

"Never?"

"Never," Rhamnusia said sharply.

"Why not? I assumed every sentient and of at least mediocre intelligence person wondered about that."

"Not me, and that implies I am neither sentient nor intelligent."

Bors put his hand on her thigh but she brushed it away.

"For pity's sake, what's gotten into you? Though I guess we all have our own concerns as we grope our way up the ladder leading out of the shithole that is earth."

"Shithole?"

"That's how Irish writer James Joyce described it. See, I'm not alone in my world view."

"Nevertheless pretty extreme, even for you."

"Lots of people feel the same way, but I'm different. I know I'm different, and let me tell you, sometimes--usually in times of great stress--I find it difficult to differentiate my mental cogitations--mind's eye, views, or perspectives--from what I recognize as reality when I'm not stressed. And here's what really concerns me: what if sometime that mental perspective flipped? What if the mindset I now see as stress-induced irreality suddenly became my reality, and vice versa?   What then?   The game would be up."

"Turn right," Rhamnusia said.

"Oh, yeah."

"That ain't gonna happen, Ole," she said. "You're not going to flip.   What poppycock. But what I don't understand is why, if your condition changes when you are stressed, haven't you pooped out on me when we're in action?"

"No, no, don't you see?   I told you before, it's only afterward!   Only when I've had time to think."

"Oh."

"Thinking has always been my downfall." He peeked at her sideways to see if she had caught his sarcasm, and she had.

"Then stop doing it."

"I'll try.   Maybe a side trip over to Mount Rushmore would help.   Have you ever been there?"

"No."

She had turned quiet and terse.

"Would you like see it?"

"Up to you."

"Then we'll go tomorrow before we get down to work."

Work.   He had much groveling to do to make amends for opening his deepest feelings to her, but he had always been capable of seeing things unequivocally notwithstanding his rare flights of imagination, and he was certain she would never forsake him.

Flights of imagination was, albeit, a way of putting it; of gilding his condition.

The next day they headed to Rushmore.

Rhamnusia had regained a bit of her composure but she had some way to go before she would return to normal.

They arrived at the parking lot, got out, joined the many tourists, and walked up toward the figures. When they got as close as they could, they joined the others in picture taking. Rhamnusia called to him just as he was thinking something about rocking chairs.

"This," she said, waving at the giant sculptures, "makes me want to return to simpler times."

"Me too. Life is too complicated now. If I could have lived in any era it would have been the 1920s, before the depression. *The Roaring Twenties.*

"And I would live with you."

"We would live happily ever after. I would be an F. Scott Fitzgerald type, and you would be like his wife, Zelda, the original flapper. I'd write marvelous books and----"

"Zelda went crazy and spent her later years in a loony bin."

"You wouldn't do that; you're too sensible. You would be my muse."

"Sexist. Why wouldn't I be the writer and you be----?"

"It's the twenties! Of course I would be the famous writer. But remember, Zelda was a liberated woman."

"Women are not equal even now."

"We're quibbling," Bors grumped.

"Plus, how about the state of medicine back then. We would both probably be dead ducks by now."

"Goodness me you are a wet blanket. I'd sooner take my chances back then than live now when civilization has advanced to where we have nuclear weapons and you take the chance of being shot by simply walking down the street! Humanity is doomed by it's own success! We're screwed, so we might as well make merry while we can."

"Who's the wet blanket now?"

"Not me. Let's continue making merry!"

They both giggled.

On the way back to their motel Bors asked again, "Who did you say our Mark I is? My mind isn't in it the way it used to be."

"Cecil Farnsworth. Mark II. But we don't have to get into that until tomorrow do we?"

"No."

They drove on.

"You don't have any secret shortcomings, do you?"

Rhamnusia's eyes widened ever so slightly. "No. Nothing worth mentioning. Why do you ask?"

"I dunno. I guess because I do I assume everyone does."

"Well, I do sometimes go weeks without showering, and I could do a better job of cleaning my dentures."

"See, that's a fault right there. Your weird sense of humor."

"I'll do my best to----"

"Seriously, nothing more?"

"Nope."

"Good. It' nice to work with, and, and, you know, get along so well with someone who's flawless."

"You are so lucky."

"And I have fine tastes when it comes to women."

"You sound like you would if you were buying horses."

"Remind me to check your teeth."

As they neared Rapid City Rhamnusia turned in her seat to face Bors. "I do have some baggage from my past though."

"Oh?"

"When we're through here I have to return to Indiana to see my Mother. She's ninety-nine years old and they're going to pull the plug on her when I get there."

"I'm so sorry."

"Don't be. I have no more of an attachment to her than you did for your mother. When I was in my teens an uncle molested me, and she did nothing. Wouldn't even listen to me. Blah, blah, blah, the same old story. Anyway I went off to college, my father died, and I haven't seen my mother since he died. I won't belabor my past--it's not my way--but I had to tell you, and I hope you won't ask me any more about it. Okay?"

"Okay."

Neither of them spoke for a good five minutes.

Then, "If we were were living in the 1920s it wouldn't have gotten to the point where you would have to pull the plug."

Chapter Thirty-one

The spirit of Alecto

Rhamnusia had been promoted.

"They moved me up, and you also, by association," she joked. "You have been elevated."

Bors didn't know much about the levels, and he didn't care. "Did I get the elevator or the shaft?"

"Oh ha, ha, ha! And ho, ho!"

They were on a rented forty-two foot sailboat anchored in the Abacos, Bahamas, not far from the town of Marsh Harbour. It was about seventy-five degrees with a gentle east wind, and there were no clouds.

He and Rhamnusia were friends and lovers, but the spirit of Alecto always floated in the back of his mind, and surely it always would. The best he could hope for would be some degree of filiation between the two: Alecto and Rhamnusia.

"Why the promotions?" Bors asked. "And why are we here?"

"I thought you would never ask.   The answer is, I have no idea."

"What?   You're putting me on!"

"Ha, ha, ha!   Yes, I am."   She sat openly enjoying his discomfiture.

Bors' shoulders sagged.   "What then?"

"We're here to become rejuvenated. Don't laugh, that was the word they used.   And so I could tell you about their extended sphere of influence."

"That shouldn't take long."

A large power boat churned by and threw up waves.   Most of the boats coming to the Bahamas for the winter were sailboats.

"It won't," Rhamnusia went on, "but I'm persuasive and I talked them into this extended stay so I could seduce you."

"You already have.   But you have no decorum in such regard."

"Oh.   You noticed, eh?   Okay, be that as it may, remember some time back when I told you Ragnarök was going to expand operations to other countries?   Well, the time has come. They have always known that as bad as things are here in the States they're worse in many other countries.   Monarchs, dictators, religious zealots, ... , all kinds of odious leaders, not even mentioning the non-political thugs, terrorists, and all.   And then add the foolish, ignorant, and downtrodden masses of humanity who through their simplicity or mendacity contribute to worldwide misery."

"Reminds me of that guy up home in Montana.   He feels the same way as that."

"As what?"

"Like those Ragnarök mucky-mucks who are apparently intelligent enough to know how bad things are."

"Who is he?   The nut in Montana?"

"An elderly neighbor named Harald Nordraak.   Still one-hundred percent Norwegian after four of five generations.   I've only heard of him, but I'd like to talk with him now.   I'm not so sure he's a nut; I think he's some kind of genius in some way.   When I'm through with Ragnarök I'd like to hide out up there on the High Plains where there are few people to----"

"Don't you mean when *we* hide out up there?"

"Oh, well yes, of course.   I will need somebody to look after me."   He stuck out his lower lip and pouted at her comically.

"You will.   I can't imagine how you have gotten along without me thus far, much less as you fade into old age."

"I don't plan on reaching old age."

"Baloney!   Everybody says that but when their time comes----"

"I'd build a stronghold up there, disguised as a farmhouse, with secret tunnels, safe rooms, escape routes, and so on. If I--we--survive Ragnarök I sure as hell don't want to be taken out by some old nemesis who holds a grudge for me having cut off his balls or something."

"Why would he hold a grudge for something as trivial as that?"

"Because men become *attached* to them."

Rhamnusia chortled. "Fine, but there's an old saw about hiding out: if you want to hide, go to some highly populated area, not to some sparsely-populated place where every yokel around will know everything about you. For example when you have the house built don't you know that the workers, inspectors, and everyone else involved in the construction will blab, and as far as being withdrawn goes, you'll be the talk of the community."

"There isn't much of a community."

"Listen, I grew up in such an area, and there's always an extension. Distances are greater, so whereas in a city your neighbors are close but you're lost in the multitudes, on the prairie the communities are expansive. Farmers, ranchers, and others are apt to know people fifty miles or more away."

"And you can see people coming from that far away too."

"Is that so?"

"I'll work it out."

"I hope so, because if you drag me up there I'm no more eager to be topped than you are."

Bors moved slightly to his right under the bimini. "Maybe we should forget about Montana and live on a sailboat. I'm mostly Norwegian and you know my ancestors were Vikings. I'm pretty sure I'm descended from Eric Bloodaxe. We could go around looting, marauding, burning, and so on, and I could do a little raping on the side." He smiled.

"Then rape away, but count me out of boating. I get seasick."

"You do look a little green, and it's only our second day."

"I can't stand the waves and the rocking of the boat."

"What waves? We haven't seen a wave over a foot high, and sailboats are supposed to rock people into heavenly peace."

"Crap."

"Did you take your seasickness medication?"

"Yes."

"You must have desert nomads in your ancestry, or maybe a DNA test would reveal some Mongolian----"

"I'm as Mongolian as the pope is."

They sat and watched a catamaran in the distance. Cats were fast, but not good to the wind.

"I guess I do feel a little better," Rhamnusia said, then they were quiet for a long time, until dark, and Bors turned on their anchor light.

Bors broke their reveries. "Don't squeal to the higher-ups, but I'm a getting a little sick of what we're doing. Setting upon and killing and maiming people. Not that they don't deserve it, but I'm less vengeful."

He expected some words of comfort or agreement, but Rhamnusia remained silent.

Bors tried again. "If we lived on a boat we wouldn't be able to outrun anybody who might be after us, but at least we would die happy. And if we lived and got old together, instead of dying in a nursing home or a hospice we could just head offshore, open the thru-hulls, and go down together."

"Drowning in cold seawater isn't my idea of dying happy."

"We'd get pickled on Norwegian Linie aquavit first."

"What's that?"

"Kind of like mountain dew, but much better. Linie--pronounced *lee-nee*, which means *line*--is shipped by boat from Norway down across the equator--the line--and back, in wooden casks. That's what's supposed to give it it's flavor."

"Is it any good"

"I don't like it, but it would be fitting as a Viking's last drink. I'm a Viking and I'd make you a Viking too; or a Valkyrie."

"Lucky me."

Silence.

Then, "What is it?" he asked.

"I feel the way you do," she said. "Less vengeful."

"You do?"

"Yes."

A longer silence, then Bors gathered himself.

"That guy up in Montana--Nordraak--got to me. I haven't met him, but he's a writer and I've read one of his books. He's a supreme realist, and he doesn't seem to have much hope for humanity. He wrote a book about it: *Rattail Curves* and that's the one I read. It's autobiographical creative nonfiction. It isn't particularly uplifting. So that's what's got me down: here we are fighting against those who prevent us from improving the world, and what use is it? See, Nordraak is dismayed at human stupidity, and how can we improve--ugh, I hate to say it, *the human condition*--in the face of such stupidity? Even in democracies there are two main impediments: stupidity, and the corruption by the more clever. I didn't say more intelligent, simply more clever."

As the sun set they heard the sounds of several conchs being blown. It was tradition to drill a hole in a conch shell thus making a small horn.

"You're becoming a philosopher."

"No, just a realist like Nordraak, and it may kill me."

A few anchor lights began to appear around them, but not close, and a dog on one of the boats yapped.

"Do you feel remorse for beheading that guy?" Rhamnusia asked out of the clear.

"No, not a bit. Only for not following orders. He should have been decapitated years before. But no matter how hard we try to fight evil, we can never prevail because there are too many malevolent human beings."

"Is there nothing to be done?"

"I don't think so."

"What about your hero author up in Montana? Doesn't he have any answers?"

"He ain't my hero madam, and no, he offers little in the way of ameliorating life's perplexities. Or I should say miseries. The best he does is propose a new political organization like a political party; one in which the members are smart enough to pass the entrance exam and stuff like that. A model that he hopes would have some influence. I would tell him good luck with that. As you know I am a master of sarcasm. Well, he would in all probability admit I was right, and that he would have liked to have included in his book my proposal that all democracies would administer intelligence tests to voters; but he was not eager to undergo intellectual tarring and feathering. Maybe he did include that, I can't recall."

Rhamnusia winced. "Voting tests do sound extreme and antithetical to democracy. Whether it's forming a new political party of the elite, or voting tests, or whatever, who decides?"

"The usual question, according to Nordraak. I would like to ask him, though I think he wrote that we simply have to begin somewhere; that's the way all successful new countries, institutions, inventions--anything--are begun. Just like creating a revolutionary new anything, you have to start from scratch. You have to stop the momentum of the past and start over. And here's the essential part: you have to have the creating done by ultra-intelligent people, otherwise the creation will be doomed to failure. And the most important thing in countries is their political system, and how the hell can you embrace a democracy which comprises far too many dunces and villains? An institution that's becoming unworkable.

Look at all of the political money, corruption, chicanery, ... A confederation of nincompoops and malefactors."

"Well, well. Then there are no other solutions?"

"None I can think of."

A dog barked, and off to the west a streak of lightning flashed.

"Before anything else I am going to have it out with Eppers," Bors rumbled. "Not Scorpion, but Eppers personally."

But he thought of how slaughterhouse people got sick of the killing, and he compared them to the WWII German concentration camp killers; those higher-ups who had never felt the slightest remorse.

For a short time there was complete silence, then, out of nowhere, Bors asked, "Do you think I'm daft?"

"No. Do you think you are?

"No. Do you think you're daft?"

"No. Do you think I am?"

"No."

They both giggled.

"From what we just said, I'm sure we're both daft," Bors said.

Chapter Thirty-two

Demetrius Eppers

Bors knew that to engage Eppers in a duel would be quixotic. And difficult, because, like the saying *No honor amongst thieves*, there was no honor among homicidal executioners the likes of Demetrius Eppers. It would therefore take some doing to lure him into a showdown.

The only way to deal with Eppers was to convince him that he--Eppers--had the complete upper hand, and Bors felt that he could play the victim to the hilt. Rhamnusia was uncomfortable about his approach, but he was determined.

"You're going too far," Rhamnusia cautioned. He had been rambling about it all morning.

"Then get Ragnarök to okay it."

"I can't. I don't dare to even try because I know how they function. They would never okay it; it would be a heads-up to them, and Z would know you were going rogue."

Bors and Rhamnusia had lost themselves again in New York City. Bors hated the city, but there they were, back on another park bench.

"Then you help me. You're still the senior partner and you must have some unofficial connections."

"I do have a few, but not enough, and in any case they wouldn't get involved in a crackbrain endeavor like this."

"But hear me out. I have it outlined. We let it slip to Eppers that I'll be alone somewhere, then when he comes to assassinate me we have a group of toughs nab him. Now, here's the best part. Eppers and I fight a duel with Japanese katanas! Like the folding sword I waved around in Central Park that time, only with the real thing. A genuine duel. I make a mess of him, then I finish him off."

Rhamnusia sat stone still with tears in her eyes.

"What?" Bors asked.

But she just sat, crying quietly. A pigeon defecated on her head but she didn't notice.

"You've gone under," she said. "You need help. You don't know what you're doing. God in heaven, now I know for sure that your days in Ragnarök are limited." She moved closer to him and put her arm around his shoulders. "Let me help you again. I did once and I can again."

Bors slumped forward with his elbows on his knees and his hands covering his face, and he couldn't stifle his sobs. He remained still, crying quietly.

"It'll be okay," Rhamnusia whispered. "We'll fight it together, and when you recover we'll ask Ragnarök to release you, and if they don't we'll disappear together. Simple as that. We'll conceal our money, change our identifications, and do whatever else we have to do, short of plastic surgery. You needn't worry, I have planned our escape for quite a while."

"You have?" Bors murmured through his fingers.

"Yes. I've seen this coming. I should have stepped up sooner but you're headstrong and I knew I would be unable to reason with you. Until now. But I'm strong too, and when you're better we'll have a light at the end of the tunnel, and I'll lead you to that light."

Bors sat up. "When I'm better?"

"Yes. You have to trust me completely like you did before. Will you do that?"

"Yes."

"Then, when you have regained your equanimity we'll further our plans."

"Can you tell me anything now?"

"Norway. Only that we'll go to Norway."

"Norway? Why Norway?"

Rhamnusia smiled slyly. "Where else? It's your homeland. Well, your ancestors'. In fact you're the one who brought it up."

"Brought what up?"

"Norway."

"Hum. I guess you could pass for Norwegian."

"I hope so. I'm mostly Irish."

"Shall I start calling you O'Rhamnusia?"

But he felt he had said something asinine again. He clamped his jaws together and remained silent. It was all he could do.

Rhamnusia slid closer to him and put her right hand to the nape of his neck and her other hand to his chest. "I swear I'll help you back. And if there's any good in all of this, it's that you do--even at your weakest--have a smidgen of humor, however dopey. That's the quality in you that sustains my hope."

Two winos weaved by but she warned them off with a look.

"I have never told you," she said, "but one of my college degrees is in psychology. With an emphasis on abnormal psychology, and since you evidently retain some wit, I think it's safe for me to say that you are without question abnormal."

"I didn't know you----"

"You know little about me, but I intend to dibble out my secrets in bits as the need arises."

"Why?"

"I'll tell you when the need arises."

There was a long pause.

"Now, let's go and get you fixed up."

Something in her voice and demeanor emanated hope.

Part III

Chapter Thirty-three

Free at last

Bors and Rhamnusia sat on the grass not far from the parliament building in Oslo, Norway. They were in exile, but free. Ragnarök had not released them, but they were free. Rhamnusia had cut her raven-black hair short and she was ever more beautiful, as if she were aging in reverse. Bors allowed he too was pretty good looking, notwithstanding that he had not cut his hair or done any other modifying.

"Well Mr. Montgomery, how do you feel now?" Rhamnusia asked.

"Great, but call me Uther."

"Uther Pendragon Montgomery," she giggled.

They had gotten around to using their real names.

"Call me Gertrude."

"Ha! No way."

"Then how about Gertie?"

"I'm not wild about that either."

"Venicia?"

"Oh, please!"   She wrinkled her nose.

"I'll think of a good Norwegian name,"
Uther said.

"What's so bad about Gertrude?"   A
pigeon dropping hit her head.   "Oh!   Again!   I
attract pigeons."

"And young Norwegian hunks.   I see
them staring at you."

"Nonsense."

Suddenly Uther burst out, "Lene!   I
hereby name you Lene."

"How do you spell it?"

"L-e-n-e.   Lene."

"That spells, or should sound like, Lena,
like in the old Ole and Lena jokes."

"No, the first *e* is very soft.   Leh'ne, and
to get picky, the *e* at the end is almost silent but
with slight *r*.   That's you, Lene!"

"Well I don't know----"

"No, no, I won't hear of it.   You have no
choice.   From now on you are my dear Lene.
Lener."

She wiped the pigeon poo from her hair.
"Maybe I'll get used to it, even if I can't say it."

Uther spat on his handkerchief and
handed it to her.

"I had considered *Honeysuckle* but it
didn't quite fit."

"Oh dear Jesus, thank you Lord!"

They watched people walk by and Uther noted how similar they looked to the ones back up in his part of Montana, only not as fat.

"Old Nordraak up home in Montana used to tell people his great, great grandparents on his father's side had come from near here," Uther mused. "They were farmers. His mother's people came from here too."

"Hm."

"His grandmother's maiden name was Rud. Pronounced Ruud. On his mother's side his grandmother was a Rygg, and his grandmother's surname was Greina."

"Why are you telling me this? I thought you don't know much about Nordraak?"

"As I said, I knew the family when I was a kid. I don't know why I remember this stuff though; when you're a kid you don't care."

"Um."

"What I was leading up to is that if we intend to stay here you'll have to start learning Norwegian. They might look askance at a lady with a Norsk birth document who can't speak the language."

"I thought you wanted to return to Montana."

"That's our backup plan in case *you-know-who* finds out where we are."

Lene stared at him. "Let's see now, did you ever discuss these plans with me?"

Uther flushed. "No. But that's what I'm doing now. I'm just trying to keep us alive."

"What do you think I am, a dunce?"

"Of course not." Uther looked down at the grass. "If you have any suggestions I'd like to hear them."

"I don't, but from now on I would appreciate being in on things."

Uther took her hands in his and kissed them. "You're right. I'm sorry. Only---- Only I've never been in a situation like this."

"Do you think I have?"

"I don't know, but from the way you ask I presume not." He tried to coax a smile from her, but she was stiff and impassive. Even stronger than he had thought.

"You're right though," he admitted, "I was thoughtless, though it was your idea to come here to Norway."

She relaxed, but only a little. "Well, I'm not going to kick you out of bed over it."

Bors felt like saying that was the main thing, but he checked himself. He was trying to break his habit of always wanting to have the last word, or being a smart ass. He wasn't in a contest with her.

Birds twittered overhead as they passed, but they weren't pigeons.

Uther kept quiet for a good long while. When he dared to speak he tried to be lighthearted. "I would like to treat you to some lutefisk sometime."

"Treat? I know what it is, and I've even had some, and if you think I'm going to have more you are sorely mistaken. I don't think the Norwegians even eat it anymore. You can smell it a hundred yards away, and the only ones who eat it now are back in the States, and it's what has made most of them feeble minded. You can take your lutefisk and----"

"Whoa, simmer down! It was a joke. Well, I would have some and you could eat something else, like----"

"What else, raw fish? They like that over here. Pickled herring? Or----"

"Meatballs and mashed potatoes. I'm just trying to be accommodating."

"Then go and accommodate that young lady over there; the blond with pigtails down to her butt."

They returned to their apartment.

That evening Bors brought up Ragnarök again.

"I thought we weren't going to dwell on them," Lene said.

"We aren't, but I had an odd thought. We know that Ragnarök is expanding worldwide, and since much of the misery, avarice, witlessness, and wickedness in the world results from the machinations of world leaders, why not go right to them. Why monkey around with the small potatoes? Instead, or also, go after the dictators, kings, princes, religious killers, and all such malefactors?"

Lene simply stared at him.

"What? You think I'm going off my rocker again?"

"No, but I do think you have to let go. Stop obsessing about our past. I'm sure that's the first step in reinventing our lives."

"Alright. I will."

Chapter Thirty-four

Reunited

Uther was at one with himself. Norway was his spiritual home. *But you are not a spiritual person*, an almost-audible voice reminded him.

"I will make some allowances," he said.

"What?" Lene asked.

"Hm? Oh, nothing. Just thinking about how at home I feel here."

She scrutinized him in her unique way that made him self-conscious.

They were sitting on the grass in a little park, it was a beautiful day, birds were singing, and . . . . The only damper Uther felt was the aftereffect of his last-night's dream. It had been disquieting; ghastly, and it had taken him until then, 10:30 in the morning, to restore himself to where he felt self-possessed enough to revive himself, and then his first utterance had been the response to an internal voice; *I will make some allowances.* He cleared his throat and prepared to speak; about anything, simply to ease Lene's mind.   She had been giving him the eye all morning.

"Ahh, this is the life," he began.   "I think we are----"

"It's too soon to tell."

"Wha . . . ?   I only----"

A homely teenage girl came by and her small, gray, short-haired dog tried to urinate on an old lady's food cooler.   The lady kicked at the dog and swore at the girl in Norwegian that Uther didn't understand; he wasn't up on all of the latest slang.   The dog looked like a giant rat.

"You only, you only.   Do you think I don't know when you're troubled?   Give me some credit."

Plainly he had not fooled her one bit and now the aftermath was worse than if he had just come out with it.   Often the repercussions were worse than the misdeed, if a bad dream could be referred to as an misdeed, or offense of some sort.

The girl stubbornly returned, the dog defecated next to the old lady, and a real row ensued, with people gathering around and jabbering in a dialect that Uther found difficult to follow.   Some of their insults would have made even a World War I doughboy blush, and one old man shook up a beer can and began spraying the dog, who--as an innocent bystander--began barking and whining. The girl spat on the old man, the old lady struck the girl on top of her head with her umbrella, a tall young man grabbed the old lady by her pigtail and pulled; and a fat lady tried to intervene and was attacked by the dog who started nipping at her ankles.

Uther and Lene gathered their things and moved away to watch the performance, and Uther saw the whole thing as a reprieve from Lene's wrath. Not wrath; she was never wrathful with him. Never disgusted either because she never felt so in the slightest. More like concern.

They sat down and tried not to laugh out loud. After more insults and half-hearted slaps and kicks all of the scufflers got tired, and with some final invectives they dispersed.

Uther and Lene looked at each other and giggled, then she sobered and asked him, "Where was I? Weren't you behaving strangely or some such?"

He decided to be proactive. "I was. I was about to tell you about the dream I had last night. One of my nightmares. But I didn't want to burden you with it as you have your tribulations too and I didn't want to----"

She knitted her brow in an almost-frown but the crisis was over. "I apologize then. For what I was about to do."

"What?"

"Chastise you for being so sullen this morning."

"Sullen? I wasn't sullen! I was----"

"Well, I am sorry I----"

"Nothing you can do. You know, I used to ride bucking broncs in rodeos, and it's like that, or like riding a tiger; you're afraid to get off so you have to keep on until----"

"You're full of it," she said. "You've probably never been on a horse in you life, and that tiger line is so, so old. And nothing I can do? I told you, one of my degrees is in abnormal psychology, so don't you think there is some possibility I could help you? No guarantees, but still."

Uther was struck mute.

"Helsike," he at last uttered.

"What? Now you've taken to swearing at me?"

"Uh? Oh, no, lord no! It just means hell, and I didn't mean you. But here comes another old lady with another rat dog."

The lady, tall, thin, and bordering on the color of her dog, approached and sat near them. She made a point of ignoring them, and Uther wondered why, then, had she come?

Lene paid no attention to the lady. "Again, what does Helsike mean?"

"Nothing. It means *darn*, that's all. At least it did in the dialect my parents spoke when I was young. Gracious, that had nothing to do with you!"

"Oh. I'm sorry. I guess I'm getting edgy too."

They moved closer together and they were good again.

They watched people for a while, and Uther kept an eye on an old man with a small mirror on the palm side of his onyx ring; the kind poker cheats used to use to read cards as they deal them. Hard to tell what he was looking at from time to time.

The rat dog had fallen asleep on the lady's lap and Uther decided that the lady was so decrepit she couldn't harm them even with an automatic pistol; she'd be too weak to pull the trigger.

As they walked home Lene pulled Uther over under a tree. "I've already presumed upon you too much today, but may I gently and with all the love I possess for you, ask about your dream? No, wait, something else first? But related to the dream. Not directly, but indirectly as a----"

Uther took her face in his hands and kissed her. "Slow down and breath deeply. What the hell are you talking about?" he smiled.

She shrank slightly.

"Okay, first, secrets. Are we going to come to an agreement on secrets?"

Uther was caught by surprise. "I thought we had."

"Oh, no, only about everyday things like our Ragnarök activities, and later about birthday presents and trivialities like that. I mean real, deep-seated secrets."

"Such as?"

"Oh, you know, dreams for instance." She smiled slyly but self-consciously.

"I see. Last-night's dream."

"For example."

He kissed her nose then moved his hands to her shoulders. "I have always made it a point to avoid burdening you with such annoyances. No use dumping my problems on you. How would that help either of us?"

"There. That's the real problem. Not your perceived problems, but not *dumping* them! First, I've confided my problems to you, and----"

"You haven't."

"Yes I have. Now here's the real deal. If you won't listen to tactful persuasion, I'm sure you will listen to hard facts, and the main hard fact is that if you share your concerns and issues with me either of two things will happen. One, I won't be able to help. Or two, I will.

Cold hard logic. In either case you will be no worse off."

Uther felt stung on both cheeks as if he had been slapped, hard, and he couldn't find the right to answer her.

"Don't let me rush you," Lene said, "No hurry." She had said it not unkindly, but seriously.

Uther felt his right cheek. "It's very personal."

"Fine. I don't care. And if it's about Alecto it's all the more urgent for us to take care of this now instead letting it fester any longer."

Uther put his head on her shoulder and he felt like crying, and he wondered whether she thought he was.

When they got home Lene sat down on the sofa and patted the spot next to her. Uther sat down beside her.

"Now then," she started, "listen to me. We're going to get this sorted out. First off you had better know that no matter what we discuss here and now, nothing will change the way I feel about you. I love you, and I will never leave you."

"Unless you do."

Lene stood so quickly that he hardly saw her move, and she slapped him on his left cheek harder than he could have imagined any woman could have; not even Alecto.

"How dare you!" she screamed, almost like a wild animal. Then without pause she slapped him again even harder. "How, after all we have been through, could you ever say such a vicious, vile thing to me?"

Without breaking into tears or showing any other so-called womanly emotion she simply stood glaring at him with utmost scorn the like of which he had never seen in her before.

Hours later Lene came out of the bedroom and sat on the sofa beside Uther where he had been waiting quietly, stunned and abashed.

He was unable to read her face. "Am I in the doghouse?"

She looked at him incredulously. "In the doghouse? The f-ing doghouse? No, the doghouse is too good for you."

But he read an ever-so-slight glint in her right eye. He slowly reached for her hand and was relieved when she didn't pull it back; and as he held it close to his heart it was limp and he surmised she had to put one last remonstrance on him before relenting.

They sat in silence for over a long time.

Uther was the first to speak. "Well I don't know about you but I'm tired of sitting here quietly on the *sofa of remorse*."

"Your remorse, not mine, but yes it is getting tiresome, so let's call it the *sofa of reconciliation and love*. Okay?" She put her hand to his cheek.

"Yes." It was only beginning to get dark outside, but through an open window he heard an owl, and like all other birds and animals there it sounded to Uther like it had a Norwegian accent. "Hoo-er, hoo-er."

"I am so sorry for slapping you and for the way I behaved," Lene began. "You weren't----"

"I had it coming."

"You didn't, and----"

"I did, but enough; it's over. From this exact moment we move on. It is possible to extinguish the past. I should know; I've done it."

"But----"

He put his hand over her mouth, and tears filled her eyes, and they were reunited, in a way that was stronger than ever.

The next day, now sitting on the *sofa of renewal*, Uther and Lene were holding each other tenderly when again through the open window the owl hooted.

"It's morning! Broad daylight, there's that owl!" Uther cried. "He must be off his trolley!"

"Off his branch, and you don't know if it's a *he*. Besides it's a Norwegian owl and if----"

"No, no, no, I speak *Norwegian owl*, and it's a he. I can tell by the inflections."

"Yes, of course, I hear it now."

"Besides in Norwegian there are letters of the alphabet that we don't have in English."

"What difference does it make? How many different letters does it take to say *hoo*, or *whoo?*"

They laughed, joked, and generally carried on for some time.

Then, simultaneously they turned serious.

"My dream," Uther said.

"Yes. The dream that led to our squabble. We have to discuss that. Not the dream, really, but the trust we are building and the openness with each other."

The cuckoo in the clock announced nine and the owl answered, though the owl only hooted three times.

"The dream was of Alecto and it was---- It was horrid. Grisly."

Lene held him tighter.

"I'll tell you everything about it, holding back nothing, but will you grant me some time?

A few days?   I just don't think I can go through it now.   Am I asking too much?"

"Certainly not.   And after you tell me I may be able to help.   Maybe so, maybe not, but in either case I think you will feel better just for the telling."

Chapter Thirty-five

Bonkerness

Perhaps for the first time ever Uther thought life was good, though he allowed that maybe he didn't know what *good* was. He simply couldn't remember anything better. Lene had saved him from his mental desolation more than once.

He and Lene were doing their best to lead normal lives no matter how difficult it was for them--abnormal as they were--to do so; accordingly it was necessary for them to come up with some idea of what so-called normal people do.

"First off--and we should know--there are no normal people. How does one define *normal*, and----?"

"Stop," Lene snapped. "Don't get into another of your dizzying definition discombobulations. Don't fly away; stay here on the ground with me."

They were at the picnic table behind their apartment and Lene had a pencil and a paper tablet before her. Uther sat back in his chair, clasped his hands behind his neck, and looked up at the clear sky. A bird called from far away but he didn't know one from another. It wasn't an owl. He had liked owls. They were smarter than most people, and as far as he knew they didn't kill each other. Moreover they were----

"I just don't see why we have to write all of this down," Uther grumbled. "It ain't rocket----"

"Humor me." She kicked him lightly under the table with her bare foot. "And help me out. This is serious you know."

He sat up again. "Yeah, I know. Where do we start? You first, as you are more normal than I am."

"I suppose we can begin with everyday things most people do when they're not working. Hobbies, sports, the kinds of entertainment they like, and so on. Then once we've made a list we can work backward to try to figure out their frames of mind. It shouldn't be that hard."

"Alright, put American football first. Most red-blooded men like to sit in front of the TV with a can of beer and a bowl of pretzels and----"

"Sarcasm ill becomes you, Lene said.

"Yeah, you're right.   Anyway put down football.   And baseball, and the most usual sports."

"Right.   What else?"

"Try to think of some of the movies that average people like."

Lene concentrated and wrote for a while. "That ought to be enough."

"Books," Uther said.   I have known adults who still read comic books, and then there are the ones--very few--who read classic literature and the like.   And pulp fiction, and I can tell you right off that most of them are awful; the books, not the readers.   Literary writing is becoming a lost art now that any ninny can crank out a book and self-publish it."

Lene scribbled away, apparently adding to his suggestions.   At last, "What else?"

"What do people do?   Not what they like, but what they actually do.   I like good books, and some movies, but that's just vegetating, not sustaining a good life."

"Right.   But we have to agree on what a good life is before we get to the *what do people do?* part.   Tell me what's good, then I'll tell you what I believe is good."

"You sound like Plato," Uther said, "but I don't think it's all that complicated.   You simply do what you want to do without listening to what others think, and as long as you're not an awful person. And----"

"Stop right there! We are awful people. Look at all of the Ragnarök stuff we've done. If there's a hell of some kind I'm sure we have reservations there."

"Not at all. I won't hear of it," Uther argued. "We worked for the good of mankind! But forget our past. That's what we're trying to do. What other guidelines can you provide?"

"Only one, and that's----"

The bird was closer now and loud enough to interrupt him.

"Go back and shoot that bird; he makes it hard for me to concentrate, and I can't understand him," he said.

"There you go again. You're right back to our former lives; shoot, shoot, kill, ... I don't know----"

"You persist in attempting to complicate matters. Regarding what good people are, you know perfectly well. Let's move on from the *what do regular, average people do?* part, dispense with the philosophical gibberish, and concentrate on what intellectuals like us do!"

"You don't want to hear my opinion first?"

"No, let's agree to differ on the preliminaries and move on to the point of all this; not this, that, or the other, but what *we* are going to *do* for the remainder of our lives."

Lene grumped, "I guess you're right."

The bird piped up again.

Uther winced. "That bird sounds like a Montana crow who's had too much home-brew."

Lene, slightly miffed, held her tongue.

"Then let's get started," Uther began. "Recreational, hobby, pastime, or quotidian activities that are enjoyable to both of us and that are substantial."

Lene stopped sulking and started writing.

"Golf, stamp collecting, hiking, karate, ..." she breathed as she wrote.

"Golf?" Uther butted in. "It'll be a cold day in----"

Lene raised her other hand and *shushed* him as she continued writing.

"Archery, bridge, chess, cooking, collecting old beer cans, fishing, woodworking, jogging, ..."

Uther couldn't contain himself. "Hold it! Fishing? That'll be a sad day when I spend my time trying to outsmart a fish!"

"Knitting, sewing, ..."

"Some of that strikes me as the kind of hobbies and pastimes that common people take up."

"What's wrong with that?"

"Nothing I guess, but we aren't common .
. . ."

"And I threw in things like stamp
collecting and collecting old beer cans only as a
reference."

When Lene finally finished her list she
looked at Uther, he looked at her, and she
crumpled her notes and threw them back over
her shoulder.

The next day Uther and Lene were back
in the park where the ruckus between the old
lady and the dog girl had taken place.

"I'm chagrined at having actually sat there
and made a list," Lene said.

"No matter.   I'm surprised that I sat there
and helped you.   How desperate are we?"

"Moreover, how screwy are we?   That's
what concerns me even more."

"Kind of the same thing I guess," he said.

"Umph."

Uther lay back in the grass and clasped
his hands over his stomach.   Suddenly he sat
back up and felt the back of his head.

"Oh for the love of----   Dog shit!"

He wiped his hand on the grass. "I'll bet it was that little rat-dog from the other day. Do you have a tissue?"

"No, but it'll take more than a tissue. What a mess!" She tried to suppress a smirk. "There's a washroom over there," she pointed.

"Dog shit isn't as bad as cat shit. When we were kids a cousin and I were wrestling and we rolled in cat shit. Oh, lordy! It's worse than dog, cow, horse, chicken, or anything."

"You have such a delicate way of putting things."

When he got back from the washroom he looked around for the rat-dog girl but she wasn't there.

"A dog that looks like a big rat but shits like a moose," he grumbled.

"You are obviously an expert on shit," Lene taunted.

Uther sat back down, carefully. "I take great pride in such knowledge," he said without humor. "But you well know how I think, and there's usually something lurking behind my everyday thoughts."

"What, then?"

He drew a deep breath. "I'm drawn back to our disorientation. Lene, what are we to do? You've noticed me lying on the bed in the middle of the day, thinking. I don't know about all of the hobbies and such that we came up with, and if none of them are for us, then what? I'll tell you what. Some people are devoted to their work. They work till the day they die, or are forced out. In the United States work is a stronger ethic than in most countries. Some people win a lottery and keep on working. And all that. So, you can see it coming, here we are and we can't even return to work even if we wanted to. Up the proverbial *Shit Creek* without a paddle."

He took another deep breath.

"So, again, what are we to do?" He lifted his hand to hold her silent. "I don't expect you to answer that--you can't any more than I can--but I am saying if only there were some occupation other than Ragnarök which we could take up, we might find our calling. There's no reason we would have to have actually done it as long as we could learn and do it. Whatever *it* is, or would be. I think we have to find the big *it*."

Lene, still sitting, twisted to face him; and, eyes wide, she studied his countenance.

"You think I'm bonkers!" he burst out.

For a time she didn't speak but there was a spark in one eye. She was tormenting him in her delightful way.

"Alright, what?" he demanded.

"Despite your *bonkerness*, you do come up with some good ideas."

"Whenever you say such things I get leery."

"Don't.   This time you are onto something."

"Oh?"

"Certainly.   All we have to do is figure out what the big *it* is."

"That may not be so easy."

"Considering that I am already a registered nurse, I could----"

"RN?   I didn't know you are an RN!"

"Of course you didn't.   I am your big enigma.   How do you think I was so good at patching you up when you got in trouble?"

"For the love of----"

"So I could go back to school and become a brain surgeon, and then I could take care of your----"

"You're not my big enigma, you're my big enema."

"You don't believe me?"

"You're really a nurse?"

"Yes."

"I feel faint."   He hammed it up by putting the back of his right hand to his forehead.

"So do I.   Here comes the girl with the dog."

"The rat-dog girl?"   Uther sat up. "Great."

The girl passed to the other edge of the park.

Uther started over. "You have always been the creative one; really, what could we do? What occupation-like life could we lead?"

"You could farm."

"Oh I could never do that now. Not enough land; farms are much bigger now. And I know nothing about it anymore. It's not the kind of thing you can pick up just like that; it would take years. It would be like your joke about becoming a brain surgeon."

"Was I joking?"

He didn't bother to answer.

Weeks passed, then a month, then two, and Uther saw Lene's depression and he knew she had seen his; yet their love--if changed-- was stronger. And they were strong, and there were periods of happiness.

"We must remain strong," Uther said one day, "or we'll go down like the Titanic."

"I'm your life preserver," Lene said.

Chapter Thirty-six

Suspicion

Uther and Lene were walking hand-in-hand around Vigeland Park in Oslo.

"How are you feeling, Viggo?" she tittered. She called him that whenever she was in a good mood.

"Okay."

"Okay? Not great, fantastic, wonderful?"

"Better by the day. You, Lene?"

"Great, fantastic, and wonderful. I hope we can live out our days here."

They stopped by the sculpture of *The Angry Boy*, and they both laughed. It was the universal angry child.

Lene said, "We deserve this way of life."

"Well, *deserve* is a----"

"Tut-tut. Don't get philosophical on me again. Definitely not the old author up in Montana crap. I think he's a little nutty."

"He makes more sense to me than anybody else does. To a higher degree. I guess he doesn't write for lowbrows. And as

usual throughout human history, when smart
people come up with new things--radically new
machines, concepts, medicines, or such--that
can be proven to be practical and beneficial,
average and lower people usually reject them.
In view of world problems, to them the status
quo is comforting, and they sit in their own
little spheres and hope things will get better.
Well, well, well, guess what. Often they
don't."

It was easy to tell the tourists from the
locals. Most of the people were tourists, and
most of them were either overweight or Asian.

"Where were your people from?" Lene
asked.

"From around here. Maybe some were
from the Bergen area."

"What does *Bergen* mean?"

"*Berg* means hill, or mountain."

"What did your ancestors do?"

Uther laughed. "You already know!
They were Viking raiders; the worst of the lot.
And they were exceptionally handsome,
especially the men. When they went abroad
most of the women they attempted to rape and
carry off not only went willingly, they
volunteered! Why my great, great, etc.
grandfather Torvold was overwhelmed with fair
maidens most of the----"

"You are so full of shit!   You pulled that one on me once before."

"Dritt.   I'm full of dritt."

"Yes."

"But it's hereditary.   The same attraction applies to me.   I'm sure you have noticed how the women flock to me."

"Ha!   Anyway, you should find a way to make yourself less handsome."

"Impossible.   There is no way."

They passed a sculpture of some fair, young maidens.   "Things sure are different here," Lene mused.

"They were poor farmers," Uther said.

"Huh?"

"My people.   From Bergen and from near Oslo, they were just farmers.   The oldest son inherited the farm, and the rest of the children had to move on."

A group of teenage Japanese tourists passed by and most of the boys ogled the nudes.

Lene suddenly turned to Uther.   "How safe are we here?   Tell me the truth.   We both have our strengths and weaknesses, and I'm not good at judging things like that."

Uther winced.   "It's hard to tell."

"What?   I thought----"

"I have to admit that I'm always jumpy."

"Uff-dah."   It meant *Oh, oh,* or *Darn*.

"They don't say *uff-da* much here anymore; it's pretty old-fashioned, like us saying *Okie-dokie* or *Cat's Pajamas*."

Lene frowned. "Don't change the subject on me."

"I was collecting my thoughts."

"Bunk. One thing I excel at is reading people I know."

They stopped and leaned against the base of one of the sculptures.

"Alright, I'll level with you," Uther began. "I hope I'm wrong, but I'm not sure we're safe here. At first I felt secure, but the longer we've been here the more uneasy I've been. And that's such a shame because I--we-- really like it here. I would have told you sooner--I have always tried to be open and honest--but you have to believe me when I tell you that until now I thought it was just one of my paranoias." He began to perspire.

"Goodness."

"I'd give almost anything to be wrong, but like your ability to see through people, I have an extraordinary sense of danger. It's unexplainable. The only reason I know about it is that I have had it ever since I was about ten or eleven years old, and that instinct, or whatever, is nearly always right. You think I'm unhinged?"

He expected her to question him, but all she said was, "No, you're not unhinged."

They remained silent for several minutes, watching the tourists take photos.

"After all of my stuff about forthrightness and all, I have my own confession, and I am ashamed of myself," Lene blurted out.

Uther felt like he had received an electric shock. Then, "Well, this isn't a time for us to start quibbling with each other. Out with it."

A fat, blond, middle-age lady took a picture of him.

Lene took a deep breath. "As I walked down Karl Johans gate yesterday some old guy staggered and bumped me. He had a pen or something in his hand and I wondered if he was trying to stick me with it, but right then an old lady stumbled and fell into him."

"What?" Uther shouted, and people stared at him.

Lene grasped his elbow and led him to a quieter place.

"Calm down. I too thought I was imagining things. You aren't the only one. One day I noticed an old guy with a tiny mirror on the palm-side of his ring finger. Card sharks used to use them to read cards when they dealt. They don't anymore but I suppose undercover agents and other villains might. I could be mistaken but . . . ."

Chapter Thirty-seven

Cuckoo

They sat in their small apartment, Uther and Lene, and they had not spoken that morning. Their cuckoo clock cuckooed ten times.

"Now when I think back, I may have been stalked too. I dunno. Was your guy about fifty years old, thin, slightly below average height, with gray hair and a goatee mustache? Resembled Kaiser Bill from World War I?"

Lene's eyes widened and she nodded.

"Then the game is up," Uther grumbled.

He ran his eyes over the wall decorations involuntarily as he tried to think. Cloth wall hangings, pictures of Norwegian scenery, a shelf with porcelain knick-knacks, ... He wished Lene would offer some advice, but apparently, and uncharacteristically, she had none.

"You're not throwing in the towel are you?" she asked.

"Most certainly not." He tried to appear optimistic. "Then off to Montana for to throw the hoolihan," he sang in a lilting voice.

"What?"

"A line from an old western song. Roping."

"Oh."

"Lene, I never thought we would wind up like this: on the run. But we don't have to be, and now it's time for our--my--backup plan."

"I'll be with you till the end." She spoke faintly. "What's *our* plan?"

"You got on me once for not sharing, so feel free to speak up."

"Okay, but I was in a bad mood then, and right now I'm short of ideas. And men are better in situations like this."

"We are not! How can you----?" He stopped. "Ho, ho, that's a good one. Zing, you got me. Or, we could practice our yodeling and go to Switzerland." But she had been serious, and it was all on him now.

They listened to the tick of the clock and the yapping of a neighbor's dog next door. A chihuahua, the worst kind of yapper.

Uther began. "It may not be that dire. But cheer up, you said you always wanted to go to Montana again."

"I did not! I have never said that. And the desolate, dry, dusty, northeastern part?"

"Well I know you were thinking of it."
He winked.   "Hold your bladder."

"You damn----"   Then she succumbed to
his dry humor, and to his plan of redemption.
Cast in that light--redemption--she regained her
hope and confidence, and *I et* øyeblikk (in an
eyeblink) as the Norwegians said, a soft blanket
of peace descended on her.   Moreover she
would welcome isolation from the human race.

"I told you that I still own the farm up
there.   About five-hundred acres.   An old
geezer named Oscar Midland farms it.   You
saw how there's nothing much left of the
buildings so we'll just burn everything down
and rebuild."

"Wait.   Won't Ragnarök know about the
farm?   They seem to know everything."

"I doubt it.   That goes back a long time
and it doesn't seem like they'd care about it."

"They might start digging now though."

"Hmmm.   They could but it seems like
they'd eventually give up.   And we'd be hard to
trace; my parents lost the farm once, and they
started over on another farm.   The courthouse
burned down and many of the records were
lost."

"Let's hope they do give up."

"We'll build a fortress house like I have
all planned out in my head, and it's hard to
sneak up on someone out there."

Lene focused hard on the cuckoo clock. "Are there any Ragnarök people other than me who know anything of your past?"

"No. Not that I---- Well there is one guy who may know a few things."

"Who?"

"His name is Haskell. His organization name. I met him two or three times but nothing ever came of it and we never worked together. Too bad, I connected with him. We had much in common."

Lene looked as though she were willing the clock to cuckoo again. "Strange. So you were never suspicious of him?"

"No, not really."

"What do you mean by *not really?*"

"What are you getting at?"

"You first."

Uther felt an inner spasm. "Now that you mention it----"

"Mention it!"

"It did seem a little strange that----"

"A little strange?"

"I assumed no one could impersonate a Ragnarök member."

"You assumed?" The clock announced 10:15.

Uther hung his head. "Maybe he was a plant. I hope not."

Lene was seldom incensed but this was an exception. "I hope not too. I think not, but jeez Mr. Bors."

When she called him that he was deep in hot water.

Bors gathered himself. "Now that I think back I'm sure I said nothing about Montana. Even with Ragnarök people I have always been tight lipped; it's one of my good qualities, and it's an especially good quality to have in our line of work."

"You have many good qualities." Lene was regaining her composure." It's only that, that----"

"That what?"

"That occasionally one of your good qualities is undone--or undermined--by one of your, eh, less-good, um, tendencies."

"You are too tactful."

330

Part IV

Chapter Thirty-eight

Montana

Uther walked in the pasture behind his house. Being a child of the dry, barren, sparsely-populated plains of eastern Montana had been alright, but as he had grown older the geographical isolation, compounded by his natural introversion, had led him to develop inwardly, which he had done by immersing himself both in his own fantasies, and in the fantasies of whimsical writers. Possessed by a powerful imagination, he had the common--and in elevated ways uncommon--ability to create his own internal realities: common in that most people do it, knowingly or unknowingly; and uncommon insofar as his creations were of a higher degree of refinement. He had become aware of his special ability some time after his twenty-first birthday, when he had read, for the first time, the Bible, accidentally discovering what he considered to be one of the most fantastic of all human creations. Later he abjured that baseless belief.

He stopped on a hill, beside a ring of
rocks that the Indians had used to anchor their
tipis. A gap for the door faced east, and in the
center were a half-dozen fireplace stones.
Assiniboine, mostly, and later, Hidatsa and
Sioux. Many times as a child he had come
there to think. He hadn't been back to the farm
since he had left as a youth--except for when he
and Lena had camped there--and he wouldn't
have returned now if Ragnarök hadn't imposed
it on him. There was no quitting. They were
all in for life: *Till death do us part* was the
cynical creed. But now he, he and Lene, were
out for good, and to hell with Ragnarök's rules.

Uther retracted his previous musing about
not moving back to the farm; it was possible he
would have returned, but only if Lene agreed.

He scanned the bluish-gray western
horizon thirty miles away. In 1913 his great
grandparents had homesteaded there on one of
the hilliest, rockiest quarter sections around, in
an arid land that should perhaps never have
been farmed. They had gone broke in the Dirty
Thirties, but had recovered, as much as anyone
there could recover. Then his grandparents,
Graham and Petronella, had subsisted on the
farm. They were the best people he had ever
known, and he would always miss them. He
would stop at the cemetery again sometime.

Then his parents. He didn't want to think about them.

"You're no James Bond," Lene had told him before he had left, "and I was never one of your Bond girls. When you're off in Montana it may come to you that we're not in a movie, and Ragnarök wasn't a game."

Of course it hadn't been a game, and that wasn't what she had been telling him. She was telling him he should be more careful in the future.

He watched the prairie grass sway and ripple in the wind. Always the wind. Homesteaders had gone mad from it. Even for those who had stuck it out there, life had been hard, filled with poverty, droughts, grasshoppers, cutworms, illnesses like influenza and typhoid fever, ... And ever since the first influx people had been leaving, and they were still leaving. Hardly any left now.

Throughout his life people had seen his compulsiveness as a virtue. Determination, and stick-to-intuitiveness. But to him it was a handicap, he had always hoped his obsession-compulsion wouldn't kick in very hard. But occasionally it had, resulting in hopelessness and self destruction. It was the mark of a perspicacious obsessive-compulsive: the ability to see the consequences of the malady, and being a bit of a visionary, but being unable to stop.

But confound it all, he had won her. Rhamnusia. Lene.

Northeastern Montana had become almost the Australian Outback of the United States: small, dying or dead towns, many along abandoned railroad lines; vanished farms, some gone with no trace; and the remaining farms were islands on the vastitude that had once been touted as a promised land of opportunity. Dry, rolling fields and prairie; old ramshackle buildings, clumps of trees marking farmsteads long gone; dirt roads overgrown with grass and weeds . . . . Some miscreants thought it was a good place to hide, but those people didn't know the area. For them it was one of the worst places to try to hide out because the locals knew everything that went on. But for him it was an excellent place to hide, as he knew things like where to lie low in emergencies, the peculiarities, mores, and customs of the people, ...

Charity was practically deserted. The school was closed, as were the grocery store and the bank. The only real businesses remaining were the Silver Slipper bar, a gas station, and the post office; and most of the people left in town were old, retired farmers and farm widows, waiting to die. It looked like a ghost town.

Alecto flashed to mind. There had been something in her past that had made her almost abandon life. Uther stooped and picked a stalk of buffalo grass and put it in his mouth. She had abrogated her past as much as possible then, and Ragnarök had been her obsession. Dark-haired Rhamnusia--Lene--had cautioned him about Alecto.

Lene had been always been attracted to him. Alecto had told him, but he had known it. Alecto had been an enigma, but with Lene he had been on more familiar ground, though at first he had had no strong feelings for her.

Oh, god, he had to blot out Alecto.

A whirlwind twisted by, across the brittle grass, picking up loose weeds and dust. In the beginning he had known that he was right for Ragnarök. Destined for it. He hadn't had to set rules; only to carry out his assignments: meting out punishment. Of course later on it had all become difficult and more complicated.

Uther remembered standing there on his tipi-ring hill long ago, dreaming of Camelot; the city and the castle. King Arthur's castle--built on a hill overlooking the Camelot River--with its main hall; and its great hall of justice, where a court of knights administered justice. Trial by ordeal was often used, and cases were sometimes decided by combat.

Their home--his and Lene's--was more of a fortress than a conventional house. Large, it was constructed of one-foot-thick reinforced concrete, full basement, and hidden tunnels within and without. The security devices were beyond those commonly available, and there were many other safety features as well.

Uther no longer had personal ties there. He didn't know the people anymore. No relatives left. Still, he knew *of* them as only one who grew up there could. For now, until he could make some friends, only memories floated in the prairie wind. Sometimes you can't go back. Most of the time you can't. But he knew he could, and thank god for Lene.

Chapter Thirty-nine

Harald Nordraak

Uther had learned some little about Harald Nordraak, a fifth-generation Norwegian who could often be seen standing on the hill northwest of his house, there on the godforsaken high plains of northeastern Montana. His hill, he had told Uther. He had come there often since childhood, and now he was an old man. Over the years he had observed that there on the lonesome prairie people tended to stand on hills.

Harald had been around--college, army, business, farming--and had found in the end that his greatest ability was writing. His writing was excellent, and it was his passion in life, according to the locals, but the downside was that he had come to appreciate not much else in life, and had become a recluse.

Harald's paternal grandparents had homesteaded there in 1912. Charity had once had a population of over five-hundred, and farms had abounded, but the town had shrunk and the farms were fewer and larger, and

Harald's nearest neighbor, other than Uther, was two miles away, and the next nearest five miles. Everything had changed.

Uther recalled some guy telling him that Harald had two college degrees, had been drafted during the Vietnam war, had worked in radio and television, had owned a small-town radio station, had farmed for a while, ... He and his wife, Marie, had brought their two young daughters to the farm to raise them, but the girls had grown up and left, and he and Marie were alone and reclusive.

That was the essence of what Uther had learned of Harald.

Uther was younger than Harald, but his grandparents had homesteaded about the time Uther's great grandparents had. As for anything else about Harald, Uther didn't care. He had decided that Harald was merely an old cuckoo.

Uther was walking again, and as he paused, Harald approached, saw him, abruptly stopped, looked around, then reached for something in the small of his back. Puzzled and nervous, Uther waved, and gradually Harald seemed to sag, almost melting, and he waved back. He slowly approached, and Uther just as slowly responded until they were across the fenceline from each other. Uther thought everything was backwards: it seemed Harald was far more nervous than he was. They had of course met before, but this time was different. Uther guessed Harald's eyesight wasn't good.

"Nice to come across you," Harald said as he extended his hand.

"Likewise." Harald had relaxed.

They shook hands.

Harald was well into old age, but the kind wherein Uther could tell he had been exceedingly good looking.

"I've seen you out here from time to time," Harald said, "but never in town."

Uther frowned, then, "Never seen you in town either," and he smiled at his odd joke that Harald didn't seem to get.

"Come over for coffee sometime," Harald said. "Strong Norwegian coffee that you can stand a spoon upright in, if it doesn't dissolve the spoon."

"Hm." Uther almost smiled at the old joke, and he had to give him credit for adding the *if it doesn't dissolve the spoon* part, but after all he was a writer. He liked Harald from then on, but he didn't trust him. "Well, perhaps sometime. Maybe better if you came to my place."

"Any time," Harald replied. "Give me a call."

Uther backed away and Harald saluted and walked on. Uther didn't look back for some time, but when he did Harald was hurrying over the last knoll close to his house.

Uther mulled it all over. He had never been a conformist, and neither had been most of his friends; the ones he had had. Now he had no friends, except Lene, and she was far more than a friend.

Actually Uther had been in Charity twice recently, in The Silver Slipper bar. The first time he had gotten as boiled as an owl. Kept on muttering all sorts of other gibberish was all he could remember. Somebody had taken him home and dumped him outside his partially-built house. The second time was the next day when he had shuffled into the bar with a terrible hangover and had tried to ask nonchalantly what he had said the night before. Someone had told him a few things, and said nobody had known what the hell he had been talking about.

Chapter Forty

Uther

"Ah, there you are Nordraak!"

"Yeow!" Harald cried as he jumped to his feet. "What in the name of----?"

"Ahh, hah hah! What's the matter, you got a guilty conscience?" Uther smiled, he knew, a little too sadistically.

"Jesus! You move like cougar."

"Thank you. You jump like a kangaroo. May I sit down?"

Harald motioned limply at the lawn chair beside him. He was sitting under the tallest of the three blue spruce trees immediately behind his and Marie's house.

"Ha!" Uther said as he sat down and watched Harald steady himself. He supposed Harald would think he had been drinking.

"Well how are you, big cat?" Harald said somewhat sarcastically. "I thought I was coming to your place. What brings you here?"

"Sociability my good man. I've decided I should be more sociable, and since you're the only one around who I know, and you seem to have a modicum of brainpower, I am blessing you with a visit."

"I am indeed blessed."   Harald's hands had stopped shaking.

A hawk flew over.

"So what have you been up to?" Uther asked.

"Huh.   Same things I've been at for decades: reading, writing, and rotting."

"Rotting?   Good heavens, things can't be that bad can they?   You appear to have a good portion of mental equilibrium."

"You youngsters don't know what it's like to get old.   Nothing but physical and mental decay, and----"

"Now, now, I can tell by just looking at you that you're not nearly so bad off. Physically at least.   The mental stuff is none of my business.   How's Marie?"

"She's like a spring chicken.   Keeps trying to get me to do this and do that, or go here and go there.   She's my age but I can't keep up with her, bless her heart.   I wouldn't change anything, but an older wife wouldn't be pushing me so hard.   Anyway, have you been staying out of trouble?"

Uther put a hand to his right cheek, but only for an instant.   "You don't know what trouble is."

"How do you know? I've had my ups and downs. Being a diagnosed depressive isn't much fun."

Uther was silent for a moment. "Nevertheless. I could tell you stories, but then, as the saying goes, I'd have to kill you." He knew he shouldn't be talking that way but he couldn't stop.

Harald chuckled, apparently not appreciating the gravity of their conversation.

Uther flushed ever so slightly, and fidgeted with his walking stick.

"I only meant," he started. "Well don't mind me. Perhaps someday I'll let you in on some things. I---- Things come out wrong sometimes." He tried to smile, but it was more like a grimace.

"No matter. I do the same now and again. We muddle through don't we? I recall once I was . . . ." Harald prattled on about the time he had put his foot in his mouth about something or other, and about the time he had mortally insulted a neighbor, who had not spoken to him since.

"I worked for an organization," Uther blurted out. "Non-governmental. Fighting crime."

He stopped and his mouth twisted involuntarily. He felt like a puppet; like someone had their hand up his ass manipulating him, and putting words in his mouth. He quickly rose and grabbed his strange-looking walking stick. "I'd best be going."

"Did I see a woman over at your place the other day?" Harald called after him.

Uther felt his legs stiffen and he called back "No! Soon though."

"Bring her over," Uther heard as he walked away. Ostensibly Harald was as lonely as he was.

When he got home Uther plopped down onto the camp cot he had been using until the house was finished and Lene was there to help buy furniture and decorations. He wished she were there now.

Chapter Forty-one

Refuge

Uther had, reluctantly, moved Lene from Norway to Denmark while he went to Montana to build their new home. As he sat looking out a window on the upper level, he snorted softly. Some *home*.

It had taken him two months to burn and tear down the remnants of the old homestead and round up builders. Construction companies were scarce there, but money talked, and they--he and Lene--had more than enough of that. Money, and each other. Wasn't that enough?

He thought again of Alecto. She was-- had been--a type who would have probably liked it up there in *The Treasure State*. God, how could he suppress her memory? And he hadn't even known her real name. Hadn't even known her real name. Lord almighty, hadn't even known her real name. Hadn't even . . . .

Uther had had some misgivings about the whole building project when he had remembered Lene's warning about hiding in a sparsely-populated place. But cities weren't his thing, and he hoped Lene could adapt to the area. Area? Hell, it was to be a home that they would seldom leave; a prison. Damn Ragnarök, why couldn't they have just let them go? If someone got sick or too old to do their jobs they would release them, so what was the difference? He could only think--actually it was obvious--it was a punishment intended to dissuade others from leaving, and they were afraid of too many faint-hearted ninnies bailing out. Had he become a faint-hearted ninny? More to the point, had he and Lene indeed been set up as examples?

Supervising the actual construction had been interesting and it had occupied his mind, which was essential since he always had to have something to do. Sitting around, even in Norway, had become extremely tedious.

The one-story house was conventional looking, but there were certain unconventional features, like the special room in the basement. Uther explained to the workers how he had always had a fear of violent storms like tornadoes, and they seemed to accept that. One thing about the locals was that they were accepting of others' foibles, and not at all free with their advice. The one-hundred and fifty-yard tunnel from the safe room toward Nordraak's fenceline that ended in a rock pile surrounded by a clump of trees was a little more challenging. It was to be lined with galvanized culvert material, and that alone made the story much more difficult to concoct, but Uther made up an explanation which was at least plausible: that he was afraid of being trapped in the basement after a nuclear blast.

Uther would make some additions of his own after the house was complete: cover the windows with bullet-proof and blast-proof glass, lay explosive-protection material in the attic in case someone dropped a small bomb, install poison gas detectors, and so on. No use doing much fencing or putting up *No Trespassing* signs; anything that would prompt even more speculation. Instead he would vet any locals with Nordraak before even answering the door, except for the obvious one, then they would try to meet people. Maybe Lene would even enjoy that, and after all, the name Montgomery was still known locally by the old-timers. His father, Milo, had been nuts, and one manifestation had been that he hadn't liked his Norwegian name, so he had changed it-- probably without any legal process--from Hans Larson to Milo. Milo Montgomery. And actually Uther liked the name better than Larson; the only thing his father had done right as far as Uther was concerned. *Montgomery* had a classier ring to it.

The area population was declining, the farms becoming fewer and larger, and the small towns smaller. Still mostly Norwegians and Danes whose great and great-great grandparents had homesteaded there on the barren prairie in the early 1900s. Stodgy people who liked the solitude. The thirty-below zero winters. Uther hoped the winters would keep out Ragnarök, even if they could find him and Lene. Well, if found they go on the run again.

Uther picked Lene up at the airport in Williston, North Dakota, and they practically made love right there in the baggage area; and on the forty-mile ride home they were like children in their excitement. Possibly they would find peace at last.

"You have a beautiful nose," Uther said.

"Whaat?"

"Your nose. I have always admired it. I love you for your nose."

"Are you losing your mind?"

"Possibly." He laughed.

"Well in that case I may as well confess that I love you for your big----"

"Now, now."

They bounced along the gravel road for a while.

When Lene commented on Uther's far-from-new Ford pickup he explained that their aim now was to fit in, and it was essential not to be too ostentatious; leastwise not at first. Selling the construction of their new home had been difficult enough. And she was to join him in meeting people, but only those whom he had checked out.

As they drove he filled her in on some of the other efforts they would needs undertake, like attending some of the local events, learning about the local crops--wheat, lentils, peas--in order that they could show an interest, being sure to express concern about rainfall, weed infestations, and so on; and to generally become part of the community without being over-enthusiastic. Uther knew that--if the people were the same as they had been when he was young--they were not dull, and they could spot a phony or an outsider a mile away. They were survivors. People had been leaving ever since the early 1900s, and only the strongest and brightest remained. He thought of it as a sort of Darwinian shakeout.

"But aren't you somewhat phony yourself?" Lene asked. "Making such an effort to become part of local society simply to save our necks."

"Tut-tut my dear. I am not that crass. I look forward genuinely to taking up a new life. And by the by, what's wrong with saving our necks?"

"Whatever, speaking of necks, don't take me amiss, but isn't it a touch disingenuous for a man who has decapitated people to speak in that way?"

"Hurruph! It was one person, and he deserved what he got! Worse in fact."

"What could be worse."

"You know well enough. But cease and desist about my mistake. We're starting over. Don't you ever forget?"

"Mistake? Such a mistake is difficult to suppress."

They drove on.

"Why are you in such a huff all of a sudden," Uther asked.

"Huff? I'm not in a huff. I don't know. I didn't know I was." She looked away from him, out her open window. "I guess I'm just nervous. This is a pretty big change for me you know. It's going to take a while for me to get used to it up here."

"You grew up on a farm; that's a plus."

"I suppose so."

"Oh, I asked around about my mother. A year after my father was killed she took up with a local rancher and by all accounts he was a decent sort."

They hit a big bump in the road.

"Unfortunately he was killed by a bull a year after they were married."

"No!   You couldn't make up a story like that!   Are you sure that's not a lot of *bull*? Then what did she do?

"Good news, bad news.   She inherited the guy's ranch but she couldn't handle it by herself--and they say she had had enough of men--so she sold it and moved back to the old home place where I grew up.   She lived there alone for about five years, then she died."

"From what?"

"Cancer."

They hit another bump.

"And you said you never saw or heard from her after you left?"

"No."

"Pretty flint-hearted weren't you?"

"I guess so.   But I inherited the farm. She did that much for me."

Chapter Forty-two

Settling in

The front doorbell rang and Lene got up from her recliner to see who it was. It was the first time since they had settled into their new home that it had rung, and Uther could see how uneasy she was. There were two doors--inner and outer--and the inner was heavy and blast proof. As there were no peep holes, Lene looked first at the TV monitor, then out a window at a mirror that had been aimed at the front step.

Uther stepped closer to the monitor and saw a somewhat dumpy, blond, middle-aged lady. She was heavyset, with slightly buck teeth and men's clothing: denim shirt and pants, and round, wire-rim glasses. Uther nodded and Lene moved to let her in. There was no way this one could be sinister.

"Hi there, I'm your neighbor from two miles south of here. Sallie Mortinsen." She held out her hand, then Lene led her in.

"My husband, Uther," Lene said.

"Our old dog, Fido, is missing," Sallie smiled. "You haven't seen him I don't suppose. Big, gray mongrel type?"

"No, no dogs," Uther answered. "Sorry." Lost dog hell; she was only curious and trying to be neighborly. "Fido? Really?"

"Hah. Ha, ha! My husband, Andros, has a strange sense of humor." She giggled. "I'm glad he didn't name me."

"Fido?" Uther chortled. "Now surely your husband wouldn't have named a classy lady like you Fido?"

Sally leaned over at her waist as she laughed, and Uther and Lene laughed too.

"Come into the kitchen," Lene invited after they had recovered. "We still have hot coffee. Or do you drink coffee?" She knew all guests gathered around the kitchen table up there.

"Ha, do I drink coffee? Do bulls chase cows?" She tittered and sat down.

"Do Norwegians eat lutefisk?" Uther added.

"Cream or sugar?" Lene offered.

"Oh, no thanks, and I hope it's strong enough to cure ulcers."

"I don't know about that, but strong enough to give you ulcers."

"I remember the Larsons," Sallie said. "Old Milo and Gina. Changed their last name to Montgomery as I recall. I assume your last name is still Montgomery?" She looked at them, apparently assuming they were married. Uther wished they were.

"Yes it is," Uther answered as Lene poured. "What do you and Andros do?"

"Oh, you know, farm and ranch. Mostly farm. Still hanging on."

Uther didn't ask how large their farm was; that was a gaffe that only outsiders made. Another custom was to avoid talking politics, not that he was inclined to anyway, in view of President Einstein and his party cronies and reprehensible associates. He had nicknamed him *Einstein* because to most perspicacious people he was a low-level moron. Or he could just as well have named him *The Baron of Bedlam* or *The March Hare of*----

"No stray dogs though?" Sallie asked again.

Uther subtly put his index fingers and middle fingers to his temples. He had been disturbed by flights of thought having nothing to do with anything.

"No," Lene answered. "But if we find him we'll let you know. If not we'll bring over someone else's dog."

"Have you met old Harald Nordraak and his wife?" Sallie asked.

"I have," Uther replied.   "Seems nice enough."

"Oh, yeah."

She seemed less than enthusiastic.

They chatted about the weather and the usual subjects, then, "What brings you here?"

"Oh, hah!" Harald laughed.   He had prepared well for the inevitable question. "We're both retired from government work. Boring as spit, and always in big cities, so we wanted to spend our days in peace and quiet. That's all there is to it, and I guess some of us never get over their childhoods up here, although Lene is originally from Indiana. We're both prairie people at heart."

"Well I hope you weren't working for the CIA or the FBI or anything like that.   You never know what secrets Milo and I might have," Sallie giggled.

She was prying.   Politely prying, and Uther didn't mind in the least; he even welcomed it as a way of becoming a part of the local populace.

"Lene was in social service and I was a lower-level State Department worker. Paperwork mostly, though I did have a secret security clearance and there are a few things I'm not supposed to discuss.   Unless you get me plastered in the bar.   Seriously, I can tell you it's nothing of importance, yet I'm enough of a patriot that I wouldn't reveal it to anyone.   I wasn't a spy or anything like that."

Sallie returned his half smile.   "Oh, gracious no, I never thought for a moment!"

She was obviously satisfied, but Uther smothered a laugh, knowing how the tongues would wag now, and that they would wag in the right way rather than sinisterly or as contributing to any phantasmagoric rumor machine.

"As Uther mentioned, we just want out of the hustle and bustle of the big city, and we're tired of poking computers," Lene said.   "Maybe I'll have a garden--I've always wanted to do that--and Uther might get into refurbishing a 1950s MG sports car.   Whatever we do we don't want to ever see another computer. Though we do have a few out of necessity."

Sallie fixed her look on Uther.   "You do talk with a slight Norwegian accent.   No one would call a real accent; but some hint of it. And your words.   *Plastered*, and your wry sense of humor.   Hmmm.   I guess you never get this part of Montana out of your system."

Time passed uneventfully.   Lene planned a garden for the next summer and Uther puttered around working on the house; making sure all of the safety features were in order, and adding amenities which would make their hideout more homey. They were content; Lene more than he.

Social events were not what they had been; not as Uther remembered from his childhood, though he had not been allowed to go to many of them anyway. The town was all but dead, but occasionally someone had scheduled something: a pie social, a church supper, ... Eventually there were too few pies, too few church members, too few of everything; and most social intercourse was limited to neighborhood visits.

Uther and Lene had managed to meet several couples their age or older: Axel Larsen and his wife, Lilly, who lived on their farm six miles north; and Fergus Barnard and his wife Eunice, at their summer home seven or eight miles to the west. They were from Daytona Beach, Florida, and why they wanted to live on the godforsaken prairie was a mystery. They seemed to have some horse sense and that was a plus. Fergus had evidently worked as an electrical engineer, but he was evasive as to details. Uther had asked Harald Nordraak about them, and Harald had said that Axel and Lilly had lived in the area forever; the Barnards for five or six years .

Autumn that year was short and winter arrived abruptly and ferociously. Uther and Lene, often snowed in, often sitting before their fireplace, were at peace.

Chapter Forty-three

Philosophy (including religion)

Most of the people in the community were average; the way Uther liked it, and Lene felt the same; living simply, without the incessant, punishing worrying. Some people-- not necessarily boneheads--content themselves throughout their entire lives by devoting themselves to modest pursuits. It must be nice, Uther thought, but he well knew such mindsets were innate and immutable, and he and Lene were not of that mold; and in truth they were far from it. What then? Being unable to change their dispositions, was there any recourse other than isolating themselves and trying to fit in? Could such a metaphysical approach be possible and doable? Uther knew that he was not a deep thinker, however *knowing that he knew* was a plus. He began to feel a little lightheaded; a giddiness that came upon him when he was about to take one of his silly flights of fancy. In a few minutes he had taken off, and the first thing that came to mind was the vision of a crystal ball such as seers use, and

the apprehension that he could view his--his and
Lene's--future. Being well familiar with his
dream state he relaxed and allowed himself to
be carried along by his flow of consciousness,
which consciousness encouraged him to see
deep into the ball, and what he saw was
wondrous and comforting: a pastoral scene
similar to the rural area where they now lived,
but which scene was greatly magnified as to
beauty and serenity. It was not like a painting
however; it was three-dimensional and
animated, with wildlife, bright and vivid
flowers waving in a gentle breeze, and so on
and on. Uther was in a state of perfect life, and
somehow he understood that it was not the
commonplace absurd afterlife as anticipated by
the masses of humanity; religions that are no
more than continuations of myths and
superstitions of the past. Religions; blights on
humanity because they hold people in the grip
of falsity and unreality that precludes
participation in any rational human advances.
Rather--as in Uther's case--an inspiration which
comforts, if not protects, the living. That
posits a higher force, then relinquishes it's
control upon the death of living creatures.
After all, the fancy that we live forever in a
heaven or some such, apart from being
ridiculous in this day and age, was not at all
appealing. Uther recalled the saying

Everybody wants to go to heaven, but nobody wants to die. Ha! He didn't want to go to a heaven, but he didn't want to die either. If given the the choice he would choose death, but not too soon.

No one would say Jon Applegate was the most prominent of all of the luminaries in Charity and its surrounds. The further catch to that approbation was that not many of the local luminaries were exceptionally luminous.

Jon's life represented to some extent the life Uther wanted, but he wanted it without the dull intellect and the religion; merely a peaceful existence embracing only his particular mind and personage.

"Be careful not to become too aloof and arrogant," Lene had admonished. "You tend to look down on average people and their faults and foibles, but we all have them: faults and foibles."

"Most people have more faults than----"

"There you go again. Yes, but still. They can't help it."

Uther paid heed to her admonition, with the reservation that many can help it; they just don't want to.

Jon Applegate. He couldn't help it.

Jon--short, stout, dark, bearded, and well-past middle age--was a mostly-unemployed carpenter; mostly unemployed because there wasn't much building going on in Charity. Still, he piddled away at small jobs there and in nearby towns, enough to keep the wolf away from the door. His wife, Candice, had died several years ago and his three children were grown and gone, so his expenses were minimal. He drank and smoked, but had no other serious vices, and he lived modestly, watching TV or sitting on a bench on Main Street looking at nothing in particular, as there was nothing much in particular to see. He was a lonely soul who fervently assumed he had such an attribute as a *soul*, and he could be a bit of a nuisance to anyone who passed by who wasn't in his same condition. He was generally regarded as a good person, but who, because of his religious beliefs tended to proselytize in a town--and area of the country--where proselytizing was frowned on, but where too many did it anyway under their naive assumption that they were subtle and that they were obligated to spread their *good news*. Jon had often been reminded gently--or sometimes not so gently--to mind his own business, but more often he was ridiculed behind his back.

Uther sat on Jon's bench, and something about his limited, mundane surrounds had tempted him to float away on one of his psychical voyages throughout which he could only describe his condition as half dreaming and half awake. And there was the crystal ball, but as he struggled to keep looking deep within, it faded, and he was left sitting watching a scrawny, dark-tan dog lift its leg and mark a streetlight pole.

As he was on Jon's bench he naturally applied his musings to him. What did the crystal ball have to do with Jon Applegate? Uther guessed it was that he didn't want to end up like him, in a ludicrous mindset; but at the same time he envied Jon's simple and apparently contented life.

The dog marked another pole, then strolled slowly away. An old lady came around a corner, waved, and turned down an alley alongside the grocery store. The store had been closed down long ago, but Uther remembered how, when he had been a child, it had thrived.

Well nuts, Uther thought he could just as well go home before Jon showed up. After what he and Lene--and Alecto--had been through, boredom was perfect peace, but on this occasion communing with Jon would be too perfect. It was true drudgery.

Fæn. There came Jon around the corner of the old bank building, and when he spotted Uther his face lit up and he walked faster.

Uther regarded him as a herald of
conversational doom, but as there was nothing
else for it, he decided to get the jump on Jon by
laying a little of his own brand of doom on him.
It was Sunday morning.

"Uther! How nice to see you on this
beautiful Sunday morn----"

"Jon. How are you? I thought you
would be in the front pew." Jon appeared
sober enough.

"As usual I didn't see you----"

"You will from now on. I was watching
an evangelist on TV this morning, and all of a
sudden I saw the light. Now that may sound
strange to you, but it was a divine revelation.
There I was, at my age, a firm atheist, and the
light came on just like that!" Uther snapped
his fingers.

"You don't mean to say----?"

"Yes! I was so overcome I went down
on my knees in front of the television set and
confessed my sins, and believe me there were a
lot of them. Lene thought I had lost my mind,
but by the time I had explained everything to
her she was on her knees also!"

"Uther, I never thought I would see the
day when you----"

"It's been a joyous day, Jon. So joyous
that I must go home and resume my studies."
He got up. "I've opened the Bible for the first

time in years!   I'm only here in town because I had to take a break from the rapture."   He started to walk away.

"Bless you, Uther!"

Chapter Forty-four

A long winter

As winter wore on Uther and Lene read; first all the classics that they were interested in, then modern fiction--which was generally pretty lousy--then nonfiction. Then there was a pause in their reading, for want of anything above middling level. With the advent of the Internet--and the increased availability of self-publishing options--the quality of writing had, they felt, declined drastically.

Commercial television was, in Uther's opinion, *a vast wasteland;* a term coined by former FCC chairman Newton Minnow in 1961, and it had probably worsened since then, though that was splitting hairs. Occasionally there was something good on public television, but the older Uther got the more bored he became.

Uther had encountered about everything he wanted to. Not to say he knew everything--preposterous--but he was approaching a point in life where he simply didn't want to know much more. Transitioning from a life of action and danger to plain existence had been blissful, then challenging, then difficult, then nearly unbearable; and he could see the same tedium in Lene. They had based their lives on trying to improve--ugh, the *human condition*--and look at them now. Maybe they should had stayed in Ragnarök, but . . . . A form of PTSD, or something similar? That he and Lene had succumbed at the same time was a blessing and a curse. The blessing of course was that they understood each other perfectly.

Uther got up from his recliner and stirred the logs in the fireplace, then he sat back down. Lene was downstairs doing something or other. It seemed that despite their alikeness they were communicating less.

Meeting neighbors had been okay but it had only gone so far. The same old; they seldom had much in common with anyone, and talking about crops and weather had gotten old fast. Not dumb people, but there had been no going back to what Uther had remembered of the area. Times had changed, and the main change--aside from the tenacity of those who remained--was that in years past there had been a greater diversity, and much more activity and bustle.

One solace was that there, in their house-fort, they were safe; though were they really? When would a large drone come over and drop a bomb on them? One that would penetrate the attic shield. Or come down the chimney. He should put a grill over it; then he got ahold of himself and took in the extent of his absurdity. Absurdities, for he had not made much sense of himself lately. Or of many externals either.

Lene was changing too, but he couldn't pin down the changes. On the surface she was quieter and more withdrawn, and she had lost interest in most things. Her internals were mysterious to Uther and when he attempted to bring her out she was evasive. And once she had even cautioned him to mind his own business. Another time she had not even answered him.

One twenty-below-zero clear day when Lene was more upbeat Uther sat down beside her on the sofa and put his arm around her shoulders. She leaned her head on his chest.

"Are we getting cabin fever?" Uther asked softly.

She looked up at him. "I think we are."

They sat quietly while the grandfather clock next to the fireplace struck twelve.

"I think I know what's happening to us," Uther began. "Old Nordraak told me once how it had happened to him. He modestly confided his notably high intelligence--by different measures--and his clinical depression. Depression has been called, in some, *the genius disease*, because most really intelligent people can see the history and forward path of humanity, and the past and the future are darn dismal."

Lene considered for a few moments. "How did, does, he cope? How are we to cope?"

"Well, he didn't have much to offer, but the main thing is to stay busy."

"What? Stay busy? That's it? That's not much of a solution!"

"Unless you're a member of the hoi polloi and are counting on wafting up to some sort of heaven, or are passionate to an extreme about collecting three-prong blivits, or are immersed in other equally mundane enthusiasms, I guess that's about it." Uther had to smile at her reaction.

"I was happier in Ragnarök," she responded crisply.

"Bite your tongue! You can't mean it!"

"Well, not happy--I have seldom in my life been happy--but, oh you know, I was fulfilled at first."

"I was likewise, but here we are, brought down by our Ragnarök crusades; and our own vainglory. Damned if we did, and damned if we didn't. Shell shocked if we continued, lost now that we're out. Nordraak wrote a WWI novel about a shell-shocked guy from up here: *Men With Broken Faces*, and----"

"I always thought we were so strong."

"There's no accounting for it," Uther went on. "I'm disillusioned, and I tend to wallow in my disillusionment and, I may even say, despair."

"So do I. Despair."

"I knew that the world is going down the toilet, and I still think so. It's obvious: nuclear war, famine, global warming, ... It's unquestionable unless one is a moron, or living in some kind of mental fog. And it seems equally apparent to me that if there were any hope at all to turn things around it would not be due to the efforts of mundane do-gooders, dullards, and hopelessly optimistic simpletons. But I never thought our secret and drastic Ragnarök machinations would fail."

Lene considered. "Who says they're failing?"

"They're bound to fail. Why? Because just as with conventional activities, the stupidity of the masses is against the brilliant few, regardless of the severity of those few. Simple as that."

They held close to each other for a long, long time.

Then Uther spoke. "Sitting here is like being the bull's eye on a target. Sooner or later someone is going to hit us, even if he, she, or they are rotten shots." He involuntarily bent his head down. "They'll hit us by chance. Through persistence."

"What, then?" Lene whispered.

"There are two challenges for us. First, we have to spend far less time here, or leave altogether. And second, we have to develop a mutual passion."

"Passion?"

"You know, something we can both become absorbed in: stamp collecting; growing the world's largest pumpkin; seeing all of the county's attractions, like the largest ball of string."

Lene stiffened. "You are so full of dritt your eyeballs are brown. See, I know some Norwegian already."

"First, the getting out of here."

"That didn't work out so well in Norway."

"No, but we sure liked it there until we found ourselves in the crosshairs. What we could do is pull off a double bluff by going back."

"Yes but that's a risky bluff."

"No riskier than going somewhere else. We have to figure out a way to be more anonymous."

"I don't want to spend the rest of my life wearing an old-lady wig and dress, strapping down my boobs."

"Surely not," he pinched her left breast, "but we'll come up with something.   I'm not enthusiastic about wearing a gray wig and hobbling about with a cane either.   We'll think it all through."

"And what of our passion?"

"I'm as passionate about you as ever," Uther said, and he pinched her other breast.

"Stop that!"   She slapped his hand.   "I am not joking."

"We'll forge on.   We have to or our goose is cooked.   First we must keep up our anonymity.   Only then can we move on to Norway."

Lene swallowed visibly.   "Remember our *no secrets* agreement?"

"Of course."

"Well I have one I haven't told you." She held up her hand to quiet him.   "The reason I bring it up now is that I have just remembered it."

"Oh.   Okay."

"I have often wondered why Ragnarök hasn't given up on finishing us off by now, then a friend came to mind.   Hildegard.   She was a couple of levels above me and----"

"Above you where?"

"In Ragnarök, and----"

Uther groaned. "I think I know where this is going."

"She was a pretty good friend and----"

"How good?"

"I trusted her. Let me finish. About the time we were thinking of bailing out I swore her to secrecy and asked her what she thought about it. She seemed to think it could be done, but she urged me to stay, and now looking back I don't think she was----"

"Uh?"

"I wonder if she ratted me out, and you too by default."

She sat up straight, but he drew her back into his arms.

"I made a mistake once too," he cracked with a not unkind smile. "Let's see, it was a long time ago and hard to recall, but----"

Lene gently slapped his face.

"Ouch! But no use going back to what we can't change, so what will we do now?"

"I don't know. What?"

"We'll go forward!" he laughed.

She slapped him again through her tears.

"We can't lose all sense of humor," Uther persisted. *One Monday morning Ole was walking down the sidewalk with two big black eyes and he met Lars. Lars said, 'Uff-dah Ole, vat happened to yew?' Ole replied, 'Yew know big, fat Lena Torkelson don't yew?'   'Yeh, everyone knows fat Lena.'   'Vell I vas sitting behind her in church yesterday morning, and ven ve stood for da first hymn I noticed dat her dress was tucked up in her cheeks, so I . . . .'*

As he told his joke Lene whispered, "No wonder I love you so."

Chapter Forty-five

More locals

Uther enjoyed the ten-below-zero as he trudged through the two-inch veil of snow on the deserted country road. Usually when it was that cold there was little or no wind. He had chosen the road because even in summer there was seldom any traffic. He pulled the hood of his winter parka tighter around his face and lifted his scarf to cover his nose. Nobody there ever wore a scarf over their face--it was a sign of weakness, and of frozen faces--but he did.

He had met Ivor Nordby in town the day before. Ivor, he had learned, was one of the remaining oddballs in town. Many years ago there had been quite a number of Ivor types. Back then there were no genetic tests for paternity or maternity, but people just knew by looks, mannerisms, and gossip. It was well known that Ivor was not one-hundred percent Norwegian at all: his real mother had been part Chippewa Indian and part French. Francis Dubois. They said that Ivor didn't know, and none of the other half-legitimates did either.

Uther trudged on and he felt safe, though he was in about as open a landscape as possible. Unlikely that even a nemesis would be out in this kind of weather; most of them were tough, but city tough.

There were no birds, no animals, no people, . . . , just the way he liked it, and besides he wouldn't stray too far from home, partly because if he had a heart attack or something he didn't want to freeze to death. He had his cell phone but he didn't like to use it for fear of his calls being traced. It could have been paranoia because he knew next to nothing about phones.

A Chinese pheasant burst out from under a small caragana bush and flew noisily as far as it could to another bush. Pheasants were not native to the area, and only if it weren't too severe a winter and if they could find shelter belts to hole up under could they survive. As far as that went, caraganas--Siberian Pea Shrubs--were non-native too, but they were tough.

Damnation. Uther heard a vehicle approach him from behind and far away. He turned and made out a newish-looking pickup a half-mile back. No place to hide and no place to run. All he could do was cock the old WWII Colt 45 in his coat pocket and wait. Still probably nothing to worry about.

The red Dodge pickup bumped closer. When it reached him Uther stopped and saw an elderly man, obviously local, but he didn't recognize him. He waved and the man got out and approached him. He had on an old blue winter cap and insulated coveralls.

"You okay?" the man asked.

"Yeah, thanks."

"Don't see many people walking this road even in summer."

"Yeah. Just had to get outta the house."

They shook hands.

"Uther."

"Oh yeah, old Milo Montgomery's kid. But I don't recall you being called Uther, though I have to say your family was pretty----"

"And you?" Uther interrupted.

"Gus Bensen. We--my wife Gunilla and I--live east of town a few miles. Retired from farming ten years ago. Praise the lord for that."

Uther smiled. "I could say the same of you; I don't see many people driving this road either, winter or summer."

"I heading down to the old Elmer Smith place to check on it. They live in town in the winters now and they can't get around like they used to. He worries that somebody will trash the place or turn it into a meth lab or something."

"If you run into some meth cookers what'll you do; the nearest sheriff's deputy is twenty or thirty miles away?"

Gus reached into a pocket and pulled out a revolver that was so old Uther didn't recognize it. He waved it over his head and grinned. "I can take care of myself!"

"Hum. A big one. You could beat them to death with it."

"Say, pardon me, but you look kind of anxious."

"Oh? If so it's probably because of my former occupation. I was in secret government work. Fighting the bad guys and so on, and now that I'm retired it's taking some time to come down, and this seems to be the place to do it. Don't mind me."

"So that's it. Explains why people wonder about you. Don't worry though, it takes a while to get to know people here, but as your people used to live here the locals will come around sooner than they do with outsiders. Some of those without roots here never do fit in. Why hell, I've known some who moved here fifty years ago and they're still *new*."

Uther mused to himself, then, "Nevertheless be careful if you run into any bad-looking characters. I can't talk much about my past--security you know--but I've had to deal with some pretty rough customers."

"Ha!   I can handle myself alright."   He brandished his revolver again.

"I'm sure you can, but they'd be after me, not you."

"Speaking of which I'd better get going. Stop in and see me and Gunilla sometime. We'll put the coffee on."

"I will."   Uther smiled a genuine smile. He hadn't quite gotten the *Speaking of which . . . part.*

Gus clunked--Uther assumed that he clunked confidently--away on his mission.   He seemed nice, but Uther had been around Harald Nordraak too much, and he had become more a a touch cynical as he shared some of Harald's opinion that most people are numbskulls.   Not necessarily there, but in general.   According to Harald there are likable and not-so-likable numbskulls, and all in between, but the problem with assessing them was, how can one see dumbbells who contribute to the mess humankind is in as likable?   Further, Uther had had his own view reinforced by Harald's conviction that democracies worldwide are failing.   We pick the most capable people we can to remove our gallbladders, advise us on the stock markets, etcetera, but when it comes to perhaps the most important function of all--

running the country--every nincompoop can vote, and they too often vote for smooth-talking nincompoops. Merciful heaven! And when he had fallen into the usual response of asking Harald what form of government is better, he had been chastised for his question. *What's better? Dear me, you too? Next I suppose you will give the moth-eaten reply, 'Make me a dictator.' That's the usual suggestion.*

Uther stopped himself from falling into further philosophizing, except that his whole train of thought had led him back to Ragnarök. They had given him all manner of intelligence and personality tests, as he assumed they had done to all other applicants. From that he assumed that the higher-ups were at least as quick-witted and apprehending as he; and surely if they couldn't succeed in their overriding mission--albeit one based on force and violence, like communism--of ultimately uplifting humanity, how could anyone else or any other group succeed?

Uther turned and trudged back toward home, wishing against hope that Ragnarök would just leave him and Lene alone. He kicked what he thought was a lump of snow but unfortunately it was a snow-covered rock. After shouting a few choice curses into the void he commenced his walk.

Chapter Forty-six

Paranoia?

Uther came home and slammed the door shut. "Good lord I thought I saw Zabov!"

Lene, standing beside the kitchen sink, whirled around and gasped.

"I came around the corner by the bar and almost bumped into a guy, and for a moment I thought it was Zabov."

He slumped down onto a chair at the table.

Lene took a deep breath. "Well you crucified him and I don't think he will be resurrected."

She poured him a cup of hot chocolate.

"Yeah, yeah, that's not the point. The point is----"

The cup shook in his hand.

"I know." She took his other hand in hers.

Uther looked up at her. "You're stronger than I am, and thank goodness for that. Sometimes I look back on the first time I saw you, in that old warehouse. You were a tough

cookie then, and you still are." He smiled
wanly at her.

"Maybe then, but I'm not so sure now.
Then I was only an order-giver, not an enforcer.
I had orders coming down and fewer decisions
to make. As I think back I feel that much of it
was an act. Life is different now, and harder.
In the event, I have you, and it may surprise you
to know you are tougher than you think."

She was wearing an old-fashioned
tortoiseshell-adorned necklace inscribed with
Greek writing. He couldn't read the
inscription, and she never wore necklaces.

"Tougher? You're talking to the one who
had a complete meltdown, and almost had----"

"Anyone would have gone under after
what happened to Alecto," she whispered. It
was one of the first times since Alecto's death
that Lene had uttered her name.

Uther sat confounded for a minute, then a
lighter feeling came over him and he
understood how facing reality was better than
suppressing it; and he felt stronger for it; and he
knew he could be strong again like he had been
before. Before Alecto. Now he only hoped
nothing like that would happen to Lene.

Lene led him to the sofa before the
fireplace. After a lengthy period of meditation
she said, "We might as well stop avoiding
speaking of Alecto. Holding it in is worse."

"You're right."

"And again, about your Norway idea.   I still don't understand.   We were threatened once there, so why would we go back?"

"As I said before I think of it as something of a ruse.   What do you think?   You are a better thinker than I."

She thought for a while.   "You may have a point.   Besides, where else could we go? Switzerland?   You mentioned yodeling once."

"I'd feel more at home in one of the Scandinavian countries like Norway or Denmark.   I can get along speaking Danish too. It feels like it's in my blood; my heritage.   And I've never been a good yodeler."

"Have you done much yodeling?"

"No, but the other day when I was walking I kicked a lump of snow which turned out to be a rock, and I did some yodeling then."

As close as he and Lene were and how much he valued her advice, one fine, sunny day Uther went to sound out Harald Nordraak.   It was but a fifteen-minute walk, and as he walked Uther felt somewhat sheepish, as it seemed he had taken to running to Harald whenever he was distraught.   A tinge of embarrassment and guilt that he couldn't muddle through on his own, and with the implication that Lene wasn't enough. Yet there was something solid and ultimate about Harald, as though he were the ultimate authority on life in general; a realist who had reached the pinnacle of human understanding. One of the few who had thrust aside all of the nonsense of most human thought, and was left with what little absolute knowledge remained. Uther was not a philosopher, and certainly not a genius, but he had always maintained his good sense, and he was sharp enough to recognize Harald's acuity. Funny thing was, Harald was reluctant to use the word *genius* in any context, and he seemed to abhor the word in regards himself. What then? Realist? His highest encomium? Ipso facto it made sense to seek his advice in spite of the fact that he had probably never lived in any world even remotely resembling that of Ragnarök.

Marie answered the door and after the obligatory chit-chat she sent him down to the basement den where Harald did his writing.

"Herr Larson!" Harald greeted. "Or is it Herr Montgomery? Let's step into the family room."

Harald sat down in an old Victorian high-back chair and waved Uther to the recliner. The wood/coal stove was fired up.

"You didn't bring Lene. Pity. Marie instinctively likes her, though we know little of your former lives. Someday I'm going to get you snooted on aquavit and find out all about you," Harald joked.

Uther smiled back. Harald was harmless. "I have never liked it much. Give me rye whiskey any day."

"I would have never imagined a guy like you would turn down Norsk white lightning. Some of the old Norwegians used to call it truth serum. When you've had enough of it you either tell the truth or you start making everything up. No middle ground. Just like the dumbest of humanity do when they're stone sober: invent truth. But there I go again."

"Twenty below last night," Uther said.

"Yeah. The homesteaders would have frozen to death in their tar-paper shacks if it hadn't been for the little lignite coal mines around here. My grandmother said the drinking-water pail used to freeze up at night. So cold they used to lay old newspapers under the mattresses and pile blankets and quilts a foot high over themselves. Even if they couldn't stand to cuddle with their wives they got really close at night in the winters." Harald reminisced on about the old days for a while.

Finally Uther said, "Harald, I need advice."

Harald didn't bat an eye. "Of course you do. Everybody does; even me. Fire away; it's easier to give advice than to take it, and I'm ready."

"Huh?"

"You didn't come up to this godforsaken place for the healing waters."

Uther was too stunned to respond.

"Good grief," Harald said, "I remember when you said if you told me about yourself you'd have to kill me."

"You remember that?"

"Certainly. One can't forget a threat like that."

"But I was only----"

"Bull. And you should also not take me for an intellectual country bumpkin. I too have been around, and I have done things which might impress even you, so don't think I would be an easy mark. Now, then, with that out of the way you may feel free to tell me anything, and I assure you that your secrets will be safe with me, not due to any nobility on my part, but because I most likely won't give a diddly-damn, and even if I did I still wouldn't be eager to be knocked off by you; should you feel confident enough to try. How do you know you aren't sitting on a grenade right now? A deadly version of the old remote-control whoopy cushion?"

Harald smiled again, but a different kind of smile.

"So relax," Harald added.

Uther leaned back in the recliner. He had to consider for a moment.

"Take your time," Harald said, "and by the by don't take for granted that I am as brilliant as you may assume. If I have any quickness it is because I have two main qualities: I am allergic to bullshit, and I consider most people to be altogether stupid. Actually, to control arrogance, I should moderate the *stupid* to mediocre, or even average, simply because average isn't a trait to be admired."

Uther closed his eyes, and he felt more peaceful than most people in his position would have. Suddenly he sat up.

"Alright, I trust you, but if you----"

Harald became rigid. "There, there, none of that. I don't threaten you, and you should not threaten or in any way try to intimidate me. Please remember, I am a severe, clinical depressive--under medication--and I have no constraints. That, and the fact that I have no extraordinary affinity with life."

"Of course," Harald relented, "It just seemed like you were egging me on. But now we understand each other. Neither of us is pernicious, and talking with each other may be mutually therapeutic."

"I don't know, but I hope so. And I wouldn't be so sure about pernicious. Or mutually."

"I hope you will allow me to ask what you know of me and how you know it," Uther began.

Harald threw back his head and laughed heartily. "Why it's elementary my dear Watson! I make obvious deductions, first, and then I make probable suppositions. I have already deduced that you aren't here because this place is your idea of retirement bliss. Further, your house may fool the others, but it's obviously something of a fort. Then there's the----"

"How can you be so sure of----?"

"Don't interrupt. You are edgy most of the time, as is Lene, if that's her real name, and I'm sure it isn't. Now, as to all of the malarkey about you having worked for a secret government group, I don't believe a word of that either. Our federal government here in the U.S. is corrupt in many ways, but if anybody gets on a bad list they don't send out goons to assassinate them. We haven't gone that far yet. Therefore I know you have been in some sort of other clandestine organization. What kind? If I read you correctly you're not in it for the money. You seem to be more of an idealist."

"How can you possibly know that?"

Harald held up his hand. "Intuition Watson. Often that's all we have to go by. Some people's intuition is highly developed-- probably inherited--and most people's intuitions are not. Maybe it's related to overall intelligence, I dunno, but that's another topic. Let's stick to your story. You're on the run, apparently, because you come and go frequently."

Harald leaned his head back on the chair, closed his eyes, and put his fingertips together.

"You were in Norway for a time, and you yourself said you liked it there. Liked it very much. Then some event caused you to leave."

Harald was quiet for a while.

"What else?" Uther asked.

"As an idealist you must have been working for some virtuous organization, though I suspect your methods were not altogether, um, proper, otherwise you would not be in your present predicament."

"Anything else, Sherlock? How do you know about my--our--methods?"

"How indeed? Simple. If you worked for an association whose members are bound to kill you, what else am I to make of your methods? Moving on, I hazard a guess your wife or girlfriend, or whoever she is, was in the same organization. If not she has to be a secular saint to stick with you through all of your tribulations. Now enough from me, it's your turn. Tell me the main points, and hold nothing back; I may not know much more about you from my modest deductions, however I will know enough to discern any, ahem, untruths. And relax, you have nothing, hem, nothing more to lose."

"Your modest deductions? Good heavens! You have it all, and I fear I can only add simple--however gruesome--details regarding our former organization, Ragnarök, our methods, and our--my and Lene's-- downfall. And personal tragedy regarding one of my co-workers. And my own foibles, though *foibles* is no doubt an understatement."

Uther began by telling of his ideals and his cynicism about the fate of humankind, and about how he had apprehended the futility of fighting evil on evil's terms.

"Then our work got too gruesome, and simultaneously I didn't give a hill of beans for what we were doing, then I began to hate it. Our work."

When Uther had talked himself out Harald stared intensely at him. More than that, a penetrating stare.

Partly in order to stop the stare, Uther spoke.

"So, here's my question. You have divined my inner workings and all of that, but

what am I to do now?   Lene and I?   We're
marked, and not by your run-of-the mill mob or
such.   In fact I believe we're sunk."

"I am not a psychiatrist, and worse I am
oftentimes not very practical in day-to-day
affairs.   Nor am I one to give people advice,
especially taking into account my own not-so-
stellar life.   But if you insist, come back in a
few days."

"I insist."

Chapter Forty-seven

The verdict

Three days after Uther consulted Harald he returned for the verdict. Again they were downstairs. The stove was fired up and the ornately-decorated room would have been comfortable had it not been for the seriousness of the upcoming conversation. Uther assumed it was to be serious, unless Harald had some grand solution to the fix he and Lene were in.

No small talk this time.

"Thumbs up or thumbs down?" Uther asked.

"Hurruph!" Harald snorted. He didn't look at all encouraging as he sat with his eyes closed and gritting his teeth. He appeared older than he had three days before.

Uther waited, then, "Well?"

Eyes still closed, Harald held out his right hand with the thumb out sideways.

"What the deuce does that mean?" Uther barked.

Harald at last opened his eyes. "It means you are in deep dung and I don't know what to make of the outcome."

"No shit--pardon the pun--of course I'm in a fix. It's your *I don't know* part that makes me nervous!"

Harald began. "Hum. Well let's start at the bottom and work up. Or at the top and work down. I don't know the difference." Uther winced. "It seems to me that you have to get out of the country again, to start with."

"That's what I suggested to Lene. Back to Norway. Kind of a double bluff," Harald went on.

"That's what I thought too. Are you a mind reader?" Uther began to have a glimmer of hope.

"You know more about phony passports and stuff than I do," Harald murmured. "So we cut to the next important issue, anonymity."

"Okay."

"If you play your cards right your appearances will be the only way your nemeses can find you. How do you feel about plastic surgery? You and Lene?"

"Plastic surgery? We had considered it once and decided it would be too drastic."

"Lene I presume?"

"Oh goodness! I could do it, but I couldn't stand to see her get carved up. You know how beautiful she is, and any surgery would be a declination."

"Getting bumped off would be a worse declination."

"Nevertheless."

Harald closed his eyes again and sat perfectly still.

Uther interrupted Harald's reverie. "How about facial tanning, hair dye, and so forth? Eyeglasses, but not dark glasses; they would be a dead giveaway. Canes too, for each of us. There are special canes that, well, have a double purpose. And anything else we can do to avoid the scalpel."

"It's your decision. I'm sure you know much more about that kind of thing than I do. You know by now that I'm good at reading people, but I'm reluctant to give advice. First, because I am better at detecting people's problems and foibles than I am at coming up with solutions, and second because it's my nature. Furthermore I would hate to be responsible for anyone's misfortune. In your case, your demise."

Uther waited for more. "That's it?"

"Sorry. You're in a formidable mess, and as in one of the books I wrote I philosophically observed how often there are no good answers. No solutions to problems, calamities, or natural conditions. Dead ends."

Uther found himself at a loss for words, but at last he found his voice. "I knew all of that. I've read you magnum opus."

"Don't blame me for the quagmire you're in."

"Blame you? I'm not blaming you! I only wonder how such an apparently astute person like you--one with enough imagination and creativity to write wonderful books--can lose all of his imagination and creativity when it comes to real life!"

Harald seemed to shrink in both size and mental capacity. "I hope I haven't mislead you, Uther. My misfortune is that I'm a great writer, but in everyday life I'm a dud. Even on a higher level I'm no Socrates. Marie is the practical one who keeps me on an even keel when I wander off on flights of fancy, crackpot endeavors, or eccentric behavior. She's the rock I cling to in stormy seas; the elixir I drink when . . . . There, you see? Off I went."

When Uther got home the first thing Lene asked was, "What did he say?"

"He equivocated. He read me like a book the other day, but when it came to solutions to our predicament he had little to offer; basically what you and I had already figured out: disguises, return to Norway, all

that.   As regards reality Harald is as lost as we
are.   We're on our own."

Chapter Forty-eight

Muddling on

Horace Smithers was a retired rancher who still lived on his ranch. He was probably approaching his eighties, and he was as tough as boot leather. Leather like the cowboy boots he always wore. He was tall and rangy as if he had been purposely created to fit the cowboy myth that so many cattlemen insisted on perpetuating. Good enough looking too, were it not for his above-average sized nose that hung over his mustache almost to his upper lip. Having been bucked off a number of horses he had one bad leg and the other was not very good, but he always managed to help out at branding time.

Horace's wife, Edith, was as close to being a nonentity as one could be. As plain as plain could be--or even plainer--she had occupied all of her adult life with cooking, baking, cleaning, . . . , and playing whist once a week. She had not even been blessed with children. Her only excitement was dragging Horace out of the bar once a month. He always forgave himself by telling how he had to exorcise his demons once in a while; but Uther was, first, surprised that Horace even knew what *exorcise* meant, and second, that he had enough sense of humor to call getting pie eyed an exorcism.   And what in the world could a simple man like Horace have to purge from his psyche?

"Horace!" Uther greeted.   "Come in and pull your favorite chair up by the fireplace."

It wasn't cold, but Uther had kindled a small fire as his own form of exorcism.

"It's good to get outta the house once in a while," Horace said.   He sat and rubbed his hands near the fire.

"Hmm.   Edith on the warpath?"

"Eh?   Oh, no she's busy whipping up a big turkey dinner for tonight.   Been try'n tuh fatten me up for years.   She ain't stupid, but sometimes it sure seems like it.   I don't mind though, it gives her something to do.   She's not what you'd call an intellectual."

Uther fought back a laugh.   He had been to their place once, and the only reading materials were farm and ranch magazines and old cowboy and western paperback books. Must be nice, he thought, to live simply, but not to live with someone so simple.

Horace fingered the package of cigarettes in his shirt pocket. "John Lasker said he was in town the other day, and wouldn't you know, Smith's old bulldog--or whatever it is--bit him on the leg. Hell of a row, and John was gonna sue him and everything else. Then----"

"Sue the bulldog?"

Horace didn't miss a beat. "Lasker was worried about rabies, but Smith told him the dog hadn't been outside the house for nigh onto a year. Course Lasker said it was just his luck to be walking by when it was out, and so on, and they almost came to blows. Can you imagine those two old coots going at it? It would'a been who got winded first, not who got beat up."

"Unless the bulldog took sides," Uther hawed, and they both laughed.

They were quiet for a while, and Uther wished he could, with the wave of a wand, extinguish his entire past. Not just extinguish it, but replace it with a past of his own creation, all the way back to his birth, dissolving even the good parts of his childhood. The only past he would recreate was Lene. And Alecto. Alecto would be hard.

Lene, without a word, brought them coffee, then left.

For the thousandth time Uther considered a possible age-old conundrum; how does a mature person re-write his or her past, and replace it? Can it be done? Expunge everything? Uther was well aware of having chased that fancy--that longing--before, and short of shock therapy he had not come upon anything. Ha! *Short* of shock therapy. Terrible pun. He sarcastically thought perhaps shorting out his brain circuits--his synapses-- might be better than the condition in which he now found himself. To be honest, in which he had put himself. He had always accepted responsibility for his thoughts and actions.

". . . lost a shoe, so there I was three miles from home and I hated to keep riding old Dobbin so I tried to walk, but that----"

"Old Dobbin?" Uther interrupted.

"Yeah. She's about as old as I am in horse years. I can't get on without a little step ladder, but I can get off okay. Well, luckily Hank Dodge came along and we tied Dobbin to the back of his pickup and made it home alright. Took a while cause old Dobbin isn't awfully fast to begin with, but all was well. Till Edith got ahold of me."

"Didn't you have a phone with you?"

"Naw. I read how they give you brain cancer."

"Hogwash. And anyway what if you fell off and broke a hip or something and they found you the next day dead of exposure."

"Then I would have died with my boots on, just the way I wanted to."

"Oh, for----!"

"How do you wanna die, Uther?"

"I want to die of old age. In bed with a good-looking woman. Maybe of a heart attack from overexertion."

Horace slumped his chin to his chest in disgust. "I don't know you very well, but that doesn't surprise me at all. Seriously, how would you want to die?"

Uther sank back in his armchair and reflected. "I can't answer that Horace. You're right, you don't know me very well, and there are several reasons why I can't tell you. My past is complicated; more than you could even begin to imagine. And--and it's a big *and*--my future, Lene's and mine, is too complicated for us to hazard even a guess as to what will become of us, or even what we would wish to do, much less how we want to die."

Horace looked at him strangely. "You an FBI man or something?"

"No, but it's secret stuff, and it's all for the good of the country. Hell, how did we get on this subject," Uther laughed. "No, and when it comes right down to it, when we die, we die. Probably no choice in the matter."

Horace stared at him and fingered his long, drooping nose. "Well I'm not as philosophical as you are, and I want to die on a horse."

"Haw!" But he could see that Horace was--as another pun--*dead serious*.

"And when the Good Lord takes me I hope heaven is just like here, open prairie and fields."

"What if you go down instead of up, Horace?"

"Then I'll hogtie the devil, brand him with my old brand--it'll be plenty hot down there-- then I'll climb back out of there and head for the pearly gate and make a deal with Saint Peter."

Uther put his right hand over his heart, and with a twinkle in his eye said, "I think I'm having a coronary, so I'll be standing alongside Saint Peter waiting for you."

Chapter Forty-nine

Losing hope

Uther and Lene's longing for peace and solitude on the High Plains of Montana was futile. He knew it, and Lene knew it. It had been unspoken. Their dream of living simply had evaporated when they at last admitted to each other that they could never return. It was like someone had cut away part of him; part of his brain.

Uther had graced Jon Applegate's Main Street bench again and for the last time. To most people Jon was a nuisance, but to Uther, sometimes at least, he radiated a calming effect. There was nothing to be learned from Jon, and he was not to be emulated, but despite those prohibitions there was something to envy: peace, for Jon had always appeared to be at peace with himself. The bench should have an inscription: *The Bench of Inner Peace*, or some such.

It was, then, fitting that along came Jon. "Good morning, Uther." He sat down.

"Jon."

"What a nice day," Jon said. "It's always nice on Sunday."

Uther smiled to himself. "You're missing church. You're gonna go to Hell. Hell with a capital *H*. It doesn't worry you how you're gonna burn?" He nudged Jon with his elbow.

"Ha, ha, ha! I know you, and you can't get under my skin. Back in my younger days you could have, but not now; now when I know that religions are just big crocks of crap. Throwbacks to centuries and millennia ago when knowledge limits prevented people from realizing reality. When their only concepts were through myth, mystery, and ignorance."

"Crocks of crap? What changed your mind?"

It was nine in the morning and the steeple bell of the Lutheran church tolled. There were few regulars in attendance, and there were fewer funerals because there were more private family gatherings, or those who wanted no memorial at all.

"You might not believe me, but it happened when I got drunk awhile back; went on a real bender. It was then that I saw the light. In reverse one might say. Saw it was all baloney. It took me two days to get sobered up, and when I did, that was it, and I have never had any second thoughts.

"Goodness, Jon. And your wife? She's not up there," Uther pointed skyward, "strumming her harp?"

"God no!"

"How do you stay so upbeat and cheerful?"

"I don't know. I don't think about it I guess. What's the use? It seems to me that religion, philosophy, and all that is hokum."

"That's it? As simple as that?"

"I guess so. I suppose the secret is to not think about things like overly much."

A cloud drifted over and darkened them, then it passed and the sun shone again.

"You don't believe in anything?" Uther queried.

Jon was quiet for a few moments. Then he sighed. "Goodness me Uther, you sure do ask the questions. Hell's bells. But you're right, I don't believe in much of anything, if you put it that-away."

"You just live?"

"Well, yeah," he said simply. "What's so unusual about that?"

"Jon, you do beat all. Most people have some higher beliefs: religion, witchcraft, higher moral purpose, . . . , but you; apparently now you just exist.   What do you think about in your quiet times?"

"Think about?   That's a strange question."

"It is not.   I've never run across anyone who didn't wonder *what it's all for*, or *what the meaning of life is*, and things like that."

"You haven't?"   Jon was unaffectedly perplexed.

Uther looked away, far up the street, at a gust of wind-driven dust; at a stray dog; at a stray cat; at an old man with a cane crossing the street; at a half-dozen parked cars, ...   At the absence of traffic, the stillness, the dryness, the forlornness, the old buildings--most of which went back to the early 1900s--the isolation, and so on.   And the pitiable vacuousness of those like Jon.

And Uther felt some essence of spirit and hope slip away from him, forever, but it was mostly an essence that he had never really had.

On the way home it occurred to Uther that he could do as Jon had done: get roaring drunk, but unlike with Jon he had no positive religious convictions to repudiate, so getting drunk would be futile and would only result in a monstrous headache.   Furthermore he had no firm convictions at all other than negative ones; and unless it would be possible to repudiate, or erase, his negative feelings, it would be pointless. In no way could he engineer himself to be bland and almost non-thinking like Jon even if it engendered inner peace and contentment. What would Lene think? She would think he was crazy. A few months ago he had told her that if he ever went off the deep end she should abandon him and find someone else; no use sticking with a loony loser. It hadn't gone over too well with her, but she hadn't been able to resist observing, with some humor, how occasionally the loony part was appealing.

Uther dodged some deep ruts in the road. Every time it rained--and granted it didn't rain much--Edward Grande went over to check the rain gauge on his west section, and, there being little gravel left on the road, he always made the same mess. The counties had been struggling financially for years and gravel was low on their list of priorities, especially considering the political mandates continually heaped on them.

An antelope bounded across the road in front of him. Climate change. Antelope had been rare there when he was a kid.

Uther smiled. He had always had the penchant for inventing scenarios of his different external or internal conditions and circumstances, and certainly he would have been certifiably insane had he thought otherwise. Yet, and still, Jon Applegate had gained his his mental balance almost overnight. Something to commend in those like Jon. Is it better to be a realist, or to live in oblivion?

Uther drove on and he was ashamed of himself for having teased Jon by pretending to have found religion. That's just what people do; cling to hope. And, Uther admitted, the older he got the more he found himself hoping. And then losing hope.

Chapter Fifty

The jig is up

Uther pulled their 2006 Ford pickup into the front yard of their house and hurried inside.

Lene put down her book. "You look a bit odd," she blurted.

"You would too if you had just had a bullet through your front windshield."

"What?" She jumped up. "What happened? A hunter?"

"Hunter hell. It's not hunting season. I was way out in the open and there was nobody around. Not a stray bullet coming down, but one from a long-range rifle."

"Are you sure?"

"Yes. It came from quite a distance, and the distance was the only reason I'm still kicking."

"But way out here? I thought they would have given up by now. We're small potatoes."

Uther winced. "Dunno. We've talked through it before: if they let just one go there would be others to follow. It's not the importance of the----" He moved to Lene and pulled her to the sofa beside himself.   "The jig's up."

She was strong, but she paled and said nothing.

"We'll be on the run for a while," Uther said.   "Probably quite a while."

Lene stared at him.   "I thought we had things all figured out, but it's deeper than that."

"I don't know about you, but I was an idealist.   A free-thinking idealist who knew you can't fight evil by doping around.   You have to fight evil people on their own level.   I go over and over it till I'm mentally destitute.   I don't know how they found us out.   The villains have no conscience so it doesn't phase them, but we who retain some morality suffer.   Not all, but many of us, suffer.   Oh, god in heaven, ever since we left Ragnarök it's been pounding in my mind, over, and over, and over.   You've heard it over and over.   Forgive me."

"I do.   I'm no better."

"Anyway, why did you join?

"That again?   Much the same way as you did, but I was more proactive."

"Oh."

She whispered, "You don't even know my real name."

"And I don't want to know."

"Don't want to----?"

"For your own good. Almost anyone can be made to talk."

"But I know yours."

"In the first place if they force you to reveal my name, make it easy on yourself and tell them. I don't care. You know I had to go by my real name so we could come here and try to fit in. And, I don't really care what happens to me anyhow."

"What? That's a selfish attitude. Your life is my life."

"I'm more tired than I have ever been. Sick of it all."

Lene looked stricken. "I didn't know that! Why didn't you tell me? I could have helped you. I still can."

"I doubt it. You would probably only go down with me."

"Certainly not, and anyway you have to stick with me you know. Without you I'm----"

"I'll do my best."

"Alright then, let's start figuring out what to do."

Uther felt better, and he managed an unfeigned smile. "Fine, you go first."

"As I have said, I agree we have no other option than to go to Norway or someplace like that, but not a big place like Oslo."

She stopped, and Uther waited. "That's it?"

"Yeah."

"Okay, we're on the same page but I can take it a bit further. You know I can speak the language pretty well, even though I still couldn't pass for a native. And it probably doesn't matter because there are still different dialects every here and there. We'll go north, certainly farther than Trondheim, and we'll find a little village. The villagers might be somewhat standoffish at first--as they are here-- and they might remain that way, but who cares? Maybe not. And in Norway once they find out my people were from *the old country* they'll come around. This Montana thing has been a good trial run. In any event once we get burrowed in in some little cabin I think we'll be okay."

Lene furrowed her brow. "Doesn't seem like much fun. Sounds like the main attractions there are aquavit and lutefisk, and blond, buxom, Nordic girls."

"Fine with me, but keep in mind the blond, slim and trim men up there too. Mostly athletic skiers I assume, and----"

"Not funny."

"Here's the thing then; despite my pessimism, and regardless of what we talked about a few minutes ago, I do think sooner or later Ragnarök will forget about us. They'll have bigger fish to fry, and they'll realize that all the hell we want is peace and quiet."

"We'll have plenty of that--peace and quiet--so I hope it will be sooner rather than later," Lene grumped. "I've always liked peace and quiet," she said sarcastically.

Uther wasn't used to her sudden mood swings. They had only come on recently. "Better than being dead."

Lene lowered at him, then she lightened up. "You ain't a'gonna believe this Ole, but my real first name is Martha."

"Don't humbug me."

"Ha! I'm not, I swear. Martha. It's true!"

Uther was speechless for a few seconds. "That's not Irish. Or is it?"

"I won't tell you my last name. I just couldn't help myself with the first."

"Why not the last, either recent or maiden name?"

"What? You assumed I have been married? How dare you?" But she was laughing, and she got down on one knee in front of Uther and asked, "Sir Bors, may I have your hand in marriage?"

Uther was nonplussed. "What?"

"Will you marry me?"

"Why, I hadn't----"

"Oh don't get your shorts all knotted up, you know I'm teasing you."

But he knew she wasn't. He said, "I suppose if we can get Ragnarök off our backs we could . . . ."

Chapter Fifty-one

Back to Norway

Uther and Lene had agreed about living in the mountains of Norway. They decided to go to Kjerstad and settle in; it was far enough north to offer some additional security if it would be needed. There they would outlast Ragnarök. Both of them had found it impossible to part with the farm after all, as long as there was some slight chance that they could return. In preparation for leaving Lene had arranged for Sallie Mortinsen and her husband Andros to live in their house and act as caretakers. It had turned out they were not the big farmers they had pretended to be, and living in a new, luxurious home would surely be heavenly for them. And there would be almost no chance of them being rubbed out by mistake by Ragnarok because a blind person could distinguish between them and anybody else, unless a shooter were a heck of a long way away, and Ragnarök didn't shoot unless they were pretty sure of their target. Well, except for the bullet through Uther's windshield, and they weren't so sure that had been anything to do with . . . .

"Ahh, the northern lights and the midnight sun," Lene whispered to herself, but loudly enough for Uther to hear.

They had bought a two-story, white, wood frame house near the northern edge of Kjerstad. Their first impression was that most of the homes were white.

"I feel better than I have for a long time," Uther mulled. "I'm beginning to think we're off the hook."

"I am too."

They were standing in the living room. The house was not quite what they had envisioned: not at all Scandinavian looking; no ornate wooden scrollwork, no fancy old-time wallpaper, . . . , nothing much to differentiate it from an average home in the U.S.

Lene put her arms around Uther and kissed him square on his lips, passionately, and long.

"Does our safety mean I can start calling you Martha?" he asked.

She released him and stepped back feigning irritation. "No, it does not. I always hated that name, and----"

"Hah, ha ha! I have another sore spot to pick. However I will only call you Martha when I am irritated with you, and that's not often."

"You are wrong again. You have never been irritated with me, and you never will be. And remember, you have some sore spots as well that I could start picking at. And don't call me Martha!"

"I have none. I'm made of iron, like my great, great, great, . . . , Viking grandfather Erik Bloodaxe."

"If I'm to believe that I will have to know whether grandfather Erik was full of bullshit. If he was, then I will agree that you are a descendant."

"I am," Uther admitted. "Full of it, I mean. But I take it as a compliment. So there, Goody Two-shoes."

"Uther, if you took one of those DNA tests I would bet my virginity that you are only three percent Norwegian, and that they would be unable to determine the other ninety-seven percent. They'd have to come with a new category----"

They both burst out laughing as they had never before, then, hand-in-hand they explored the house again. It was modest in size, only several years old, and from an upper bedroom balcony they had a good view in three directions. The view was striking.

Months unfolded uneventfully. Uther again passed much time reading.

Lene took Norwegian lessons at an adult education center, and she put in many hours studying it at home too. She also took up Norwegian cooking, somewhat to Uther's surprise, as he had never taken her for a domestic type. When he mentioned it she had replied how she really wasn't, but it occupied her mind whenever she tended to be paranoid about Ragnarök, though it wasn't as often now. She had admitted that she wasn't fond of many of the local dishes like cold--much less raw--fish, and some of the cheeses, and so on. Gammelost--*old cheese*--was absolutely the worst. Nobody in their right mind could stand it; if it were made as it had been in the old days it stank to high heaven, and anybody who ate it for any length of time would--in her words--start suffering from dementia, and from loss of friends due to the smell.

She also set about decorating their rooms to match her previous expectation of what a Norwegian home should look like, whether any other homes looked like theirs or not.

Norwegian-looking wallpaper, Hardanger embroidery for wall hangings; rosemåling, decorative painting, often of floral design; . . . .

Uther saw how Lene was more disposed to meet neighbors than he was. He didn't care whether he met any or not. She had a point when she hoped friends would help them if they got into trouble, but he observed that if she was referring to trouble with Ragnarök they would be in such deep doo-doo that neighbors would more than likely only add to the depth. Furthermore he wasn't in the mood for toadying around.

"The other day I met a guy and his wife two houses down there," Lene pointed, "Gina and Lars. No, I'm not making it up. He's an electrician and she works part time at a day care center. Works out well for her because she can take her two young children with her to the center. A four-year-old girl and a six-year-old boy. Gina doesn't speak English well and I of course am not up to snuff on Norwegian, but we get by and I'll improve. I took to her. I gave her our story about how our ancestors came from here and it seemed to interest her. When I mentioned that I didn't look very Norwegian she laughed and said not many do fit the stereotype. I think the ones back home in

Montana look much more Nordic than the ones
around here, don't you?"

"Remember that the Vikings carried off
the best-looking ones like you from all over;
even as far south as the Mediterranean."

"Oh for god's sake!"

"Tis true! I looked it up online once."

"Full of applesauce doesn't fully convey
your----"

One day Uther came home with unusual
enthusiasm. "I met an old guy down the street
who seemed nice, and I had a good talk with
him. Anders. He has never been to the States,
but he knew quite a bit about it. He said his
wife died a year ago. Used to be a college
professor, but didn't say what he taught.
Maybe English; he speaks it well and he has
quite a vocabulary. Nice to visit with someone
with a brain for a change. He bought a small
house and took up painting landscapes."

"Don't I have a brain?" Lene half pouted.

"Certainly, and it surpasses mine to the
point where I can't keep up with you."

"Nonsense, but thank you for saying so."

"He's a big, rough-looking character, not
someone you would take for a professor.
Seemed lonely, as one might imagine. We
should have him over sometime."

"Okay."

Chapter Fifty-two

Superego

Uther--in some small degree of desperation--had taken to pondering the invention of his own personal mindset. More than a mindset; a new intellect to which he could turn whenever he wanted to, or needed to. He was fully aware of his philosophical limitations, but he saw those limitations as a plus that would allow him to start from scratch.

His basic tenet was no doubt an old one: how all human experience is internal, not necessarily real; and he had previously boiled that down to personal representations. One such representation was literary fiction. Not literary in the sense of excellent writing--such writing had degenerated to where the words *literary fiction* had lost all meaning--but pertaining to all written fiction. He mulled over his best example: as a child he had known many people, and he had read many novels. Now, at his maturity, most of the people were dead, but both they and the characters in the novels remained engraved in his mind.

Howsomever to him they had been real.
Unfortunately his superego piped up.

*Nonsense! You, a realist, concocting
something like this?*

"I'm desperate," Uther said.

*And even if one considered your reality
people and your book people to be equally
valid, that's nonsense. Everything we know is
reality-based! You can't go by fiction.*

"You can if the fiction is based on reality,
or is plausible."

"What?" Lene asked.

She had just entered the main room.

"Huh? Oh, nothing." He put his
recliner upright. "I was daydreaming."

She left, came back with a flyswatter, and
swatted a fly on the wall behind him, then she
stood in front of him.

"What are you desperate about?"

"Desperate? Nothing. I must have
dozed off for a minute."

She scrutinized him. "Remember, no
secrets."

"Of course not."

She left and he sat looking at the wall to
his right, at the pictures they had bought at a
second-hand store; ones they had thought
looked Norwegian. No secrets. He would run
his new philosophy by her sometime to see

what she thought, so in light of that they weren't really secrets.

A fly Lene had missed buzzed around and around his head; or was it his head buzzing? The fly went away and there was no more buzzing.

One of the pictures was actually a photo of an old Norwegian fisherman standing in wading boots beside a fishing boat. It was a sailboat--about a forty footer--and there were nets all over it, drying. The man looked to be in his sixties, tall, with a beard and mustache, and he was smoking a pipe. A small, shaggy dog stood on the shore looking at him. Uther could almost smell the sea water. He had always had a good imagination.

He leaned the recliner back all the way and resumed his pipedream----

His superego had been wrong; if memories--and even current conditions--were possible, then they had as much validity as real memories or conditions. There, that's that. Ipso facto, Uther continued, one could recreate his or her own world, and he would start doing so forthwith, and after a few more meditations he would spring it on Lene with the hope she would be favorably impressed and would join him there.

Lene bustled through carrying a vacuum cleaner and Uther sat up again. She was not at

all the domestic type but she knew how to keep
busy. They each had their ways of staying
busy. She went into the bedroom and turned
on the cleaner and he could no longer
concentrate, but he had finished for the day
anyway. Too much thinking like he had been
doing could land him in the nuthouse. Better
to take it slowly for several days so if he were
nuts he could get a grip on himself and stop.
He had always known himself, and he felt that
as he had had time to recover from his previous
lapses and had become stable again, he could do
so now. Furthermore he had been justified in
his earlier breakdowns, as no one could have
stood up to tragedies like the horrific death of
Alecto. That and some of his other
experiences had reminded him of pulp fiction,
and they brought him back to his notion of the
individual creation of reality; how do you
separate the improbable from the impossible?
Therein would be the hairline separation that
would ultimately indicate the feasibility of such
an endeavor as constructing a peaceful realm of
existence.

As he got up from the recliner Uther felt a
twinge of doubt and he hoped Lene wouldn't
think he was as mad as a hatter.

Four days later Uther and Lene were sitting on lawn chairs in their back yard, having their morning coffee.

"I haven't heard your owl lately," Lene said.   She was in a good mood.

"He knows I'm crazier than he is, so I assume he flew away for good."

"She."

"I don't think so.   I have never been deserted by females and that includes owls. They *flock* to me."

Lene sputtered coffee over her shirt. "Flock?   Lord spare me."

They sat laughing.

Uther decided it was time to let Lene in on his personal philosophy.   He began and she perked up.

". . . so I figured out that if we don't know the difference between real and invented things, there is no difference.   Unless of course the inventions are so bizarre as to be impossible. A person still has to have a good grasp of reality . . . ."

Lene's face started to sag in disappointment despite his effort to be positive. The worst was not that she didn't understand, it was that she *did* understand.   His heart started thumping harder than normal and it even missed a beat now and then.   What now?   While she sat in utter dismay he put his coffee cup on the

table before he shook too much to hold it
without spilling.

Uther made himself smile. "Oh, don't
give me the *look*, I'm simply telling you of
some of the fanciful thoughts I sometimes have
before dozing off. For goodness sake you don't
think I'm serious about all of that. You know
what a vivid imagination I have! Mind games.
And don't forget that I am--I think I've told you
more than once--an ultimate realist."

She relaxed, but not completely. "I don't
know what to think when you get like that."

"Like that? What do you mean, *like
that?"*

"You know. Imaginative, or any other of
your euphemisms. You upset me, and what's
more I feel compelled to remind you of our *no
secrets* agreement. It's more than a mere
agreement, it's our sacred, secular pledge to
each other. If you renounce that you renounce
me forever."

She cried for a few seconds, then stopped
and looked down at her cup.

"No, no," Uther cried as he got up and
went to her. "I haven't broken our pledge."
He knelt beside her chair and put his arms
around her waist. "I never will, and if I ever
think or do anything even remotely close to
what you might consider a breach I will come to

you and let you judge before it gets to where it would be a real transgression!"

She lifted her head and looked at him doubtfully. "Do you swear? Because if you ever----"

"I do swear to you. You are my very life!"

She leaned down and kissed him on the top of his head. "It's over then; our little tiff. No, our little misunderstanding. You know how unsettled I can get."

"And you know how my imagination runs away with me sometimes, and I only ask you to remember how my fantasies can get the better of me if I'm not careful."

He stood and they shook hands ceremoniously and facetiously.

Even so, that night as he lay wide awake in bed Uther was troubled by his revelation to Lene. He had nearly crossed a line; the line that he and Lene had set.

Chapter Fifty-three

Carving trolls

For all of his unease and disinterest, Uther kept up on United States news, and it fell on him as something of a shock one morning to see how Ragnarök had, at long last, come out in most of the major media. In all of the years the organization had existed nothing like that had ever happened. Uther had never given it much thought, but he had--he guessed--assumed either Ragnarök had kept their activities so clandestine that nobody knew for certain; or even if there had been knowledge of their activity no one in the news organizations wanted to stick out their necks for fear of becoming targets. In either case he was doubly relieved to be out of it all.

While sitting again in the backyard, alone, Uther could not help thinking of his tiff with Lene. Bad enough to have aggravated her to such distraction, but to also put himself on the cusp of insensibility. Had he been at the point of madness? If so wouldn't he be the last to know? Undoubtedly, he thought, but maybe

it was just his thinking, and objectively how
could he possibly know even that; know what
he couldn't know? Lene would understand but
there were two flies in the ointment. If she was
aware he was on a downhill slide, his slide
wouldn't be obvious at first; and the other fly
was, in a worst case what could she do about it?

How close--how intimate; to what state of
oneness--can two people be? Lene had her
weaknesses too and it was remarkable how
similar to his they were, and Uther was tempted
to conclude that they should be better suited to
help each other, however that was probably a
tenuous conclusion, as maybe they would only
tend to go down together. Go down? Good
lord, he was turning into a croaker. Going
down, hell, they were surfacing; starting over.

Lene came outside.

Uther spoke up, "I've been thinking of
hobbies, and I have a great one in mind.
Carving gnomes and trolls. It's an obvious
pastime here in Norway; every creek and stream
used to have a troll under the bridges and----"

Lene sat down at the table and dried her
hair with a big towel.

"Were there female gnomes and trolls?"

"I, well I don't know. Probably not but
what does that have to do with----?"

"If not, you're being sexist. I wanted to
model for you, but according to you all of the

gnomes and trolls were males. More than that, I wouldn't deign to participate in a sexist hobby."

"Oh, brother."

"Have you carved much?"

"No. Well I used to whittle when I was growing up on the farm."

"Whittle?" She had put on her kind, sincere face. "Couldn't you find something a bit more ambitious than that?"

"Like what?"

"I don't know. Carving trolls just doesn't seem like you."

A lady several houses down the street was screeching at her husband again. They were elderly but they had not lost any of their vocal strength or articulation.

"If you're going to burst my bubble you should replace it with a new one. But then you'd more than likely burst that one too."

Lene's mouth twitched ever so slightly. "I only thought you would get into something more challenging, like chess, or computer programming or something. Something more suited to take your mind off things. Unfortunately one can carve and think at the same time."

"Huh."

The lady down the block was ranting about--of all things--spilled milk.

Uther settled back in his chair. "I guess I could think of something else."

"Good. This is our life now and we should aim for things more substantial. After all our adult lives have always been dedicated to *things more substantial* and we can't quit now."

Uther tried unsuccessfully to conceal a smile. "I don't know what would be as substantial, as you put it, than working with Ragnarök, but we can try. I think I'd be an excellent hitman, and you could find a good pimp and start seducing and robbing johns."

Lene threw her towel at him. "I don't think that's funny about prostituting myself. Why do you always have to be so crude? And your hitman suggestion! What the hell have we been doing over the years? You have a weird perspective of . . . ."

Uther felt like fleeing. The old lady was still at it behind him, and Lene railed on in front.

Then Lene, apparently seeing his despair, stopped. It wasn't like her to be so irate, and this was the first time she had been that upset with him in a long time. They stared at each other, then they looked down. After a long pause their eyes met again.

"I'm so sorry," Lene said. "This isn't like us. This isn't us at all. Forgive. me"

They held hands over the table, then Uther put both of his hands to his forehead. "For me life is like swimming in a giant septic tank. I can't stand it but if I get out I know I'll die."

Lene's eyes widened but she didn't explode. "Dear me. Actually I feel that way sometimes too, but I couldn't have put it so vividly." She frowned. "Are you that way all of the time?"

"No. It come and goes."

"It's the same with me. It comes and goes."

She moved her chair around the table so as to sit by him, and they held hands again, and for a while they both seemed paralyzed in some way.

"We have to find a way, or ways, to keep out of the septic tank," Lena began. She was calm now, and analytical. Her old self. "We've been trying to think of pastimes, hobbies, and all, but our ideas were superficial. Only a good start. We should be looking at our situation--our lives--from a higher perspective. I don't know, because I can't relate to other people well, but I suppose such things come to them intuitively. For me, and I guess you, we have never lived like other people, therefore we have to work at such things from an analytical perspective, but ruling out many of others'

mundane pursuits.   Points of view and
assumptions.   Like religion, politics, lifelong
goals, and so on.   I sure can't see you becoming
a church deacon for instance."

"And I can't see you becoming a nun, or a
tidy little housewife who cooks, cleans, sews,
and brings me my slippers when I come home at
night from a hard day of deaconing."

That night when they went to bed their
love was better than ever.   Lene was beautiful
in every physical way, and she was at times
insatiable to the point of wearing him out
completely.

Chapter Fifty-four

The owl again

"There's no point in denying it; we are leading vapid lives," Lene burst out one morning over coffee in the back yard. "Pointless, useless, dull lives." She took a long gulp of coffee but spilled some on her lap. "Oh jeez!"

"Heck of a note when spilling coffee is the most exciting thing of the day," Uther quipped.

She continued wiping herself with a napkin.

"I'd almost be ready to go back to work for Ragnarök," Uther said.

"You are not, and it's no funnier than when you said it to the last time. Or was it I who said it?"

"I just meant I'm so bored I'm losing my stasis."

"Your what?"

"My stasis. It means----"

"I know what the hell it means! Don't talk down to me. And don't think for a minute

that using uncommon words makes you any
smarter."

"Sorry, I just get so fed up with things."

"How does using odd words help?"

Uther felt like he was physically
withering under her heat. "I guess they don't."

The owl was back, and it *whooed* three
times. It had been away for about a week.
Lene looked around for the owl, but she said
nothing and Uther didn't dare to say anything
either until he found out which way the wind
was blowing in regard to her mood.

Lene calmed down and assumed her
analytical look. "What we gonna do, Ole?"

"I don't know Lena."

"Whoo, whoo, whoo!" the owl said.

"There he goes again, and again, I wish I
spoke Norwegian owl," Uther ventured.

"She," Lene said in a monotone.

Late that afternoon Lene entered through
the front door wearing an unusual frown; so
unusual that Uther got up from his recliner.

"What's up," Uther asked.

"Oh, I met three ladies down the street
and visited with them for quite a while."

"Well good for you, you're----"

"It wasn't much fun. In the first place I
had trouble understanding them, what with all
of their slang and stuff, and they talked so fast.

They didn't seem to notice that I couldn't keep up, or they didn't care."

"You'll pick it up with time."

"That's the thing, I'm not sure I want to."

"Why not?"

"They didn't seem too sharp."

"What of it? Nice people aren't always brilliant."

"I know that, but I'd much rather be around those who are intelligent enough for me to have a decent conversation with. Good grief!"

"Whoo, whoo, whoo!"

Lene started. "There's the owl again."

Uther went to one of the rear windows and shouted, "Whoo, whoo, whoo!" The owl didn't respond.

"You're getting goofier than I am," Lene burred. "What will the neighbors think?"

"You--Miss Smarter Than Thou--worried about what the neighbors will think?"

Lene fell back into a plush chair and was quiet. But after a while, "What's with you and that owl?"

"I honestly don't know. I've just always liked owls. Do I need a psychoanalyst to figure out why? Who cares?" He went to the radio and tuned to the classical music station, then he went to his recliner and they both closed their eyes and listened for a long, long time.

Two hours later Uther got up and turned off the radio, then he sat back down.

Lene opened her eyes and looked around perplexedly for a moment. "Such music is my only solace. The music, and you."

"In that order?"

"You, you, you, and the music."

"My solace also. You, and the music, and the music is a far, far distant second."

They closed their eyes.

"Whoo, whoo, whoo!"

Uther lifted his head and looked at Lene. She had dozed off.

But then she woke up long enough to say, "I'm not interested in associating with average people either."

"Then you must be in heaven, being around me."

Two days later Uther and Lene went for a walk down the street from their house. It was a beautiful, sunny, cool day.

Lene said, "When we talked--albeit sarcastically--about going back to work for Ragnarök, that just about says it all doesn't it? Lost souls."

She took his hand and they walked on like any other couple.

Now and then they met and greeted people, some of whom had dogs. One had a large, black, uncastrated tomcat. At such times Uther longed to be alone with Lene somewhere in Montana, but he reproached himself for thinking so. Their angst was within, and they had both accepted responsibility for the position they were in. Stoics and realists they were, but acceptance hadn't eased their distress; that was impossible to do with mere words. He had been taught that too often, throughout the beatings his father had given him, and one lesson in particular had stuck: *Sorry, sorry you little runt? Saying you're sorry doesn't change anything. Words! Just more of your damned words!*

Words are overrated in situations like theirs Uther felt. What was required was some sort of mental reorganization like a realignment or even a rebirth, but how? Neither of them had much faith in psychiatrists. A year ago Lene had brought up the possibility of hypnosis but she had not said it with much conviction, and he had received it with no enthusiasm. They were familiar with electroconvulsive-- shock--therapy but that was for severe depressives and so on. *Good lord*, he thought, *I'm going off the deep end again.*

"Ouch!" Lene cried. "You're squeezing my hand! What's going on?"

"Oh, sorry, I was just thinking."

"Well think happy thoughts. What were you thinking about?"

"Ways to get us out of our miserable situation."

"Yet again? Some religion we haven't thought of before? What have you *divined*? Pardon my wit"

"I have divined nothing. Pardon my wit."

Lene groaned.

"We'll relax for a few days, then we can put our heads together and plan our future. Recently I have been overcome by optimism."

"It must have been pretty recent."

Along came the cat lady again, from around the block, and Uther felt that she was of the sort who liked cats with balls bigger than his. He had *divined* it.

Chapter Fifty-five

Buddhism

"Buddhism!" Uther shouted as he awoke one morning.

Lene all but levitated from the bed. "Holy Jesus and Mary!! What the----?" She sprang to her feet and stood shaking. "Mother McCree, what's going on?"

"Calm yourself, I've found the answer!"

"Calm myself? Calm myself? You almost give me a heart attack and you lie there serenely telling me to calm myself? Have you lost your mind completely. Look at me!" She held out her hands. "I'm shaking like a leaf in a tornado and you tell me to fucking calm myself? I ought to----"

"Never mind, I think I've found the way out of our doldrums. Buddhism!"

Lene glowered at him. "My aunt Millie did that to uncle Milford and he died. Literally scared him to death."

"Must have had a weak heart."

"I'm going downstairs to put on the coffee."

"Be careful, coffee might make you nervous."

She gave him the finger and stalked out.

Downstairs over the kitchen table Uther tried to smooth things over.

"Your aunt Millie no doubt had that on her conscience for the rest of her life."

"Not at all. She was like you, she didn't have a conscience. They had never gotten along well anyway and she went on to marry the next-door neighbor with whom she had been dallying for years. They lived together for many years, then when they were both in their eighties she scared him to death too."

"You're making it up!"

"It's true. I heard she had gotten tired of him so she found a pair of cymbals and went into the bedroom early one morning and----"

"You don't expect me to believe----" Uther started.

"Honest truth. Cross my heart and hope to die. My point is, you could have killed me by waking me up that way."

"I'm sorry. I was only half awake, and it was involuntary." He reached across the table for her hand but she remained still and icy. "Really, I was just coming out of a dream. I couldn't help it."

She remained skeptical. "Sometimes living with you is like living with a wild animal."

"Is that a compliment?" He could see her weakening. "A cat? A tiger I hope."

"Kiss my butt."

"I will if you'll go back upstairs with me. I've always thought your butt was your best----"

"I thought it was my nose. You said nose once."

"Both. I should have said both." He was playing her and they both knew the game. "*But*, I've always been partial to butts."

Lene got up. "Let's go up on the balcony and you can tell me about your revelation."

They went up and sat next to each other.

Lene brushed away something from the rail next to her. "Owl poop."

"How do you know it's owl poo?"

"I just know."

They were at ease again with each other, if not with life.

"Are we obsessed with owls?" Uther asked.

"You are, and it must have some special meaning; some personal import."

"Nope, as I've said before I just like owls."

"Noses, butts, and owls?"

"Whatever you say."

"Yeah," Uther agreed, "but now down to brass tacks. You've heard me mention Buddhism now and then? Well I used to be into that many years ago but I gave it up."

"Why?"

"I suppose I had too many other things going on. Just living life, as young people are apt to do, and giving little thought to growing old. However I did learn a thing or two about Buddhism--and despite the fact that I renounced it in my youth and several times since--it re-emerged in my dream last night as our possible salvation."

Lene looked blankly at him. "You mean you want us to forge ahead in life as Buddhists because of a dream you had?"

"No, no, there's more to it than that!" He turned his chair to face her more. "Of course it wasn't just the dream; the dream was only the trigger that brought back everything. Or my recent thinking prompted the dream. No matter. Listen, this time I'm for real, and I want you to bear with me. Will you do that?"

She held her blank look.

"What?" Uther asked.

"I'm pregnant."

"You're what?"

"Pregnant."

"How can you be? Impossible! You're, you're, and we've been----"

"Ha, ha, ha!   Gotcha!"

"Oh, please!   Don't do that to me.
Søren!"

"Ha, ha, ha, and ho, ho, ho!   So there,
smarty pants."

"Alright, you got me, but why?   Why
now when I'm trying to save our lives?"

"Hell if I know.   Maybe I'm trying to
help pave our way to normalcy."

"You call that paving the way?" Uther
growled.

"Sure.   We have to lighten up, which
brings me to what I want to say next.   Our
connection with each other is stronger than I
thought.   I too, when I was young, got into the
Buddhist thing.   I was out in San Francisco and
I met some hippies from the sixties who, unlike
most, had hung onto their ways until they were
old and had wasted their lives.   They never
admitted to wasting their lives but they had
wasted them, and had *wasted* themselves on
drugs as well.   In the event, I was young and
didn't know much, and they made sense to me,
and some of them claimed to be Buddhists.   I
don't know if they really were, or, looking back,
how their lifestyles would have fit in with
Buddhism.   They were always saying things
like *cheer up*, and *go with the flow*, and other
meaningless mots.   I followed them for a while
until I got older and came to my senses, and

when I got fed up with their insistence on free love, which I never took to."

Lene paused and fingered her wedding ring. She was wearing it early since they weren't yet married.

"I assume most of them are dead now," she went on. "The only silver lining is that it was an interesting experience, and I learned a good deal about the Buddhist ways of life. So as you see, I am open minded, even after all of these years."

"Bless me and save me," Uther said. "How do I put up with you?"

"The same way I put up with you."

"Then pipe down and listen to me."

"Okey dokey."

He eyed her dubiously as if he suspected she was on some kind of whoopy pills.

"Whoo, whoo, whoo!" Uther threw up his arms and flapped them. "Now I'll tell you what I know about Buddhism. To start with I want no part of Zen. That's too far fetched; reincarnation and all that. Too much like religion, and we know what misery religion has inflicted. So----"

He saw Lene's lips start to move and he wagged his index finger at her. "There, there, let me finish."

She gave him a cross look, but stopped.

"It's a way of life . . . ."

Chapter Fifty-six

Fading away

Uther gradually realized where he was: in a hospital. As the fog lifted he looked around for Lene, but there was only a nurse puttering around at a nearby counter. He tried to ask her what had happened, but he only spouted gibberish. She turned and smiled, and said something in Norwegian that he couldn't understand, then she turned away.

The fog descended.

Uther opened his eyes and after a few moments he remembered he was in a hospital, and he knew it was morning. That was all. A pretty, young, buxom, blond nurse showed up at his bedside and took his pulse. He again tried to speak, but she merely smiled and patted his hand. Then the fog started to roll in again.

Again a nurse, but this time not the young pretty one; but an old, plain one who was cheerful and pleasant. She took his temperature and blood pressure, and gave him the obligatory pat on his arm.

"You're coming along fine," she said.

"What ha, happen, hap----?"

"I can't say; I'm just an old nurse. I take temperatures and so on, and I am proud to say I am sincerely compassionate, but I leave patients' questions to the doctors." She did, however, lean down and smile. "I can venture to say you look good to me though." She winked.

Uther thought he read more into her compassion than mere professional concern.

Several days later he awoke again. He guessed it had been several days because he had heard a nurse talking to a doctor; something about *telling him,* and *police.* He couldn't follow the rest of their discussion; only that it was about him, and they sounded serious. He got the impression that the doctor was a psychiatrist.

Uther gradually focused on two young police officers--a man and a dark-complected woman--who stood over him. The lady smiled and Uther took comfort in the fact that he had not lost his marbles to where he could not read people's mannerisms.

A doctor came up beside them. "What do you remember about your incident?"

"Incident? What incident?"

All three at the bedside exchanged glances, then stepped away from the bed and huddled, and the doctor looked back several times.

They returned to Uther's bedside, and a chill came over him. "Where's Lene?" he asked. Was it Alecto all over again?

The dark officer--maybe a sergeant, Uther didn't know the ranks--began. "Do you remember picking up a package at your front doorstep?" she asked tenderly.

"Package? No, I----" Then he became nauseous and a nurse came with a pan for him to be sick in.

"Do you recall a neighbor of yours named Anders?"

"Yes."

"Someone saw him drop a package on your doorstep. He said it was a guy named Anders, but he wasn't certain."

Uther clutched the pan again. When he was through he wiped his mouth with a towel. "But what about----?"

"We're getting to that," said the young policeman. He was blond and his English wasn't very good. "You have to be strong while we tell you what was in the box."

Uther's head began to swim and the room turned darker. He had gone through the same thing before, and he wished he could die.

"Is this Lene's ring?"

The police officer presented the engagement ring that Uther had given her.

"Yes."

"And is this Lene?"

He held up a large photo of Lene, eyes shut and with her body covered with a white sheet. Scrawled on the sheet was *HASKELL*.

Uther reached for the photo, but the officer pulled it away.

"It's her! Tell me! I can take it. Is she dead?"

"Yes."

It was stone silent in the room for a minute.

"We found her covered with that sheet," the lady officer said. Do you know who Haskell is?"

"Show me an uncovered photo!"

"We will, when you're ready."

"I'll never be ready so just----" As he felt himself fading he heard the doctor speculate that most likely he would never be normal again. Uther tried to speak again but he knew from the way they were looking at him he was no longer making sense. But as before, he could understand them.

"Perhaps he'll come around," the doctor said, "but I don't think so. I've only seen two similar cases and neither of them--victims of similar severe physical and mental trauma--came even close to recovering."

He was speaking normally, assuming that Uther couldn't hear.

"One died and the other was not much more than a vegetable for the rest of his life."

The room shimmered, and faded, but Uther could still hear him.

"Oh, wait, I recall a third case. He recovered to where we thought he could return to normal life, but not long after, he committed suicide."

Part V

Chapter Fifty-seven

Rat-tail Curves

Too many remembrances and too many dreams--mostly of the farm and the immediate area--to the point where they almost blended with reality. Not necessarily altogether bad dreams or full-fledged nightmares; many were only slightly irritating, and some were downright good ones like colorful sailboats on the prairie, picturesque little villages he had not known about, quaint buildings in the middle of the nothingness, ... Years before, he had realized that most of the good dreams were longings for *more* than reality could provide. And some of the dreams were so strange that he could not account for them, like the one where he approached Marie and she asked him where his disciple was. Gracious. Was he an egomaniac? He didn't feel like one, leastwise when he was awake.

Harald had written his magnum opus, *Rat-tail Curves*, a creative nonfiction, autobiographical work about real and human limits, but it had not sold well, and he guessed many people were just too limited to appreciate it. During his lifetime he felt that writing in general had degenerated, and he assumed it was because there were so many other visual and audio media now. But his mental, verbal, and internet carping and croaking hadn't changed anything. Still, for years, he had soldiered on. Writing was the only activity that lifted and delivered him from everyday existence.

Standing in front of his workshop, Harald looked to the south. His grandfather, Lars, had known an old World War I veteran who had lived down the road a few miles: Morgan Feeney. Morgan had been in the 2nd Division--the Indian Head division--in France, and had come out okay physically, but with a case of shell shock. He had, however, been brave and strong during the war, and after. Harald had written a novel about him titled *Men With Broken Faces* that had gotten glowing reviews. Perhaps his best work, as he had related to Morgan as if he himself had been in Morgan's war: the crushing death, gas, shell shock, rotting corpses . . . . And as with most of humanity, the utter barbarity, ruthlessness, and overwhelming stupidity of it all. The imbecility of human beings; the kind of imbecility that pushed the most rational and brilliant of mortals to near psychopathy and ruthlessness themselves. And by far the worst

of it were the kings, dictators, and politicians--
those who exhibited the most fury--who lead
the soldiers from behind, instigated the wars,
and were often followed heroically by
noncombatants.

Harald's neighbor, Uther, had reminded
him of what Morgan must have been like. Not
in looks, but regards inner self and strength of
character. Harald had been drafted during the
Vietnam war and had spent two years at a desk
job as a personnel psychology specialist.
Nonetheless, even as a noncombatant, he had
identified with Morgan, though he remembered
little of the old soldier; only the stories.
Maybe it was because he was a severe
depressive that he had related to Morgan. And
in some unrealized way Harald had identified
with Uther, through what little he had known of
him. But was he mis-comparing afflictions?
Harald knew both Morgan and Uther had been
maladjusted in some way; that had been
obvious. What had not been so obvious had
been the complexion of their maladjustments.

Uther and Lene had left unexpectedly
without even so much as a wave and a goodbye.
Taking into account their tribulations he
couldn't blame them, and he regretted his
inability to have helped them more. The thing
was, he believed, people are all responsible for
their actions. Most average people gasped in

horror whenever he said that, but life is harsh, and who else should be responsible? Society, family, some nebulous fate, a god of one sort or another? The only observation that made any sense is that too often there is no sense: only randomness. *Non*sense. Often there are no remedies.

Well, and well; enough philosophizing. Too much.

A large dust devil twisted across the fields a few hundred yards away. Already in the spring weather was dry and hot, and it took Harald back to the Dirty '30s that his grandparents and parents had lived through. Global warming, though there were many deniers. Too many dunces. Too many dunce politicians. The trouble with democracies.

Uther and Lene. Harald had heard they were dead, and somehow he knew it was true.

God it was hot.

Chapter Fifty-eight

FBI?

Harald heard a long, firm knock on the door and he guessed right away that it wasn't anyone local. He opened the door and there stood two tall, dark-haired, handsome men in their thirties.

They smiled pleasantly and one took out a card and presented it. "FBI," he said. "Harald Nordraak?"

"Yes." He looked at the card. "Since I'm not a criminal I'm not familiar with FBI cards and badges and stuff. Do you have a phone number I can call?"

"No. We've never been asked for that before. Just like with police detectives and so on, the IDs always suffice. We're field workers, not computer ticklers, and we're in the front lines fighting terrorist-inspired crime. Right now we're seeking information on a person or persons of interest. May we come in?"

Harald stepped back and they entered.

"I'm agent Linvold, and this is agent Smith."

"Please sit down." Harald indicated the dining room table, and they sat. "Coffee?"

"No, thanks," Smith declined with a shake of his head.

"Nice place you have," the talker said.

"Peaceful, and the winters keep away the lower elements of society." Harald looked them over. Something wasn't right.

"How do you keep from going batty, especially in the winters."

"I'm a writer, and I'm already batty. And my wife, Marie, keeps me on my toes." He stood and went toward the back door, and both men stiffened unnaturally. He took down the flyswatter, returned to the dining room, and swatted a fly on the wall.

"Pardon me, but you two seem kind of nervous," Harald said. "Is your work getting to you?"

They glanced at each other. "Maybe so. It can get interesting at times."

"Yes it can," the quiet one said, and he looked at the other one again. "I think we need a break."

He spoke so firmly and meaningfully that Harald wondered at it.

They all paused before the talkative agent asked, "Is your wife here?"

"No.   Went to town for something or
other, so if you're impostors--criminals
yourselves--now's your chance.   I see you both
have guns, and you know I don't, and it
wouldn't take much for you to overpower me.
I just hope you don't leave Marie a widow.   We
have our squabbles but I don't think she's ready
to get rid of me yet."

"Whatever gives you that impression of
us?   We're not----"

"Humm.   Not to be rude or anything, but
I expect you'll get to the reason you're here."
Harald smiled politely.

"Oh, certainly.   Then to begin, did you
know a guy named Uther Montgomery who
used to live up here?   When he was a child, and
later when he was much older?"

So, whoever they were, that was their
game.   "I knew the Montgomerys, but not their
kids.   I do seem to recall they only had one boy
though.   Anyway I haven't been around here all
of my life."

"And did he move back to the home place
recently?   Within the last year or two?"

"He did indeed.   He had a good-looking
woman with him both times."

"Both times?   He was here more than
once?"

"Yes.   Say, if I didn't know better I
would think you were after him for something

he had done, and I don't want to get him into trouble. Not that I know anything about his past anyway. We only talked politics, philosophy, and so on."

"If you didn't know better? You just said you don't know anything about----"

"I don't. Not his past. Anyway, I heard he was dead, and don't ask me how I heard it because I don't remember. You have to realize, when he--they--left here for the second time I forgot about him." Harald paused. "He was interesting though, I'll tell you that. Now you tell me, is he dead?"

"Yes, both he and his wife, Lene."

They sounded to Harald like they were lying, but----

"Too bad. I liked him. I felt sorry for him. He was someone I could talk to. Not many like him up here in the middle of nowhere."

"One last question. Have you ever heard of Ragnarök?"

"Who?"

"Ragnarök. It's an organization."

"It sounds Norwegian. How do you spell it?"

The *FBI* man spelled it.

Harald wrote it down. "I know a little Norwegian. I'll look it up later." He was curious, but mostly he was doing his best impression of a half-baked old codger." As he wrote he saw the main agent shrug slightly at his partner.

Harald got up, slowly, feigning infirmity. Even at his age he could probably have made mincemeat of both of them.

"Easy now," the quieter man said nervously.

"I'm going into the kitchen to get some cinnamon rolls," Harald said. "For pity's sake, do you think I'm up to something? What could a poor old guy like me do against you two, and why would I do anything? You want to accompany me?"

They eased back onto their chairs and Harald hobbled, intentionally, into the kitchen. He came back with a plate covered with a paper towel.

"Who wants a roll?" he asked, sitting back down and setting the plate on the table in front of him.

Both visitors declined.

"Then how about a good, old-fashioned World War II hand grenade?" Harald asked, pulling off the towel and picking up the grenade.

"Yeahoww!" the two cried as they fell backwards to the floor on top of their chairs.

Still on the floor, they pulled their guns and sat up.

"Are you crazy?" they asked in unison. "Put both hands on the table. No, put your hands in the air!" They got up.

"Sorry, can't do that," Harald laughed. "Settle down and I'll tell you what's going to happen." He pulled the grenade pin with his teeth.

"Settle down!" one of the men shrieked. "You settle down or I'll blow you to bits!"

"No you won't," Harald said calmly. "All of the outer doors are locked and you have nowhere to go, and if you blow me to pieces the grenade in my hand will go off, as will the other one under the table, and we will all be blown to kingdom come. Now, before any of us does anything rash, put your guns on the table and sit down."

"You're insane!"

Harald shrugged his eyebrows. "No. Maybe a little eccentric, and old enough not to value life much anymore, that's all. Now sit, or be prepared to meet your maker. Guns on the table, and slide them gently toward me."

Somewhat to Harald's surprise they did so, and he swept the guns to the floor beside him with his forearm.

Apparently having had second thoughts the talker turned surly. "I think we could disarm you."

"Only it you want to go to the Happy Hunting Ground." He took his other hand from under the table. "There's the old saying that two grenades are better than one. So now that there's no danger, let's talk."

"No danger?"

"Hmmm."

"Talk about what?"

"About Uther Montgomery. I'll tell you everything I know about him, but only because he's dead and can't be harmed anymore."

Harald told what little he knew of Uther's childhood and of his adult life, which was next to nothing. He then went on to expand his and Uther's conversations, and that took a while."

Harald concluded, "Now you know everything that I know about him, and of his friend--or wife, or whatever she is--Lene. Though tell me, is she still alive?"

"No. She was----"

Harald stopped him. "Spare me. You don't yet understand. I'm sorry to know they are both dead, but as for all of the rest, I don't want to know. You seem to think that I was involved with them in some nefarious activities, and I wasn't. I have the upper hand, at least for now, so why would I lie? All I want is to be left the hell alone, and I get pretty damn sore when people like you come barging in. Those like you insult my intelligence; whatever intelligence I have. Not that anyone like you two have ever accosted me; usually it's only some neighbor trying be neighborly, or whatnot. You guys take the prize."

To Harald's surprise they both smiled weakly.

"Now here's the deal," Harald said. "I played dumb with you at first, but I'm not. Dumb. I'm just an old guy from an earlier time when a person's word meant something. I've leveled with you about Uther, and I'm straight when I say I know nothing of this Ragnarök. I propose--assuming you have any brains at all, and despite whoever you're working for, and in order not to instigate some ruckus which might backfire--that you tell me, without revealing anything too much--whether or not your activities are evil. One way or another it would put my mind at rest. Then I put the pins back in the grenades, you pick up your guns and leave. Because, for the most part, I just don't give a darn what you're up to. I repeat, I only want to be left alone."

Linvold and Smith studied each other for a several seconds, then Linvold--the talker-- said, "Okay."

Harald lifted his hands--each holding a grenade--from under the table. There was a pin on each small finger.

"Here," he said, "take this one first, and the pin, and secure it."

Smith did so.

"Now the other one. And if you please, put them over there," he pointed off toward a shelf on the other side of the room."

They did as directed.

"And now," Harald said, "Your end of the bargain."

Smith, still standing, paused and reflected for a while. "We see our activities as, if not noble, necessary, to save humankind."

Harald felt his eyebrows go up. "Not a simple *good* or *evil*?"

"No."

Harald shrugged. "Fair enough. Don't forget your six shooters," he said, pointing with his thumb."

They picked up their guns and as they moved toward the front door Harald threw them the key. Linvold looked back and said, "You beat all. Being locked up with you is like being locked up with a mad hatter."

"*The* Mad Hatter?"

"No, just a mad hatter."

The two left and Harald watched out the window until they were out of sight. An owl hooted.

After his nerves had settled Harald went into the dark living room and slouched into his armchair. He had played it well, and he knew more about Uther than he had let on. It would have been easier to have simply told the truth, but he had felt a need, or an obligation, or something, to protect Uther's memory, even if he was likely the only one to remember.

Moreover, Harald knew he would be haunted by Uther's failure. If a seemingly strong person like Uther had been broken, what kind of person would it have taken to have persevered?